MY HEART BELONGS TO YOU

ANN ROTH

OLIVERHEBERBOOKS

CHAPTER 1

*S*tarr Dehl was going stir-crazy, and the day had barely begun. Her fault for coming home to Miracle Falls in cold, bleak January. But with Dahlia and Jake's wedding in six-plus weeks, it seemed a good excuse to leave LA. She needed time to design and make dresses for the wedding— Dahlia's wedding gown and the matron of honor and bridesmaid dresses for herself and Sunshine. A ton of work.

She'd attempted to get a head start in LA and had already sketched out Dahlia's dress. But the hectic pace Wes demanded for the costumes she designed for him, and his insistence that she travel with the band on their never-ending tours had waylaid her progress.

That and the panic attacks.

Those things were terrifying. Months ago, afraid she might be seriously ill and maybe dying, she'd hurried to her doctor's office for an exam. The woman's advice: see a relaxation therapist and take a much-needed break. Now, before she lost more weight and bit her nails to the quick.

It didn't help that lately and for the first time ever, her passion for designing and sewing her creations had diminished significantly. Doing both for the wedding wasn't half-bad, but to continue making a living at it? Not so much.

A blasphemous thought she quickly pushed away. She hadn't told a soul about the doubts she was having— saying the words would make them real. Besides, she was certain that after a much-needed break from Wes, she'd be back to her normal enthusiastic self in no time.

Of course she would. Without the career she'd eaten, dreamed and breathed since she'd first started sewing in fifth grade, cemented into her heart and soul with a degree at Parsons New School of Fashion, she'd be lost, a rudderless ship in a vast sea of what nexts.

At the very thought, fear and uneasiness twisted her stomach and foreboding tremors eddied up her spine.

Starr clenched her teeth. "I'm not going to quit the job I love," she stated out loud. "I'll go back to LA refreshed and ready to continue with the career I was made for, the job Wes hired me to do and depends on me for. Got that?"

The self-pep talk helped. So did the deep breaths she sucked in and released until she felt in control again. Everything would be fine.

Much better.

She'd been in Miracle Falls four days now, bunking at Mama J's, aka Mama, because to Starr and her sisters, the woman was their mother. Not biologically, but she'd taken them in after an aneurism had ended their mom's life. Sunshine had been eight, Starr seven and Dahlia six. Raising three stair-step sisters hadn't been easy, but Mama had loved them and done a good job. She was also head of medical records health information at Miracle Falls Hospital, a big deal.

On top of that, she had an active social life that kept her busy, much busier than Starr had realized. Not that long ago, Mama had been more of a homebody, her life revolving around Starr and her sisters and of course, her work. Now the woman was so busy with friends and activities in the evening that not counting dinner with the family Saturday and fussing over Starr much of Sunday, communication with her had been reduced mostly to texts and an occasional phone call.

Her sisters had equally full lives. Besides running successful businesses, Dahlia was busy planning her wedding to Jake. Much of Sunshine's free time was spent with Trevor, her smart private investigator boyfriend. The way their relationship was going, no one would be surprised if they got engaged in the near future.

Starr wasn't involved with anyone— as crazy busy as she was keeping Wes in custom-designed outfits and shopping for accessories to go with the clothes, who had time for love?

Which didn't mean she didn't want it. Someday. At the moment, she was focused on other things. Three, to be exact. First and foremost, eliminate the panic attacks by practicing the exercises the relaxation therapist had given her and cutting down on stress. The stress reduction part had begun the day she'd left LA. A close second, designing and sewing the wedding dresses. All of which were tied to number three, renting a small place where she could sew and live in peace while she was in town.

As much as she loved Mama, staying with her had to end, and soon. Setting up the sewing machine and laying out the patterns on the kitchen counter— the dining table wasn't big enough to work on and there was no place to set up the folding table Starr had brought with her— then putting everything away so that they could use the kitchen to cook and eat was getting old. Really old.

Eager to go out and look for a place, she filled a baggie with cheese and crackers, then sent a text to Mama. *I'm exploring neighborhoods and checking out possible rentals. I have no idea when I'll be back and will get something to eat while I'm out.* In other words, I haven't had a panic attack since I left LA, so quit worrying about me.

A born worrier, Starr was more than capable of doing that all by herself. After bundling up in the thick parka Mama had kept for the few times Starr visited and donning boots, gloves, and a hat, she tromped outside. Despite the bitter cold, it was a beautiful morning. The weak winter sun shone on the snow so that it glittered, and the smell of cold clean air invigorated her. She hadn't realized how much she'd missed winter. Who'd have guessed?

Jack Frost had shrouded the windows of the reliable Honda Civic she'd driven some twelve-hundred-plus miles from LA. Before she scraped them clean, she turned on the engine to warm up the car. When she finished the job, she was sweating and tired. No doubt partly due to the physical damage caused by too much stress over too long a period of time. At least her appetite was coming back.

She didn't have snow tires yet, but had made an appointment for the following morning. No matter— she'd learned to drive in ice and snow years ago. Besides, most of the roads had been plowed and salted.

But where to start? With no idea, she decided to drive around and look for Available to Rent signs, including the neighborhoods in the north part of town, which was more woodsy and rural. Winter should be an easy time to find something.

Starr hoped.

The town had grown quite a bit since she'd last visited some years ago, and she relied on the GPS to navigate. She headed north, toward several new neighborhoods that'd sprung up while she'd been in LA. When she'd graduated from design school in New York and moved to LA to design costumes for Wes and other bands almost seven years earlier, the population of Miracle Falls had been roughly five thousand. Today, more than seven thousand people lived here, and the town was still growing.

While she was scouting around one of the areas in the north part of town, she noticed a two-lane road. Woodlawn Road, Dead End, the sign said. Why not take a look? Maybe she'd find something there.

Filled with a sense of adventure, an emotion she'd nearly forgotten for too long, she started down a rustic road. Evergreens and other trees with bare branches lined both sides. Exactly the rural-type area she wanted.

Houses peeking from between the trees were far and few between. No wonder the road hadn't been plowed. Driving was tricky, and she went at a snail's pace. Then, glimpsing a cottage through the trees and a Y in the road leading toward it, she quickly turned into the small driveway. Too fast for the ice and snow. With a mind of its own the Civic veered toward the snow-covered yard and plowed into a charming life-sized metal rendering of a dog. A sharp thud and hideous *screech* filled the air, knocking the dog down before the car abruptly stopped.

Oh, no! Tense and fearing a panic attack, she shut her eyes, drew in a calming breath and held it, then released it the way the relaxation therapist had coached her. To her relief, her chest barely felt tight, and she was able to breathe without struggling. No panic attack this time. A good sign. The airbag hadn't deployed, either, making exiting the car easy. Worried about the front end and the damage to the metal dog, she quickly tromped closer to check out both.

WANTING to work on his latest whimsical creation that morning, Brady Barton had convinced Toni, a trusted and experienced employee, to swap schedules. His father wouldn't like that, wasn't much for change and preferred that his schedules be meticulously maintained. But not counting holidays, Mondays were generally slow, and Brady saw no problem with going in after lunch. It meant working till closing at eight o'clock tonight, but he didn't mind.

A few months ago, a friend of a friend who lived in town had seen one of the whimsical animal sculptures he'd posted on his Instagram account, an occasional source of sales. She'd wanted one for herself and had purchased a playful cat. Yesterday, she'd contacted him and asked for another cat about the same size in a different pose. Brady had grinned. His first ever second sale, and from a local.

After discussing the details with her, he made a sketch of what he envisioned and emailed it to her. She loved the design, and he sent her a contract to finalize the details. He was anxious to get it made and delivered to her within a few weeks. Working fulltime at the store left him little time to get it done, which was why he rarely worked evenings and never weekends there.

He was welding pieces of scrap metal together when an unpleasant noise stopped him mid-meld. As far as he could tell, it'd come from the guesthouse at the back of his property. Filled with a sense of dread, he shut off the blowtorch, tugged off his heat-resistant gloves and set his safety glasses aside. In record time, he was out of his basement studio, pulling on his hat and winter gloves and shrugging into his coat enroute.

Trees and the tall privacy fence between the two places obscured the little cottage from view. Traversing the slippery, snow-crusted ground was treacherous. Thanks to the great traction on waterproof snow boots, he crossed the meadow and a narrow stand of trees, five hundred yards in all, then unlocked and opened the gate in the privacy fence without falling on his ass.

There he paused, silently noting a woman peering through the windows. What was she up to?

The woman— her car— was parked where his beloved sculpture had sat for the past eighteen months. It lay on its side, a metal found-object homage to Shep, the joyful Irish Setter and loyal companion he'd brought home from the pound when he'd graduated from college eleven years earlier. The dog had seen him through the divorce and after, until he'd passed on last fall. Just knowing it was there made Brady feel good.

She was up on the porch. He stayed still and watched her peer through the front windows, then head around to one side. Scowling, he advanced toward her. "What are you doing?"

He was angry and his voice gruff, reminding him of his

father. God keep him from turning into that. The woman let out an audible gasp and pivoted toward him. "Inhale," he swore she murmured. She took a deep breath, then scooped a handful of snow off the porch railing and formed it into a snowball. Her cheeks were red, her eyes narrowed in warning. "Don't come any closer."

Hadn't meant to scare her. He stood stock still. His first thought was that she was beautiful. High cheekbones, generous mouth and full lips. Tall, with long legs. His ex-wife Verity had been a looker, too, and had ripped his heart to shreds. His ex was a blonde, and this woman had black hair, make that shiny black, that fell past her shoulders. "Or you'll what— lob that snowball at me?"

She looked sheepish. "It's the only weapon I have. I used to play softball, and I have a good aim."

He admired her pluck. "Just tell me why you were looking through the windows like that."

"Who are you?" she asked.

"Uh-uh, you first. Answer my question and tell me what happened to my dog."

"You own that?" Her eyes widened. "I'm so sorry."

As she headed down the porch steps to the yard, he realized how tall she was. He was six foot two, and she was at most two or three inches shy of that.

"I didn't mean to plow into it," she added. "I'm scheduled to get snow tires tomorrow morning. Terrible timing, I know. I've been driving around, looking for a place to rent for the next seven weeks that I'm in town. I saw the Y in the road and took the turn into the driveway too fast. My car went renegade on me. This place," she gestured toward the one-story, "is exactly what I'm looking for. I was trying to find out if anyone was home. You didn't answer the door when I knocked."

"I don't just own the dog sculpture, I made it."

"No way. I'm impressed with your creativity and feel like such a twit for ruining it. You were saying?"

"I don't live here. Neither does anyone else. This is my guesthouse, and it's not for rent." Now and then, he thought about renting it out, and from time to time he opened it to visiting friends or relatives in both summer and winter, but most of the time it sat vacant. Which was fine with him.

"Oh." Her shoulders slumped as if she'd been defeated. "I'd better call my insurance company."

He moved toward the front end of the car and studied it. "From what I see, there's a minor dent in the fender. If that's the only damage and you report it, your premium could go up."

"Good point. At least let me pay for the sculpture."

"Irreplaceable, but you can reimburse me for the materials I used when I made it."

"So it means something to you."

She had no idea how much. "Everything I create means something to me. This one is an ode to my dog." He paused and shifted from one foot to the other. "He passed on last year."

Her face pinched in on itself, and she glanced down. "Now I feel even worse."

Good— she should. On the heels of the thought, he felt for her. She hadn't meant to knock it over. "Don't waste your guilt on me. I should be able to repair it." It wouldn't be the same, but if he'd learned one thing since the divorce, it was to man up and move on. "I'm Brady Barton," he said, extending his hand. "And you are?"

After squinting at his outstretched arm as if not sure she wanted to touch him even though they both wore gloves, she gave in and shook. Then quickly let go and stepped back. "Starr Dehl."

He knew that last name. "Any relation to Dahlia?"

"She's my sister. You know her?"

"I designed her engagement ring and her and Jake's wedding bands."

"I love that ring!" she said, her face lighting up. Her eyes, a dark brown, seemed to sparkle. "So you're the talented jeweler. Small world."

"Smallish town. That's me." It'd only taken his father two years to give in and let him try his hand at designing jewelry, currently the only part of the job he enjoyed. "The wedding isn't for a while yet," he said, wondering what she was doing in town this far in advance.

"I'm designing and making clothes for it— the matron of honor, bridesmaid dresses and wedding gown. It's easier to do the fittings here than in LA." She paused, looked away. "Plus, I needed time off from my job."

There was more to that story, he guessed. Maybe like him, she was unhappy with the day job. He wasn't going to ask. Her life wasn't his business and vice versa.

"The woods around here are so pretty," she said. "I really like this part of town. You don't happen to know of any places for rent in the area, by chance?"

Nope, and he wasn't about to offer the guesthouse. The last thing he needed was a neighbor, especially a beautiful female, knocking on his door about one thing or another. He shook his head. "I don't."

Time to get back to the studio and work a while longer before changing clothes and heading to the jewelry store. "I'm due at work soon. Why don't I turn your car around," he offered, to keep her from inflicting more damage to his property.

"That's probably a good idea." She handed him the key and stood on one of the porch steps while he maneuvered the vehicle, not so easy with those tires and the ice.

When the job was done, he returned her key. "Thanks," she said. She reached into the passenger seat and pulled a card from her purse. "Here's my contact info. Let me know what I owe you. Again, I'm truly sorry."

He stuffed the card in a pocket of his parka without glancing at it. "Take it easy out there," he advised. As soon as the car disappeared from view, he carefully collected the broken tribute to Shep and carried it to the studio.

CHAPTER 2

*B*rady wasn't exactly warm and friendly, Starr mused as she slowly drove back the way she'd come. But then, she'd crashed into the sculpture of his beloved dog and knocked it to the ground. She felt really bad about that and hoped he'd be able to repair it. That was as far as her feelings for him went.

Looks wise, he was okay, with a firm chin and a strong nose and nostrils that flared slightly when he was angry, irritated or both. But his piercing ice-blue eyes unnerved her.

Then why was she attracted to him? Because she was. For the simple reason that she hadn't been with a man in ages.

With the demands on her time, brief flings were all she had room for. But casual sex had never been what she wanted, and awhile back she'd made up her mind not to be with a man again unless an actual relationship was involved. Which was a joke, as she hadn't been romantically involved since Nathan. That relationship had lasted from her freshman year at Parsons through the first few years she'd found work as a professional designer, when Nathan had ditched her to go back to his former girlfriend. Even thinking about that put a sour taste in her mouth.

Now, at nearly thirty, she had no idea how to go about finding someone interested in her. A man nothing like gruff, terse Brady. So what if the genuine sorrow on his face when he mentioned his dog had touched her? His advice not to waste her guilt on him and to expect an increased insurance premium if she called in the fender bender had also been unexpected. Not that she needed to worry about money. Over the years Wes had paid her very well for driving her relentlessly, and she'd put away a fair amount. But she didn't want to waste it on pricier insurance.

She liked what she'd seen through the windows of the guesthouse, the modern-looking kitchen and living room big enough for an arm chair, ottoman, and a sofa. A fireplace, too. She'd always dreamed of living somewhere with a fireplace.

It wouldn't be there. Was it any wonder he didn't like her? After what she'd done to his sculpture, she didn't blame him. Never mind, there were plenty of other streets and neighborhoods to check out. Not today. She'd wait till tomorrow, after the new tires were installed.

There was still time to sew before Mama got home, but Starr wasn't in the mood. She decided to clean the house instead and take care of dinner tonight. Something good from a takeout place. That is, if the woman planned to be home.

As soon as she parked in front of the house, she texted Mama. *Did you get the text I sent this morning? I'm home now. I haven't seen much of you and hope you'll be here for dinner tonight. What should I pick up?*

Moments later, her cell rang. "That was fast," she answered. "Hope I'm not bothering you."

"I'm taking a coffee break. Yes, I saw your text. Are you having a good day? Did you enjoy exploring?"

Starr made a face at the solicitous tone. No, she hadn't had a panic attack. "It's been interesting. I'll tell you about it when you get home. What do you want to eat tonight?"

"Starr, honey, I won't be home till late. This is my night to meet with the quilting club, and we always have dinner first."

"Oh, okay." Starr couldn't hide her disappointment. She wanted to share her day over a meal and then watch a show together, the way they sometimes had when she and her sisters had lived here.

"Didn't you see my note?" Mama asked.

"What note?"

"The one I left on the kitchen counter near the coffee maker."

Starr headed into the kitchen. "It's not here."

"Yes, it is. Look again."

She checked the counters, on and under the kitchen table, and around all the fixed and moveable appliances. "There's no sign of it."

"Well, I never. Hold on a minute."

She heard a rustling sound. "What are you doing, Mama?"

"Looking through my purse. Here it is, in the pocket where I keep the car keys. I don't know how that happened. I was in a hurry this morning and distracted, I guess. Anyway, don't expect me home till after ten. Help yourself to anything from the fridge."

Next, Starr tried Sunshine at Nourish, the popular spa she owned. Her sister wasn't in, but she did manage to score a massage for the following morning. Which she badly needed. For the past few years in LA, she'd been too busy to spend the time on herself and could hardly wait. Then she tried Dahlia, who answered.

"Hey, Starr. What's up?"

"Do you want to meet someplace for dinner? I had an interesting few hours today that I want to talk about. Jake's welcome to join us."

"That's sweet. I would, but we're having dinner with a prospective client. From time to time, we do that." A few years ago, they'd opened Dehl and Palladino Public Relations, and the marketing and promotions company was doing really well. "Maybe later in the week? I so love that you're here and that we can spend time together. If you want to talk I'm free now."

That'd do. "Great. Wait'll I tell you about my morning." Starr explained about driving around, the minor fender bender and meeting Brady Barton.

"Brady's great," Dahlia said.

"He was pretty grumpy to me, but after what happened he had every right to be."

"I guess so. Normally, he's warm and friendly. And good-looking, don't you think?"

Not with a scowl on his face and those cold eyes. "What does that have to do with anything?" Starr asked.

"Just sayin'. I don't know a thing about his personal life except that he's divorced. I didn't even know about the art thing till right now."

Divorced. Maybe that had something to do with his crabbiness. "I'm not interested in his personal life, and I know he feels the same about me. What I am interested in is the guesthouse on his property. It's the cutest! He has a huge lot and lives a fair distance from it. I think. There's a tall privacy fence and trees in front of it, and I couldn't really tell. I so wanted to see inside the guesthouse and possibly rent it, but it's not available."

"That's a shame," Dahlia said. "What's on the agenda for tonight?"

"I'd planned on treating Mama to a meal, but she has a dinner and quilting thing. She said she wrote me a note about that and left it while I was still in bed. I never saw it because as it turns out, she put it in her purse instead of leaving it on the counter."

Dahlia paused. "Get used to it."

"What do you mean?"

"Lately, she's been too darn busy. This past weekend was great, but family get-togethers are far and few between and sometimes forgotten."

Being equally busy with her job, Starr understood. "She has a lot on her plate."

"She always has but didn't used to be like she is now."

Starr frowned. "Are you worried?"

"No, just confused. Why is she running herself ragged socializing?"

"That's a good question. Tell me, is the Corner Café as good as it used to be?'

"Is snow white? It's still one of my favorite places to eat. This is the slow season, but it'll probably be crowded anyway. If it were me, I'd go there. Oh, and Main Street has added two women's boutiques with clothes that Sunshine and I love. Not that you'd buy any— you make your own clothes and they're fabulous. But just in case..." Dahlia gave her the names. "Why don't you get in touch with Robin and Savannah? The three of you used to have so much fun together. I'm sure they're looking forward to seeing you."

As much as Starr wanted to get together at some point, she wasn't quite ready. They'd expect updates on Wes, her health and her career, stuff she didn't want to talk about. "I'm not in the mood to play catch-up right now. Thanks for the shopping tip. I'll order something to go from the Corner Café and do some browsing while I wait. After dinner, I'll be working on your wedding dress."

Too bad there wasn't a place for her to spread things out and sew without worrying about cleaning up at the end of the day. The bedroom she'd once shared with Sunshine was too small, and the tiny room where Dahlia had slept, which was about as big as the closet in Starr's Brentwood townhouse, was now used for storage. It was amazing the three of them had fit into Mama's little home.

"Yay on my dress! The Corner Café is only a few blocks south of Joseph Barton Jewelry."

"And you're telling me this why?" Starr asked.

"In case you're in the mood to browse jewelry. There are some beautiful pieces in there."

"I don't need anything. Brady's last name is Barton. Any relation?"

"Yep. He's slated to run the place when his father Joseph retires. He pretty much runs it now."

They schmoozed a while longer before disconnecting.

After checking the Corner Café menu online, Starr placed an order for an hour from now, which gave her time to check out the new shops before darkness fell around four-thirty. She visited Monique and Little Black Dress, the two boutiques Dahlia had recommended. She liked both. Maybe she'd come back another day, when she had snow tires and wouldn't have to worry about driving in the dark.

Then she glanced up Main Street. The Joseph Barton Jeweler sign across the street caught her eye. It was classy, with a gold frame and black lettering. Without intending to, she crossed to that side, aimed for the store and peeked through the window. The light in there made it easy to see inside. A few customers were milling around. Brady was there, too. Unlike the jeans and thick parka he'd worn this morning, he was dressed in a sportscoat and a pale-blue shirt open at the collar. Without the bulky parka, she was able to see his broad shoulders.

Another employee, a female who looked to be in her twenties, stood behind the counter.

For some unexplainable reason, Starr watched him work with a gray-haired woman. He smiled a lot, which certainly improved his looks, and set the customer's purchase in a small box which he placed in a shopping bag. Moments later, she exited through the door with a pleased expression.

Suddenly, as if he sensed Starr staring, he glanced out the window and stared back with his brows raised a fraction. Even from outside, the ice-blue eyes were hard to miss. Talk about embarrassing. She wanted to dart away but forced a smile and a wave. Then, feeling the heat on her cheeks, she recrossed the street and headed for the Corner Café.

* * *

MUTTERING SOMETHING ABOUT NEEDING A PICK-ME-UP, Brady left the store and Isabella, one of the part-timers, and headed after Starr. She was a fast walker, her long legs churning as if she were eager to move far, far away from the jewelry store. From him.

Why had she stood outside the store and stared through the window?

No slouch when it came to striding fast, he caught up with her a block away. "Hey, Starr," he called out, loud enough to make sure she heard.

She spun around, her breath visible in the cold. "Hi."

"I saw you standing outside the store. What's up with that?"

"I was in the area and curious to see it," she said and fiddled with the zipper of her jacket. "Is that a crime?"

"You could've come in, you know."

"You were helping someone, and I didn't want to bother you when I'm not planning to buy anything."

If she thought all he cared about was making sales, she was way off-base. "People are always coming in to browse. Doesn't matter to me whether they buy or not. I was planning to call you later and pulled out your card. You mentioned designing clothes for the wedding, but not that you do it for a living."

She squared up and raised her chin as if defending herself. He had no idea why. Could be that she didn't like talking to him. He told himself he didn't care but was stung anyway.

"It wasn't that kind of conversation," she said. "But yes, that's what I do."

"You mentioned that you sewed, but not that you make a living at it. I've never met anyone who does that. I'm impressed."

"It's interesting, for sure. As I mentioned this morning, I feel that way about your art. I don't sew for just anyone. For the past almost five years, my focus has been designing stage clothes for Wes Mason."

"The Wiglets singer. Cool."

"Yes. Is there a reason why you followed me tonight?"

"You waved at me through the front window and then took off, and I got curious, too. You seem to do a lot of peeping through windows."

"I swear, I don't do it often." She bit her lip.

"Twice so far since we met this morning. I came after you because I have something to tell you and figured I may as well do it in person. I checked and have plenty of scrap metal and fasteners in my workshop to repair Shep. What I'm saying is, you don't owe me a dime."

"That's good news. But time is money, too, so if you change your mind..." She blew on her gloved fingers and shoved them into her jacket pockets. "It's cold and I want to pick up my dinner at the Corner Café and get home before dark, since I won't have the snow tires till tomorrow."

He seconded her taste in food. "Good idea. It's a great place to eat. "I should get back to the store." He meant for the conversation to end there, but the offer he'd entertained and rejected since their meeting that morning spilled out of his mouth instead. "If the guesthouse were available, you'd need it for seven or so weeks. Do I have that right?"

Her jaw dropped. "You're telling me I can rent it?"

"Don't put words in my mouth. You haven't seen the inside. When you do, you may not want it. Or I might change my mind and need it myself. You said seven or so weeks?" he repeated.

She glanced upward at the darkening sky, her forehead

wrinkled in thought, then nodded. "Yes, and I'll pay whatever you charge."

"That's no way to negotiate. What if I asked for five figures or a bespoke suit?"

She gave him a dirty look. "You'd do that?"

"No, but you ought to be careful. There are plenty of people around happy to take advantage of you."

She scoffed. "I'm not an idiot. I've been around the block once or twice. But you're right, I shouldn't have said that. What I meant was, paying rent won't be a problem. Can we try this again?'

"Why not. If the guesthouse were available, how long would you want to stay?"

"Seven weeks or so. But as you said, I might change my mind after I do a walk-through." The corners of her mouth tilted up. "Was that better?"

"Much."

"When can I see it?"

He paused and thought about that. "What time are you getting those snow tires tomorrow?"

"Nine o'clock. I have another appointment at ten."

"The store opens at nine-thirty."

"How about after work?" she said. "With snow tires, driving in the dark won't be so risky."

"Can't— I have plans then."

She looked almost envious. "At least one of us does."

"It's not as good as it sounds. I'm having dinner at my parents' house."

"You don't look happy about that."

He shrugged. "You know how it is with moms and dads. They nag, they lecture." Mostly his father.

"At least you have them. I never knew my father, and my mother died when I was seven."

Oh, man. In all the meetings he'd met with Dahlia and Jake, that subject hadn't come up. He felt for Starr. "I'm sorry."

"Yeah, that was a rough time. But things turned out all right for my sisters and me. Our mom's best friend, who we call Mama J, took us in an gave us lots of love. Can I see the guesthouse Thursday instead? I'll come any time."

"I should leave for work around eight-thirty, so eight o'clock? Text when you arrive and I'll come right over."

"Great."

The genuine smile that bloomed on her face turned her from striking to incredibly beautiful and wowed him. Not welcoming or wanting the feeling, he quickly turned away.

CHAPTER 3

*S*tarr was lying in bed waking up when the alarm she'd set went off. Too tired to wait up for Mama to get home from her quilting and dinner thing the previous evening, she'd fallen asleep early. Since arriving in Miracle Falls she'd been sleeping a lot, catching up after years of late nights and early mornings spent keeping her boss happy. This was the day to get the snow tires and a massage, and she didn't want to be late for either. She also wanted to tell Mama about the guesthouse she might be renting. Fingers crossed.

Mama was dressed for work and making herself breakfast. She seemed surprised to see Starr. "What are you doing up so early?"

"I went to bed at nine last night and slept enough. I also have that snow tire appointment."

A blank look. "You're getting those today?"

Starr recalled mentioning it after she'd scheduled it the day before yesterday. If the tables were turned, she likely wouldn't remember the day and time, either. "When I finish there, I'm getting a massage at Nourish."

"Wonderful. You'll leave the spa so relaxed." Starr pulled a mug from the cabinet and made a beeline to the coffee machine. Mama smiled at her. "You look much better than you did when you first arrived."

Starr thought so, too. "I've been eating and sleeping really well."

"No thanks to me. I'm sorry I haven't cooked much for you. Between work and my social schedule, this has been a packed week. And it's only half over."

No wonder she seemed forgetful. Whenever Starr was swamped with sewing, designing or redoing yet another outfit Wes didn't care for while she also managed the two seamstresses she'd hired to help with the nonstop fix this, do that, come up with something different, she'd been just as absent-minded. "Are you kidding? When I showed up over the weekend, you cooked both Saturday and Sunday. I don't expect anything more. I'm not sick, I'm stressed and feeling a lot better. Have I mentioned how much I like your hair style and the natural color?"

Mama touched her short 'do. "Thanks. I like it, too. You don't think it makes me look older than sixty?"

She was touchy about entering a new decade. "Not at all. The silver streaks are elegant. Did you have a good time last night?" she asked, nursing her coffee while Mama ate and periodically checked her watch. She'd always been a stickler about getting to work before she needed to. Starr and her sisters were the same way.

"As fun and fulfilling as ever. I love spending time with my friends." She fixed Starr with a concerned frown. "Aren't you going to eat?"

She wished Mama would stop worrying about her. "I will,

I promise. I just woke up, and I'm not hungry yet. Can I tell you about yesterday?"

"Of course. Did you find any promising neighborhoods and maybe an apartment or two for rent?"

"As a matter of fact, I did." Starr told her about narrow Woodlawn Road, how the car skidded in the driveway of the little house that'd caught her eye, hitting Brady's dog statue, and the rest of the story. She didn't mention the instant and unwanted attraction she felt for him. She was the last unattached sister, and Mama wanted her to meet someone. She hadn't come here for that, especially when in approximately two months she'd be back in LA. At the very thought, her stomach clenched.

"Heavens," Mama said. "Was it that bad? I didn't even glance at your car. Is it all right, or at least in decent-enough shape to get those tires?"

Realizing she was grimacing, Starr composed her face and silently ordered herself to relax. Much better. "Barely a dent. Brady says it won't take much to fix the dog— he made it out of found metals or something. The guesthouse is empty right now. At first, he said he wouldn't rent it, but when I saw him last night—"

Mama's eyes widened. "He asked you out that fast?"

"Of course not. I stopped at the Corner Café, which is just a few blocks from the jewelry store—"

"Joseph Barton," Mama said. "That's where I got the thumb rings for you and your sisters after your mother passed."

"You did?" Starr doubted either of her sisters knew that interesting bit of information. She glanced at the thumb ring she never took off. Her sisters also wore theirs always. The three identical silver rings were similar to the one their mother had worn and been buried wearing. The single open knot symbolized an eternal bond between them. "Did he make them, too?"

"No, and I don't recall who did— an older employee who'd been there for years. That was, what? Let's see, you're twenty-nine and your mother passed when you were seven... Twenty-two years ago."

Starr wondered what Brady's father was like and why he didn't want to have dinner at the man's house. "Is it true that Mr. Barton still works there?" she asked.

"I don't keep up with that, but I recall Dahlia saying that Joseph had planned to retire a few years ago but apparently isn't ready. I'm sure Brady will tell you if you ask him. Back to you seeing him last night."

"Don't go getting any ideas, Mama. I'm not here to get involved with anyone, I'm here to rest, design and sew and be one of Dahlia's bridesmaids." Also to mellow out and not worry so much. "Okay?"

With her mouth full, Mama didn't answer. "We only talked for a little while," Starr went on. Long enough that the attraction continued and her cheeks burned hot in the cold air, but Mama didn't need to know that. "He said he'd changed his mind about renting the guesthouse. I'll be doing a walk-through tomorrow morning. The outside is charming. Let's hope the inside is the same."

She thought of something else. "It might not work at all. To hedge my bets, after lunch today I think I'll look at other neighborhoods." Which might be better anyway, as living almost in a landlord's backyard wasn't the best idea. For now, she'd push the house and its attractive owner from her mind.

"Very wise." Mama checked her watch again. "Goodness,

look at the time. I called a meeting this morning and I don't want to be the last one to arrive." She stood and started to clear her dishes.

"Let me do that," Starr offered.

"If you don't mind."

"Not at all. I hope you make it on time."

"Me, too. Enjoy that massage, and have a wonderful day." Mama opened her arms. Despite the six plus-inch difference in their heights, the hug enveloped Starr in warmth and love. In her mind, her short Mama was a giant of a person. "I'm so glad you've come home."

"For a little while," Starr reminded her, because she didn't want her getting her hopes up, which she might. Mama left, and she headed for the bathroom to shower and dress. Then she made herself a hearty breakfast and cleaned up the dishes, all without a single thought about Brady. Not long after that, she headed for the tire shop.

With any luck, she wouldn't think about him for the rest of the day.

STARR HADN'T BEEN in Nourish Spa since a few months after Sunshine had opened the doors over seven years earlier— way too long since her last visit home. Even after all this time, the moment she entered the building she felt welcome and comfortable. It smelled good in here, soothing. Merchandise for sale on the shelves and skin-care products in a locked case behind the check-in area made her want to browse and buy. Credit Sunshine for that. She had a real talent for knowing what customers needed and wanted.

The person at the front desk, a friendly woman who looked about Starr's age, greeted her with a smile. "Welcome, Starr. I'm Maddy. Your sister is expecting you. Do you know where her office is?"

"On the opposite side of this floor, I think."

"The door on the right. Before you go, let me get you signed in for your massage. There's no rush— you have another twenty minutes— but I want to let your masseuse know."

As Starr crossed the spa some minutes later, the door to her sister's office opened and Sunshine came toward her. At five-foot four in flats she was roughly the same height as Mama. And beautiful, blessed with blue eyes and light-brown hair that formed soft curls around her heart-shaped face. Whereas Starr was tall, with brown eyes and straight dark hair.

Hard to believe they were sisters, and yet they were. The birth certificates of each of them stated the father as unknown. For all they knew, the three of them had different fathers. Mama had no idea, either. As yet, none had been curious enough to find out through Ancestry or other genealogical test companies.

Starr had seen both sisters Saturday when Mama had hosted a dinner for them and their boyfriends. She'd known Jake since he and Dahlia had dated in high school. She liked him. Trevor seemed nice, too. Her turn was coming sometime in the future. She hoped.

"Hey, you," Sunshine said. "You look healthier than you did over the weekend."

"Mama said the same thing. I certainly feel better."

"How are the dresses coming along?"

"I haven't worked much on them— I don't have enough room at Mama's— but once I get an apartment and can spread out some, I'll make great progress." She told Sunshine about Brady and the guesthouse. Before Sunshine could ask questions, the phone rang.

"Hang on," Sunshine said and answered. "Thanks, I'll tell her." She disconnected. "It's time to get ready for your massage. I'll give you the changeroom instructions. Let's have lunch or dinner soon."

"I'd love that." Humming, Starr headed for the changing room, already anticipating the treat in store for her.

Some hours later, more relaxed than she'd been in forever, she stopped for fast food. When she finished she drove around and checked out the neighborhoods listed on Air B&B that offered monthly rentals. She jotted down her top choices and tried to get excited but couldn't work up much enthusiasm.

Despite the nice neighborhoods and descriptions of available rentals anyone would jump at, she still wanted the guesthouse. An impossibility. Yet later, after she pulled up Mama's driveway and shut off the engine, she sat in the car, clasped her thumb ring and asked for what she wanted. "Please, let me rent the guesthouse." A silly plea.

Feeling ridiculous and determined to find an alternative to the guesthouse, she headed inside and ranked her top choices.

CHAPTER 4

*a*fter work Wednesday, Brady stopped to pick up a few items before heading for his parents' house. They lived in a swanky part of town, some five miles west of Main Street. Not that far from the jewelry store, and he pulled into the driveway right on time. The front light was on, and despite the drawn drapes it was obvious that the house was lit up inside.

Dinner with the parents was always dicey, with the tone of the evening dependent on Joseph Senior, who Brady privately referred to as "Senior." Now if Joe, Brady's older brother, were here, tonight would be a different story. The favored first-born, Joe had been slated to run the jewelry business, which had passed from father to son since it'd opened some decades earlier. Senior had subscribed to the seriously outdated tradition, or had until Joe had fallen for an exchange student from New Zealand during her junior year abroad at Princeton.

She'd stayed around the following summer to be with Joe, then returned home. As soon as he graduated senior year, he'd left to marry her and settle there instead of taking over the business. Leaving Brady stuck with the job he cared about although not that much since Senior hadn't wanted him there. Art was his thing. Still, he wanted to make his father proud and did his best to fill his brother's would-be shoes. With Joe at the top of the ladder and Brady on a lower rung, an impossible situation.

Filled with dread and armed with bribes— fresh-cut flowers from his mom's preferred florist and a bottle of Glen-Dronach 15 Revival Single Malt, his father's favorite imported scotch, he rang the doorbell with his elbow.

Moments later, his mother answered the door and ushered him in. The opposite of stoic Senior, she was openly pleased when he came for dinner and greeted him with a kiss on the cheek. As always, his father shook his hand. At one time they'd been the same height, but in the past year or so, Senior seemed to have shrunk a bit. At sixty-seven, that was to be expected. Or so Brady had heard.

His father flashed a rare smile. "Thanks for the scotch, son. I love this stuff. Join me in a drink?"

It was always good to score a few brownie points. Brady returned the smile. "You bet. Smells good in here," he said while his father opened the bottle and poured two fingers each into a pair of shot glasses.

"Dinner may be a bit late," his mother announced after they both sat down and smacked their lips. "I got a little behind when we Skyped with Joe, Jessica and the grandkids."

That explained dear ol' dad's good mood. Brady was sorry they hadn't invited him to join in the call. But with the nineteen hour time difference between here and there, he'd been at work. It didn't really matter anyway, as he and Joe texted several times a week and occasionally Skyped. They hadn't Skyped in too long, though, and Brady made up his mind to remedy that in the near future. "That's great. How's he doing, and how are my niece and nephew?"

"As usual, he's very busy," she said. "There's always a lot to do at the ranch. It was nice that he and Jessica were able to visit with us for a little while. Their kids are so cute. Lydia's about to turn three. She's full of chatter. Stuart has learned to walk and is toddling around all over the place. He adores his big sister and looks up to her the same way you did Joe from the time you were crawling."

So true. Texts were fine but couldn't fill the gap caused by his brother's absence. Brady missed him and envied him for going after what he wanted instead of sticking around to please Senior.

"I know you two are in regular contact," his mother said. "When he mentioned you, I told him you're doing a great job at the store."

On that note, his father turned somber. He hadn't forgiven his namesake for leaving the country instead of taking over the business. Sensing the good mood had vanished, Brady glanced at his mother. "Why don't I help with dinner?"

"There really isn't much to do. It'll be ready soon. Chat with your father while I finish up."

Making small talk with him was the last thing Brady wanted to do. But it was what it was, and he complied. "I expect you want to know about sales today," he said, and shared the numbers. "I can't speak for anything that happens tonight, but this was a reasonably busy day for January. The total sales were higher than they were on this day last year.

Also, two new customers commissioned me to design jewelry — an engagement ring for one and a diamond bracelet for the other." *Aren't you glad you finally let me take over the jewelry design part of the business?*

"Not bad." Senior nodded, which coming from him was praise. "I wasn't in yesterday, but I will be tomorrow and Friday."

He couldn't let go of the business and still spent three to four days a week at the store. He also weighed in heavily on hiring and promoting employees. Either he couldn't let go, still didn't trust Brady or both. Brady barely stifled his frustration. "You don't need to do that, sir. I'm managing very well on my own."

"I'll be there at nine."

"Why so early? We don't open till nine-thirty."

"I'll be there at nine."

"Whatever," Brady muttered, fighting to hide his irritation. "Fine with me if you want to open the store tomorrow. I'll come in the afternoon instead and work till closing." That way, he wouldn't feel rushed when Starr did her walk-through and would have time to work in the studio.

"That won't do. You came in late yesterday. You should be there on time or earlier."

The comment was both an order and a rebuke. Brady had expected as much. "Can't make it before nine. You know I'm often at the store well before it opens. Toni has been with the company for almost five years. She's competent and able to run the business when I'm not there and was happy to switch schedules. I think she ought to be promoted to assistant manager, don't you?"

Senior pursed his lips, an indicator that he had no interest

33

in discussing the matter. There the conversation ended. After a few tense moments, Brady's mother summoned them to dinner.

While they ate, Brady told them about Starr and her car crashing into the Shep sculpture. He omitted any information about her, including that he was considering renting her the guesthouse. Best to avoid negative comments about that from Senior. His mother voiced concern and wanted details about the damage to the artwork.

Brady told her, then set down his fork. "Is that why you came in late yesterday?" his father asked.

"No, I wanted to work in the studio on an artwork a customer commissioned. And a good thing I did. Otherwise, I wouldn't have been around when the accident happened."

"That's why you traded schedules with Toni?" Senior's snort was pure disapproval. "Your sole focus should be on the family business, not on your hobby."

It wasn't the first time Brady had heard that. "When I'm at work, it is. What I do on my own time doesn't take away from that. Creating art, including the jewelry I design for our customers, makes me happy." Kept him sane, too. "Both contribute to my doing so well at the store."

"Yes, but when you ask one of our employees to trade schedules with you for no legitimate reason, your focus is elsewhere."

In the interest of civility, Brady kept his mouth shut and let the comment slide. An uncomfortable silence fell, and his mother stood. "Who's ready for dessert?"

* * *

THURSDAY MORNING, determined not to be late to see the guesthouse, Starr left Mama's early. Thanks to several days of winter sun and the usual traffic, streets were mostly clear. Including Woodlawn Road, although by the snow piled on either side of the little driveway, it appeared to have been shoveled. Had Brady shown the house to someone else? Not likely, as he'd told her he didn't usually rent it out, but she worried anyway that he'd changed his mind. Like it or not, anxiety was part of her DNA.

Determined to push it aside, she pulled to a stop and took a few deep breaths. Calmer now, she glanced around. Aside from the cleared driveway, nothing had changed. No sign of the dog sculpture, just the empty space where it'd sat. The snow on the porch and railings seemed to have shrunk a bit.

She texted Brady that she'd arrived, then exited the car. The silence here was amazing, though as she stood near the car waiting for him, she noted sounds that had escaped her before. Squirrels scampering here and there over bare branches that creaked in the wind, a bird squawking high in the sky, its outstretched wings majestic in the wind. A hawk of some kind, or was it an eagle? The crunch of boots as Brady crossed the snow and opened the gate.

"Hey," he greeted. This time those ice-blue eyes were almost friendly, a hopeful sign that he hadn't changed his mind.

"Hi." She pointed upward. "Is that an eagle squawking?"

He glanced up and shook his head. "Eagles don't make a noise like that. It's a hawk."

"Whatever it is, wow. Just, wow."

"They're majestic birds, all right. The sounds and wildlife

around here are one reason I bought this property. That and the distance from neighbors. I like my privacy."

"Ah, you're an introvert."

"No, but I'm around people all day, and that gets tiring."

So he didn't want anyone bothering him. She filed that away for when— she was determined to think positive— she moved in. "How long have you lived here?"

"A little over two years."

Not long. Had he been married at the time?

"I moved here after the divorce," he said as if he'd read her mind.

Starr wanted details but refused to pry. "Thanks for shoveling the driveway."

"I did it just for you. Ready for the walk-through?"

Grumpy and private, but still a nice guy. More attracted to him than ever, she nodded. They headed up the steps. She wiped her feet on the front door mat and stood back while he did the same and unlocked the door.

"You probably saw the entry and living room on your nosy snoop the other day," he said.

The smile playing on his mouth softened the comment. "Glimpses only. You caught me before I got too nosy."

"I keep the heat inside pretty low, so it'll be cold in here. Probably smells musty, too."

He opened the door and nodded at her to go inside. As she passed him, she caught a whiff that smelled good. Something he shaved with? Whatever it was, she liked it. He was right about the house— it was cold and the air was stale.

Standing in the little entry, she let her gaze travel. Off-white paint on the walls and ceiling, lots of daylight through the windows. The red and navy striped armchair, brown leather ottoman and what appeared to be velvet navy sofa she'd noticed before. And the fireplace. Not gas, either, an actual wood-burning unit.

Be still my heart. "I covet that fireplace," she breathed, imagining pleasant evenings curled up in front of a cheerful blaze while she read or streamed something. "Does it work?"

"As far as I know. I've never tried it myself— I have one at my house— but family and friends from out of town who've tried it haven't complained." He checked his watch, a clear sign he wanted to leave for work soon. "Come on, I'll show you the rest."

She'd noticed the stove/oven combination in the small kitchen the other day. Now she saw a table for four in front of a window facing the rear of the house. A coffeemaker and a microwave sat on one counter above the dishwasher. Across the hall from the kitchen, a small utility room with a stacked washer and dryer. At the opposite end of the house, the bathroom and two modest bedrooms. The smaller one would make a perfect sewing room.

"I want this," she said.

He smiled. "So you said the other day."

"When it's right, you know it's right. What do I do now? Give you the deposit? Sign a short-term lease?"

He pulled a folded sheet of paper from his jacket pocket. "Here's a copy of the boilerplate rental contract I printed out this morning. I haven't had time to read through it myself, but I will. Take a look and get back to me with questions."

"Could we do that now?" she asked, eager to move in.

"I don't have time. My father has decided to show up at the

store at nine." His slight grimace told her what he thought about that. "I should get there before him."

"Dahlia mentioned that he was supposed to retire and let you take over, but he hasn't." His nose flared a fraction and she realized she'd said something she maybe wasn't supposed to know.

"What else did she tell you?"

"That's about it. Don't worry, she didn't give me any details about your divorce."

"She couldn't if she wanted to. I don't talk about that."

"That's twice in a few seconds I've irritated you. Sorry."

"Where did you get that idea?"

"Your nostrils flare when you're upset. They did the other day, too."

His eyes widened the tiniest fraction. "Observant, aren't you?"

"I work for Wes Mason— I have to be."

Brady nodded. "I read somewhere that he's temperamental."

Understatement of the year. "I can't really say. I signed an NDA."

"Working for a famous rockstar, I guess you would. Like I said, I have to leave. After you read the contract and figure out the changes you want to make, we'll go from there."

Starr was ready to move in now, but the suggestion made sense. "I'll do that as soon as I get home. I'm eager to get this done. I know you're in a rush, but do you have time to tell me how much the rent is and the amount you want for the damage deposit? I'll save any other questions for later."

He told her. Both seemed reasonable, cheap by LA standards. "I'm good with that," she said. "When can we get together again and finish this?"

"You don't waste time, do you?" He looked thoughtful. "I'll be at the store till six and don't have any plans for the evening. If you're free, let's meet someplace for drinks or dinner and finalize the details then."

She'd planned to sew tonight, needed to, but renting the cottage was too important to delay. As soon as she got back to Mama's she'd read the contract, then sew what she could. "I can do that. Corner Café, just after six?"

"See you then."

They shook hands. When she'd entered the guesthouse earlier, she'd taken off her gloves. He hadn't worn any. Despite the chill inside, his hand was warm and welcome against her cold skin. His eyes were also warm and surprisingly mesmerizing. She liked that way too much.

A moment later, he cleared his throat and broke his gaze. "Your hand is freezing."

"Yours is the opposite." Starr half hated to let go, but he was already disentangling himself. Darn her for the unexpected wayward feelings she had no business having. He was going to be her landlord, nothing else. Getting involved with him in any other way wasn't what she wanted.

She moved onto the porch. "Thanks for making time for this," she said to his back as he locked up.

As she descended the steps and headed toward the Civic, she was sure she felt his stare. Or was that her imagination? As much as she wanted to check, she didn't. A moment before she slid into the car, unable to stifle the urge, she turned to wave and managed a smile. He raised that warm hand and waved back, but remained solemn. She didn't blame him. The handshake had been awkward.

Right then, she changed her opinion of him. She agreed with Dahlia, he was good-looking, even wearing a neutral expression. Not that it mattered. She needed to forget about him and focus on sewing the wedding clothes.

But on the drive home, she forgot about sewing and thought about him and the guesthouse instead.

CHAPTER 5

*A*fter spending a trying work day under the watchful eye of his overbearing father, Brady wanted nothing more than to go home, guzzle a beer or two, and lose himself in crafting the cat his client had ordered. But having made other plans, he strode toward the Corner Café to meet Starr. A completely different way to get his mind off Senior that was welcome and also confusing.

She wasn't at all what she'd seemed the other day. She was surprisingly easy to talk to, and the expressions that flitted across her beautiful face were easy to read. The openness almost made him think she was straightforward and honest. But he was no fool, not after the way Verity had played him.

He was still smarting from the idiot he'd been. He'd always seen himself as a one-woman man with a solid marriage that lasted till one of them died when they were old. Unfortunately, he'd picked the wrong woman for that. Next time, at some point in the distant future, he'd spend a lot more effort getting to know someone before letting his heart get involved.

He wasn't about to trust Starr easily. To the point that he'd considered pulling a credit report on her and would've if she'd wanted to rent the place for more than two months.

What had possessed him to offer her the guesthouse in the first place?

He considered reneging, but backing out wasn't his nature. Besides, she'd been so excited. She'd make a lousy negotiator. For the first time in ages, he chuckled. Then caught himself and sobered. She wasn't bad at reading him, either, and he didn't like it. Although she'd come right out and told him about his nostrils this morning. He was still shaking his head, hadn't realized he did that until she pointed it out.

She was much better at reading him than Senior was. He didn't seem to notice Brady's irritation over being micromanaged. Or if he did, he let it roll off him.

As much as he wanted to make his father proud and earn his respect, he was sick and tired of being treated like an inexperienced school kid. But pleasing the man was important, plus he needed to earn a living.

Back to Starr. Was she also divorced? Did she have someone special waiting for her to hurry back to LA? She hadn't said, and her personal life wasn't his business. Yet here he was, wanting to know more about her. Solely because she was going to be his tenant. He had no interest in getting otherwise involved with her. The less he saw of her, the better. He intended to spell out the boundaries over dinner— he was hungry and needed to eat— including that she not bother him unless there was a problem with the house.

The Corner Café drew locals and tourists year 'round, including ski season. If it was crowded, they might have to wait for seats. Through the large front window he noted that the majority of tables were occupied.

He entered the restaurant, already salivating at the aroma of homecooked food. After taking off his coat and hanging it on the packed coat tree, he scanned the room for a place to sit. To his surprise, Starr had beat him there and was gesturing at him. Her smile dazzled him. As he made his way toward her, he couldn't help but return the greeting with a grin of his own. On the way, friends, acquaintances and customers greeted him. Including his close friend, Shane, who was with an attractive female who looked familiar but Brady wasn't sure. The guy went through women faster than water through a hole. Brady stopped to say hello.

"This is Aurelene," Shane said. "Meet Brady."

"We've met." She pointed to the bracelet on her wrist.

So that's why she looked familiar. "Looks good on you," Brady said. "You made the right choice."

She smiled. "Thanks."

Shane gestured at an empty chair. "You're welcome to join us."

"Can't— I have a business meeting."

His buddy followed his gaze. "Who's that?"

"Her name is Starr Dehl. She's Dahlia's older sister. And no, she's not a date. It's business. See ya."

Ignoring Shane's sly expression, he headed across the room.

"Why is that man looking at me?" Starr said when he sat down.

He glanced over his shoulder. "That's Shane. He thinks you're my date."

She snorted. "That's pretty funny."

Was he that bad? Brady frowned. "I don't see the humor in that."

"Well, I do. You're going to be my landlord, I hope. Anything more could be messy. Anyway, I'm not looking to date anyone while I'm here."

"Boyfriend back home?" he asked stiffly. She shook her head, and he relaxed. What was the matter with him? "I'm not dating, either, and Shane knows it." He set down his copy of the contract. "Did you read through this?"

"First thing when I got back to Mama J's. Can we order before we talk about that? I'm beyond hungry. Just before you came in, I asked the waitress for menus."

She was awful thin and looked like she could use a good meal. Maybe she'd been sick. Hadn't noticed when she was wearing a coat. "Good," he said. "I'm ready to eat, too."

They decided quickly, and he signaled the waitress. "Separate checks," Starr told her.

Brady didn't object. This was a business meeting.

After they enjoyed their chowder starters, he gestured at the contract. Starr pushed her bowl aside. "It seems decent enough, but I think we should specify that it's a month-to-month thing, and no more than two months. I don't expect to be here the full eight weeks, but just in case. If I leave earlier, I'll pay for the full second month."

After the main courses arrived, the conversation resumed.

"I thought about your leaving early, too," he said. "If you want to prorate the rent based on how many days you stay, I'm cool with that."

"Seven weeks is almost two full months, and as I said, I'll pay the full amount." She paused to chew a mouthful of her mac and cheese. "Don't you love the food here?"

"Sure do. This pot roast is excellent. Anything else about the contract?"

"I have a few questions. Are utilities included, what about wood for the fireplace, and when can I move in?"

He grinned at that.

"What did I say?" she said, frowning.

"Nothing you said. It's your reaction. You're so excited, you're sparkling. It's refreshing."

"No one ever said I sparkle or that I'm refreshing. I'll take it." She beamed at him.

Talk about a stunner. Friendly, too. As any person about to rent from a landlord usually was. Looks weren't everything, he reminded himself for what seemed the dozenth time since she'd barreled into his life. She had a healthy appetite. He enjoyed that, and figured if she'd been sick, she wasn't now.

Time to put an end to this meeting before he forgot he wasn't interested in her. Not long after he answered the questions and a few more that followed, the meal ended.

While they waited for their separate bills, he revised his contract to reflect the changes. They each initialed the amended information and signed on the bottom line. He agreed to get a copy to her, and she handed him a check which he pocketed.

"It came true at last," she said.

"What's that?"

"A silly little thing I do with my ring. I hold it and wish for something. It never works, or didn't till now."

Each to his own. That was that, and they stood to leave. Shane and Aurelene were still there and from what he saw, enjoying each other's company.

On the way to the coat tree, he nodded at them.

"Can I move in tomorrow?" Starr asked as they exited the restaurant.

"Slow down. Let me get my cleaning woman in there first."

"Does the house need that? From what I saw this morning, it looked okay to me."

"It hasn't been cleaned since friends of mine from out of town used it way back in the summer. Judy, the woman who cleans my place and the guesthouse, has already agreed to get it done in the morning."

"What time will she be done?"

"Impatient, aren't you?"

"You have no idea."

"Why the rush?"

"Mama J is super busy with her own life, and I don't want to put her out anymore. I also need my own space, where I can spread my work out."

Decent of her not to take advantage of the woman's hospitality. "Explain what you mean."

"I like to lay out the pattern pieces, preferably not on the floor. I brought a folding table with me, but there's no room to set it up at her place. I think it'll fit in the smaller room at the guesthouse. I'm going to use that as my work room."

"You've thought this all out, haven't you?" he said, impressed. "If you're in that big a hurry and that anxious, I'll ask her to finish before noon."

"Great. I tend to overdo the anxiety, and I'm working on that. I'm much better now that I'm away from LA. I'm eager to move in because I have a lot to do before the wedding, and I really need to get to it. Do you happen to have a key with you?"

"I didn't bring one, but I'll ask Judy to leave hers under the mat. I'll stick a copy of the contract in an envelope and leave it in the mailbox."

"Okay." She tugged strands of her shiny, thick hair through her fingers. "Or maybe I'll show up before noon. In case she finishes early."

"She's good at what she does. I'd appreciate it if you don't rush her. There's nothing worse than someone micromanaging you and breathing down your neck, making you feel less-than. Take it from me, I know what I'm talking about."

"I've managed my small team of seamstresses for three years and never once did that. I never will." She squinted at him as if trying to work something out. "I'm guessing that's what your father does to you." After a brief pause, she added, "An assumption I have no business making, and I apologize. It reminds me of Wes. When he does that, it's stifling." She shuddered, which was interesting. "Okay, I'll show up around noon."

She wandered toward her car, and Brady headed through the gate in the privacy fence. On the drive to work, he shook his head. He'd rented the guesthouse to a woman he was strongly attracted to when he didn't want to be, a tightly wound female much like Verity. But unlike his ex, Starr made him forget himself to the point that he'd forgotten to set down the boundaries he'd meant to lay out, mainly that he didn't want to be bothered unless it was an emergency. For the second time, he questioned his sanity in agreeing to rent to her.

* * *

STARR TRIED NOT to arrive too early at what she already thought of as her home for the next two months. She had breakfast with Mama, who seemed pleased for her. After enjoying a leisurely soak in the tub— the guesthouse had a shower only— she changed the sheets on the bed, gathered the dirty towels and laundered them. Next, she loaded her belongings into the Civic. She filled the tank with gas, then stopped at Beekman's and bought groceries. All that took time, yet she still managed to reach the guesthouse a good twenty minutes before noon. Too darned organized for her own good. If Judy was still there, she'd wait in the car.

As it happened, the cleaning woman was locking the door on her way out. Starr exited the Civic and introduced herself. She guessed Judy was in her fifties. "I'm looking forward to living here for a little while," she said.

"It's a decent place to live. Brady's a good man. So were the Elmquists."

"Previous owners?" Starr guessed.

"That's right. They built the main house and lived there for a good twenty years. Before that, this whole area was woods. Most of it still is."

"I noticed that. I'm guessing they built the guesthouse, too?"

"That's right. When I started working for them about six years ago, they were building it for their son and his wife and daughter for when they visited. They used it a few times, then Mrs. E. got sick. Poor woman had cancer. When she passed, her husband moved away to live closer to his son and family. Brady bought the property, and I was hired to clean it. That's how we met."

Judy was chatty. Maybe she knew more about him. "It's interesting that he's in the jewelry business and an artist, too," Starr said.

"He's good at both. A talented man. I like his art. I clean for the Wallaces on the other side of town. They have a sculpture of a horse of his about this tall," she used her hands to sketch a small object. "It sits on their mantlepiece. I'm real careful when I dust it. It isn't nearly as big as the sculpture of Shep, but it's every bit as good." She eyed the now-empty space in the yard. "I wonder what happened to it. He made it right after the poor dog was cremated."

She would have to ask. "I didn't have snow tires yet and skidded into it. Brady's going to fix it. Was Shep sick?" Starr wondered.

Judy shook her head. "It was his time. He was old and in a lot of pain. Brady loved that dog more than anything. I expect he was missing his ex-wife, too, and I imagine making the sculpture gave him comfort she wasn't around to give."

So he still had a thing for his ex. Like both Nathan and Jimmy from high school.. Starr tugged her merino wool slouch beanie over her ears and mused over this tidbit. It explained why he wasn't dating and probably meant that, despite a few warm looks at her, he had no interest in their getting together.

Where had that come from, when she felt the same toward him? No interest whatsoever now that she knew he still carried a torch for his former wife. Been there, done that. Twice.

Never again.

Such a relief that she didn't have to worry about any attraction between them. "Why didn't he put the Shep sculpture in his own yard?"

Judy shrugged. "You'd have to ask him. All I know is, that sculpture meant the world to him."

Feeling terrible again for what she'd done, Starr kicked the toe of her boot into the snow. "What happened was my fault. The road was slippery and I lost control of my car and knocked it down. Brady says it won't take much to fix."

"I hope that's true. What brought you all the way out here? Did you come here to see him? He doesn't usually invite a woman over except for the rare customer who needs to get their hands on his art right away." Judy gave her an appraising look. "It'd be nice if he was seeing someone."

"I'm not a customer, and we're definitely not dating. I'd never met him or seen his work until I skidded into it. I was looking for a place to rent, and this house caught my eye."

"It's a real nice place."

For the first time since exiting the car, Starr noticed a stack of wood near the door. "Did you put that here?" she asked.

"I don't get paid to do that. Brady did. He left a note for you in the kitchen, something about a fire."

Aww, so nice of him. Starr had the feeling Judy would hang around all day with the slightest bit of encouragement. But time was passing, and she was eager to take her things inside and get to work.

She said goodbye to the housecleaner, then began the process of moving in and setting up her sewing room.

CHAPTER 6

ondering if Starr had moved in, and more importantly wanting to tell her what he'd forgotten to say the night before, Brady phoned midafternoon, during a coffee break.

"All moved in?" he asked.

"I am. I met Judy. She's talkative."

This made him wary, not that the woman knew much about his personal life. Even if she did, there wasn't much to tell. "She can be. What'd she say?"

"I now know more than I wanted to about the couple who owned the house before you, and that one of the people she cleans for has a sculpture of yours."

Completely innocuous. "Did she mention that I'm a sloppy housekeeper?"

"Is that so?" Starr sounded amused. "She didn't say a word about that. She thinks the world of you and had nothing but good things to say."

"I like her, too. She's fast and thorough, and she stays out of my studio. The last thing I need is to have anyone tidying up and moving things around in there." The thought of anyone doing that bothered him.

"I guess I wouldn't want her in my work room, either. She did a great job with the guesthouse. It's spotless. Oh, and thanks for leaving some wood for me on the porch. How thoughtful of you."

Her gratitude made him feel good. "I know you're wanting a fire, and I happen to have a big woodpile here. Even bigger after I added to it last November when a tree was uprooted during a big snow."

"What a shame about the tree."

"Sure was. You grew up here and know how our winters are. Bet you haven't missed that."

"Big surprise to me, I have. I like the cold and snow. We don't get any of that in LA."

She had a point. He cocked his head. "I hear water running. Let me guess— either you're in the kitchen or doing laundry."

"No laundry yet. I came with a suitcase full of clean clothes. But yes, I'm in the kitchen, taking a break from sewing to sip a cup of tea. How's your day so far?"

"Not bad." Try dull. It was a slow, really slow day, and he wished he were working in his studio instead. "Did you find the contract?"

"In the mailbox, right where you said it'd be. I like this place and being out here in the country, Brady. I've only been here a few hours, and already I'm making progress on Dahlia's wedding dress."

There was a smile in her voice, and he found himself smiling in return. "So the quiet agrees with you?"

"I love it."

MY HEART BELONGS TO YOU

He laughed. "You sound so happy. And you thought I was the introvert."

"Believe me, I'm not one, either. I'm a people person, but there's something about the quiet and the scenery that lifts my spirits. You can't find that in LA. With no one but me here, I feel at peace. I'd forgotten how much I enjoy what I do for a living."

He envied her that, wished he felt the same about the jewelry business. "You're lucky."

"Aren't I?" Another smile in her voice. "Well, my teacup is empty. I should get back to work. Unless... Is there another reason you called besides to find out if I'm here?"

Good thing she'd asked. The instant she'd answered the phone, he'd gotten lost in listening to what she said and had forgotten why he'd called in the first place. "As a matter of fact, there is," he said, and cleared his throat. "Don't take this personally, all right? But please, don't call, text or knock on my door unless it's an emergency."

After a brief hesitation— was she taken aback?— she responded. "I'd never do that. The other day, you mentioned something about valuing your privacy. I'm the same way, yet for the last few years I've had far too little of it. Being here is a real treat."

Hadn't expected that and should've been relieved, not oddly disappointed that she wanted privacy, too. He scratched his head at that and thought about her comment. She must've been living with someone she didn't get along with. "Bad roommate?" he asked.

"No, a super-demanding boss." She paused. "Ack, I shouldn't keep saying negative stuff about him."

"NDA— right," he said, and imagined Wes bugging her day

and night. At least his father didn't go that far. "It's good that we're on the same page about the privacy thing."

"Yep. Bye, Brady."

She disconnected before he had a chance to respond in kind, like she couldn't wait for the conversation to end. Exactly the way he wanted it.

Then why was he frowning?

* * *

AFTER DINNER THAT NIGHT, Starr decided to relax in front of the fire. Brady had left newspaper and small pieces of wood in the hearth. So considerate of him. She wasn't sure why he hadn't used the bigger logs from the porch, but since it was there... May as well start small and build up. She found a match and struck it. The newspaper caught quickly, and as the flames caught on the wood she smiled to herself for all of two seconds.

Suddenly smoke gushed into the room. Her eyes watered, she coughed, and did the only thing she could think of. Rushed outside in the cold, leaving the door open so the smoke could get out, and phoned Brady.

To her relief, he answered right away. "You said not to call unless it's an emergency," she started, sounding breathless to her own ears. "This *is* an emergency. I need help now."

"What's the problem?" he asked, sounding somehow both concerned and annoyed.

At the moment, his attitude wasn't on her radar. "The living room is filling with smoke, and I don't know what to do."

"Did you open the damper stop?"

MY HEART BELONGS TO YOU

"What's a damper stop? All I know is, I'm standing on the front porch in my socks and no coat, freezing."

"Go get both and put them on. I'll be right over."

Worried about the sewing, she dashed inside and shut the door of the sewing room to keep the smoke out. Pausing only long enough to grab her coat and slide her feet into the slippers she'd left in the living room, she dashed outside again.

Brady arrived moments later. He must've run to get here so fast. Breathing hard, he left his boots near the mat outside and entered the house. Starr followed him. "You're right, it's pretty smoky." He grabbed one of the fire tools from the brass holder beside the fireplace and poked at what was left of the dwindling flames. "I'll bet money it's the damper stop," he said as he crouched down in front of the hearth.

Clueless, she joined him. "I still don't know what that is. Are you looking at it now?"

"The stop is a clamp that locks the damper open until you shut it. When it's open, the smoke goes up the chimney. Otherwise, it causes what we have here. Follow the poker and you'll see it."

So that's what the long tool was called. In order to see the end of the poker, Starr had to move closer to Brady. Despite the smoky odor, she caught a whiff of the shaving cream or whatever it was he used. Did he have to smell so good?

He pointed the poker toward the rear of the hearth. "That black lever is the damper." He set the poker beside the fireplace. "Hand me the right-handed glove in the metal basket beside the toolset, will you?" She did and he pulled it on. The thing reached half-way to his elbow.

"I wondered what the gloves are for," she said.

"They're heat resistant. The damper is likely hot and I

don't want to get burned. Watch this." He reached his gloved hand into the hearth and felt around. "It's definitely closed."

"I can't see up there. It's dark and there isn't enough room."

"Then move closer. Don't worry, I don't bite."

Maybe not, but his delicious scent and the warmth emanating from being so close proved a potent combination. Unwanted feelings, hot and dangerous, swirled inside her. Doing her best to focus on the hearth, not him, she watched as he manipulated the damper. "I'm pushing it back now. There, it's open." Instantly the remaining smoke rose up the chimney.

Starr realized her mouth had gaped wide and closed it. "I had no idea," she said, feeling like a complete dimwit.

"You grew up here and were so excited about building yourself a fire, I assumed you did."

"I wish. Mama didn't have a fireplace. Some of my friends did, but I never paid attention to how they prepped things before they made the fire." Starr groaned. "First, the sculpture accident, now this— I hope you know how bad I feel about both. I'm sorry I bothered you, Brady, and after you asked me to leave you alone."

"Knocking the sculpture over was an accident, and I've put it behind me. Tonight, you were right to call. Your timing was great— I'd just finished dinner. And now, you know what to do next time. A few more pointers. Before you go to bed or leave the house, be sure to close the fire curtain in case for some reason something pops and sends sparks onto the rug. When you wake up in the morning, check to make sure the fire is completely out, then shut the damper until you want to make another fire. That keeps the cold air out."

Not about to bother him ever again if she could help it,

Starr listened closely. "To make sure I do it right, I pull the lever outward."

"Exactly. Leave it that way. Then when you want another fire, open it again before you ever set a match to the newspaper."

"Got it," she said, chafing her arms. With the front door open, the room had grown much colder. "The smoke is gone. I think I'll close the door."

"Why don't you wait a few minutes to air it out in here." He ditched the glove and lobbed it into the metal basket.

"Good shot," she said and put her coat back on. "Can I ask you a question?"

"Shoot."

"I appreciate that you put newspaper and little pieces of wood in the hearth, but why didn't you use the logs on the porch, too?"

He gave her a funny look. "I get that you never learned how to make an indoor fire. What about a fire pit or a campfire outside on a clear night with the stars overhead?"

"Any firepits I've been around were started and maintained by other people. I've never built a campfire myself, either, but I toasted hotdogs over a beach fire when I was in high school." She'd enjoyed that. "What does that have to do with now?"

His brow wrinkled slightly and he studied her. "You really have no idea how to build a fire?"

"Sadly, I don't. It didn't seem that hard— light a match and that'd be that." Disappointed in herself, she sighed. "I guess enjoying this beautiful fireplace is out." She'd been so looking forward to using it while she stayed here.

"You're giving up? I won't let you. That'd be a shame."

His can-do attitude was contagious, and she raised her chin in determination. "You're right, I'm no quitter. I'm sure I can learn how on YouTube."

"A better way is to learn from someone who's in the same room with you."

"You're offering to teach me?" She couldn't help her excitement. "But you're busy. I wouldn't want to put you out." Hadn't she done enough of that already?

"Not a problem. Let's do it right now, while I'm here. Then I won't have to worry."

He stood and gave her a hand up. She felt the warmth of his firm clasp everywhere from her own hand to parts of her body that hadn't been touched in too long.

Unsure she wanted him to be here when she felt things she shouldn't, she frowned. "Don't you have to work in your studio tonight?"

"It'll keep. You need more kindling than I left for you. I have plenty at my place. Hang tight, and I'll be right back."

She didn't have time to think about that before he went out, put on his boots and started for the gate.

If anything romantic happened between them tonight, and she truly didn't want that, but if it did, it'd be a rebound reaction for him. No, thank you. Getting involved with him in any way other than as his tenant was out of the question. She'd call and tell him not to come back. That felt right, and she reached for her phone. Then put it down again. She wanted to learn how to make a fire the right way.

Never mind the heat simmering inside her. While he was gone, she'd pull herself together and forget all about the crush she had on him.

That shouldn't be too difficult. She hoped.

CHAPTER 7

*G*rateful for the pathway lights between the guesthouse and his place, Brady tromped through the gate to get more kindling for Starr. And questioned his sanity. Inviting himself to teach her the ins and outs of making a good fire? He shook his head. She didn't need him for that, could learn how through a YouTube like she'd mentioned.

What'd gotten into him?

No need to be a genius to figure that out— he was way too attracted to her. He regretted the offer and considered canceling, but changed his mind. Purely for safety reasons, he'd follow through. Then he wouldn't have to worry about another fire-related safety mishap. He'd stay just long enough to coach her through building a decent fire, then come straight back home.

Resolved, he loaded a fair amount of kindling into an empty grocery bag, added a pile of newspaper, and returned to the guesthouse.

She was standing at the window— no drapes drawn in the

brightly lit living room— and appeared to be watching for him. As he crossed the yard, she raised her hand and waved, like a lover waiting for him to come to her.

Shocked that for a split-second he'd enjoyed the idea, he shut it down with a dose of reality. He didn't know jack crap about her, except that she could design clothes and worked for Wes Mason. And a little about her family. An attractive woman like her had her pick of men. For all he knew, behind the pretty smile and big brown eyes, she was as devious and fickle as Verity.

The last thing he wanted was to get involved with her. Minimal contact, period, was more than enough.

Tell that to his sex-starved body. Fallout from the divorce had sapped his libido for over two long years, and regardless what his head told him, the rest of him was more than ready to rock'n'roll with Starr.

As he climbed the front steps, she opened the door. "After you left, I shut it because it was and is freezing in the house. I turned up the heat."

"It'll warm up fast, especially after you build a fire." Despite the below-freezing temperature, he was already too warm thanks to the heat sizzling inside him. "The airing out helped. It doesn't smell too bad in here."

She stared at the bag in his hand. "That's a lot of kindling."

"You won't need much of it tonight, but I'm assuming you'll use it up in no time. I tucked newspaper in here, too. If you build a fire often enough, you'll soon need more of both. Give me a sec to store most of this kindling beside the wood pile. I'll leave enough in the bag for tonight." He made quick work of the task, then returned to her. "Ready to start over with a new fire?"

"You want *me* to do that?" she said, twirling and untwirling a lock of hair around her finger and wearing the tightly pinched expression he'd seen the day they'd met.

"Well, yeah. You can't learn if you don't try. Don't worry, I'll be here to coach you the whole way." Then get the heck out of Dodge.

"All right, but I'm a little nervous."

Some minutes later, under his guidance, she started a small fire. "This is exactly what I did before, only now the damper stop is open." Her gaze followed the path of the smoke. "Look, it's going up the chimney. You have no idea how relieved I am. You're a good teacher, Brady. I'm surprised."

"What'd you think I was gonna do, get mad? Don't tell me my nostrils are flaring."

She laughed, a great improvement over the anxiety. "Not even a little. I didn't expect you'd be so patient."

Must've come off as the opposite. He wondered at that. "You're quick to learn and easy to coach. Keep an eye on how fast it burns," he advised and hunkered down beside her. "This kindling is good and dry. If it's too green— you want to use seasoned wood, not green when you make a fire— it burns slowly or doesn't catch at all. This stuff will burn up fast and could go out if you don't watch it. You don't want that, so feed it a little more kindling. Since it's burning so well, add a couple of the bigger pieces."

A few minutes later, satisfied with her progress, he went on. "Once the new kindling is going strong, add a log. But not too soon or you'll snuff it out. And don't add more than a log or two at a time or it might get too hot in here. You want to feed the fire slowly and stop feeding it in time to die down before you leave the house or go to bed."

Her forehead wrinkled a little. "So much to learn."

"You're catching on fast. In no time, you'll be a pro."

Soon she had a nice fire blazing in the hearth. "This is what I imagined would happen earlier tonight," she said, brushing her hands together and standing up.

He stood, too. "You did it, Starr. Good job." Now he could take off.

"My first fire ever. I'm not a fire-builder virgin anymore."

Standing proud, she turned toward him with a brilliant, 24-karat-gold smile, and he forgot about leaving.

"Thanks, Brady. Without you, I couldn't have done it." Either her flushed cheeks came from being close to the fire or she was blushing.

"Happy to initiate you in the joys of fire-making. Now I don't have to worry about you smoking the place up beyond repair."

"Very funny." She got quiet and seemed to be struggling with something.

"What are you worried about now?" he asked.

"I was thinking— do you want to stay a while and enjoy my first self-built fire with me? I can make popcorn. It's the least I can do."

He wanted to. A lot, and saw himself sitting beside her watching the dancing flames together. Sharing a bowl of popcorn and maybe more…

Bad, bad idea. "I appreciate the offer, but I should get to work on an order for a customer." Which was true but could've waited a day or two.

"Oh, of course." Her weak smile flickered, and the fire seemed somehow less cheerful. "I totally understand and hope what happened didn't put you behind schedule."

"Don't worry about that. Before I forget," he said and dug into his hip pocket for a key. "This unlocks the gate. It automatically locks again when it closes. Hold onto it in case you need it."

"Thanks, and good night, Brady."

WATCHING the fire and munching popcorn was fun, even if she was all alone, Starr told herself. Only it wasn't, not really. Could she help it if Brady had turned out to be a really good guy? She'd gotten past his gruff exterior and he was easy to be around, and she would've enjoyed sharing the popcorn and the fire with him.

Then again, it was a relief he'd chosen to leave, and much safer for her, now that she'd decided to really get to know a guy before getting physical. That part of her life was behind her. Besides, he was still pining for his ex-wife.

Yet despite both no-no's, being around him tonight had tested her resolve.

There was a moment when his smile had reached clear to his ice-blue eyes and they'd burned as warm as the blazing fire. Thinking about it now and the corresponding heat inside her body had stirred a longing she didn't want to feel. Not for him.

She was grateful for his help. Without it, she wouldn't have figured out what had gone wrong or how to fix it. He'd been a good sport about that, taking his time explaining how to make a fire that lasted and encouraging her as she went. But she wouldn't bother him again. She wasn't about to make a nuisance of herself or have him worrying that she depended on him. She didn't and wouldn't.

Something else she hadn't thought of till now and bonus for her, she hadn't come close to having a panic attack. Not even when smoke had flooded the living room and fear had sent her scurrying outside without a coat or shoes.

"Yay, me!" she said out loud.

With Brady gone, she felt... Starr struggled to put a name to the unfamiliar hollow feeling inside. Then it hit her. Lonely. She was lonely. How long had it been since she'd felt this way? Not for ages, and no wonder. Between Wes constantly riding her to get this done, do that and repeat, her need to manage her tiny staff, and the near nonstop travel to concerts all over the U.S. and the world, she'd been too busy to notice much of anything. Any solitude had been spent sleeping, with occasional meaningless sex. Ugh.

Now, long-neglected emotions crowded her chest. Yet it still felt empty. Crowded and empty at the same time. Imagine that.

The only way to get rid of the loneliness was to reach out to family and friends and have a real relationship with a man.

Maybe she'd start dating. Not while she was here, but when she got home. Finding time for that wouldn't be easy. In order for it to happen, she needed to make a few changes. Talk to Wes, convince him to hire another employee to share the workload and take someone else on tour so that she had more time to herself.

The mere thought of rejoining the rat race and dealing with the man behind it made her feel sick and threatened a dreaded panic attack. Refusing to suffer through that again, she pushed thoughts of the job and her boss from her mind and thought instead about tomorrow night.

After she and Brady had signed the rental agreement at the Corner Café and parted ways, she'd FaceTimed with Dahlia, Sunshine and Mama all at the same time and invited them to come over and see her temporary digs. Mama couldn't make it— she had plans with friends at a cheese and wine painting event —but Dahlia and Sunshine had eagerly agreed to come for takeout and a look at the sketches for their bridal party dresses. Also to decide on fabric that went with the dark green and bronze Dahlia had chosen for her dress and the overall color scheme. Starr planned to pick up fabric samples in the morning.

She'd gone a step further with the wedding dress. Between the hectic routine a few days before leaving LA, she'd talked with Dahlia about the style and color of dress she wanted and had followed up with a sketch she envisioned. After a bit of back-and-forthing, Dahlia had okayed the design. Working in the sewing room, Starr had begun stitching a mockup in muslin, which she always did before starting on the real thing.

That took care of tomorrow night. Now for Saturday. She'd been playing phone tag with Robin and Savannah, but was finally able to reach them both. Those were fun conversations, and by the time they ended, she felt somewhat reconnected. They each had kids and busy weekends scheduled, but they agreed to meet for lunch the following week.

Good enough. She went to bed feeling much better and ready for what she knew would be a good night's sleep.

CHAPTER 8

hen possible after work, Brady unwound with a pick-up basketball game at the Miracle Falls gym. As soon as he finished work Friday, he drove straight there to meet Shane. In the locker room, his bud was already suiting up. "I noticed some of the regulars on the court," Brady told him. "Looks like we're in for decent exercise."

"After sitting in front of the computer all day, I could use that." Shane tied his sneakers, then squinted at him. "I'm not the only one, man. You're as tense as a wire about to snap."

Thanks to another irritating day of being micromanaged by Senior. The man hadn't let up, not even when Brady warned him to back off. He really needed to blow off steam with a rigorous game, followed by relaxing with a beer and food someplace. "How can you tell? Are my nostrils flaring?"

"Huh?"

"According to Starr, I do that when I'm annoyed."

"Oh, really."

Brady didn't appreciate the guy's speculative smirk. "Spit it out, Shane. What are you implying?"

"She must really be checking you out."

"FYI, she pointed it out shortly after she crashed into the Shep sculpture."

"She did?"

"That's how we met." Brady explained.

"And you're renting the guesthouse to her." Shane shook his head as in, why would you do that?

"Yup." Not wanting to get too far into the weeds, Brady padlocked his locker and nodded at the door. "Let's get out there."

When they hit the showers a good hour or so later, he felt much better. "I needed that," he said, wadding up the stinky gym clothes and stuffing them into his duffle bag.

"I hear ya. I'm ready for a cold beer and dinner. Pizza Time or Chet's?"

As good as the pizza place was, it was miles away and sure to have a guaranteed waitlist for seats. "Chet's is closer to the gym and bigger so we'll be able to get a table." The sports bar also had good eats and a great selection of beer. "See you there."

They met up in the parking lot and headed inside. On almost every wall, big screens displayed sports competitions of all kinds. Being a Friday night, the place was busy, but as Brady had predicted they had no trouble finding a booth. They were both starving and settled in to watch a hockey game while enjoying a pitcher, bacon-wrapped jalapeños and parmesan tater tots. Next, they moved on to ribs, mac & cheese and coleslaw. Chocolate chip cookie sundaes for dessert.

Full and content at last, Brady sat back and rubbed his happy belly. "I feel like a new man."

"Can't beat good beer and good food. What's with Starr? Has she rammed into anything besides the Shep piece?" Shane cackled like he thought he was being clever.

"Good thing you're not a comedian. You'd flop."

"You never said why she rented your guesthouse."

"Her sister Dahlia's getting married. Starr is here to make the wedding dress and dresses for herself and the other women in the wedding."

"She sews, huh?"

Brady filled him in about the costumes she designed for Wes Mason. His bud seemed impressed. "How cool is that? Is she involved with Wes, maybe doing more than sewing for him?"

Shane could be a real jerk, but Brady refused to take the bait. Not about to divulge the few comments she'd made about her boss, who sounded demanding and hyper-vigilant, he shrugged. "All I know is, she works for the guy."

"Is she involved with anybody else?"

"We haven't talked about that stuff. Why would we?" Except when she'd said she wasn't dating. "She only moved in yesterday. Our conversations are about the guesthouse. Other than that, there's not much to say." That Brady cared to tell his friend. He didn't mind sharing about the little smoke problem, though. "There was an incident last night at the guesthouse."

"Oh, yeah?" Shane raised his eyebrows.

"One reason she wanted to rent it is the fireplace. She was excited about that but forgot to mention that she had no idea how to make a fire." Brady shook his head, remembering. "She didn't know about the damper and left it closed when she put a match to the paper and kindling I laid for her. I did that as a welcome, the same as I've always done for family and friends who visit during winter. I had to go over there and straighten out the situation. You wouldn't believe the smoke."

"Oh, man. She knocks the sculpture down, then screws up the fire? That's one accident-prone woman. I hope the smoke didn't mess the place up too much."

"At first it smelled, but it wasn't around long enough to do damage. Opening the doors and airing the place out took care of the stink."

Shane shook his head. "I'll bet she won't do that again. Wonder what kind of accident she'll have next."

"None, I hope. I taught her the ins and outs of fire making."

"What else did you do with her?" His friend flashed a knowing smile.

"Knock it off, will ya? Not a thing." If you didn't count fighting the urge to get real comfy with her in front of that fire.

"Don't BS me. You like her, and she likes you."

Brady snorted. "What gave you that idea? Like I said, we just met."

"Who cares when you met? The way you looked at each other at the Corner Café is a dead giveaway."

"You must be blind. That and your over-the-top imagination will get you into trouble. Unlike you, I don't put the make on a woman right away. There's nothing like that between her and me," Brady assured Shane— and himself. "You already know we were talking business. She was happy about the spare bedroom and has set up her sewing operation there. She didn't mind the rent, either, wrote out a check right there in the Café. She moved in yesterday, and last night I taught her to make a fire. End of story."

Not quite. Brady was unhappy about his overly warm reaction to her. She wasn't for him. He didn't want to talk about her anymore and did his best not to think about her.

"If you're not interested in her, maybe I'll give her a buzz."

He didn't care for that at all.

His bud sobered and held up both hands, palms out. "If looks could kill… Chill, Brady. I was pulling your chain."

"Well, stop. What's the deal with you and Aurelene? Tired of her already?"

"Not at all. I'm not one to predict the future, but so far, so good. I like her, and she seems to like me. The chemistry between us is crazy good." By the dopey expression on Shane's face, he was smitten.

Brady hadn't seen that before. Uh-oh. "How long have you known each other?"

"Almost three months. Why?"

"Just be careful, okay?"

"You think because you married Verity a few months after you met and then got burned for it, I will, too? Not gonna happen. You know me— I don't go in for that love stuff, and Aurelene knows it. She happens to be the same way."

Brady had his doubts, and his face must've given him away. Shane eyed him. "What's with you, Brady?"

"I don't want you to get hurt. Trust me, it sucks."

"I saw what it did to you. Why do you think I date a lot of different women and always have? Because it's risk-free. As long as I don't get serious, I can't get hurt. You ought to give it a try."

"Maybe I'm not ready. Anyway, it's not my thing." Brady changed the subject. "How's work?"

"Not bad. I got a nice raise this month, plus I'm up for a promotion."

"That's great." He envied the guy for that.

"How's business for you?" Shane asked.

"I sold another piece of art, a second purchase from a customer. She gave me a deposit, and I'm working on it now."

"Way to go. I meant your real job, the jewelry business."

"Don't ask."

"Your dad still on your back all the time?"

Miserable, Brady nodded. "I don't know how to get through to him. It's like he doesn't trust me. I'm thirty-two years old and I've worked on and off in that store from the age of fourteen. I've pretty much run the business since Joe left, but you'd never know it."

Brady was so fed up, he wanted to walk out. Of course he wouldn't, and Senior knew it. Joseph Barton's Fine Jewelry was and always had been family-owned, and Brady was proud of the store's reputation and success. He even liked working there when his father wasn't around.

But if Senior continued to dog him… He wasn't sure how much more he could take.

Thank God for art. Creating it kept him sane.

When he got home later, still needing to vent, he texted his brother, the only person besides his mom who understood.

* * *

STARR HAD BARELY FINISHED STITCHING the muslin mockup of Dahlia's wedding gown when the bride-to-be and Sunshine knocked at her door Friday evening. Once her sister tried it on for fit and Starr adjusted and marked the sizing, she'd start work on the real thing. But first things first.

Her sisters had brought wine and dessert. Starr had ordered takeout and expected it to be delivered soon. "While we wait for the food, I'll show you around my temporary home."

"What a darling place," Dahlia gushed as Starr led them through the guesthouse.

"You did good renting this," Sunshine seconded. "Too bad Mama isn't here."

Starr spread her arms in a what-can-you do? gesture. "Between her job and all the stuff she does afterward, she's super busy. I never realized how busy till this past week. Bridge, quilting, wine and cheese tastings, movie watching with friends, and who knows what else. Every single night it's something different. Keeping track of which event on what night and who with would drive anybody crazy, even with the help of a calendar. That's probably why she seems forgetful. What's with all that socializing, anyway? She's always had friends she gets together with, but she never used to be this busy."

Her sisters shook their heads and looked as puzzled as she was. "Or forget anything, especially getting together with one of us," Sunshine said. "Not long ago, I invited her out for drinks after work because we hadn't seen each other in a while. She forgot."

Dahlia nodded. "She did that to me when I asked her to help me pick out flowers for the wedding. The Mama J we grew up with would've jumped at that. When she didn't show up, I thought something bad had happened and called her. She was out to dinner with friends. She apologized and said it'd slipped her mind."

Starr didn't like what she was hearing. "That's not good. I wish we knew what's up with her."

"That makes three of us," Sunshine said. "Let's continue to keep each other posted, okay?"

"You haven't kept me posted. Why didn't one of you tell me about this when I was in LA?"

"It's a newish thing that started a few months ago," Dahlia said. "At first, we didn't think it was any big deal. From time to time, we all forget things."

Sunshine nodded. "I know I do."

"Then, when it started happening more often, you were traveling or working," Dahlia went on. "When we did have a chance to talk, it was about my wedding or Sunshine's hottie boyfriend Trevor. A lot of the time, Mama was on the call with us, and it didn't seem like a good idea to bring it up. I don't think she's forgetful about other parts of her life." A pause. "Which reminds me, about then you were having panic attacks you failed to mention until just before you came home."

"I was too scared to talk about that till I knew what it was," Starr said. She felt guilty for putting her work life, which she'd long considered her everything, first. "I was wrong not to tell you. We used to be so close. I've missed that so much. I swear I'm turning over a new leaf— I promise to get in touch a lot more often. Let's make a pact to do that. So please, from now on, no matter how busy I am or where I am, send me an SOS and keep me in the loop."

"You're here now, so that'll be easy," Sunshine said. "When you're back in LA, we'll definitely share more often."

Starr's stomach gurgled. She checked her watch. "Dinner won't be here for another thirty minutes. Are you as hungry as I am?"

"You're always hungry lately, and I'm glad," Dahlia said.

Sunshine nodded. "You look healthier than you did at the spa the other day."

"I'm getting there. Good news, Dahlia, I finished the muslin mockup of your wedding dress. Do you want to try it on while we wait for the food? I want to see if it fits and mark any changes. By the time we finish, dinner should be here."

Dahlia was giddy with excitement, and with Sunshine watching, Starr got to work.

Mere minutes after she marked the changes and helped Dahlia out of the muslin, the doorbell rang. The food had arrived at last. They ate, sipped wine and laughed, which felt so good. Starr told them about the fire fiasco from the previous night.

"I felt like a fool for not knowing about the damper," she said. "But I know now. I'd planned to make a fire before you arrived, but I needed to finish the mockup and ran out of time. I can do that now, if you want." She was eager to show off her new skill.

"I would, but it's been a long week and I don't want to stay out late," Sunshine said. "How about next time? Do you like Brady? I have a hunch you do."

Was she that easy to read? Starr sighed. "What gave me away?"

"When you talk about him, you get that moonstruck look on your face. Like when you dated Jimmy Kellogg in high school."

Starr made a *pfft* sound. "I wouldn't know a moonstruck

expression if I saw one. Anyway, that was ages ago. We broke up at senior prom because he wanted to be with Caroline Anson, his ex. Who was already pregnant, remember?"

"Oh, I remember, and don't try to change the subject," Sunshine said. "The same thing happened with that guy you met at Parsons— Nathan, right?"

Starr nodded. "Similar bottom line, but different story. He expected me to be at his beck and call and didn't like me working so much. Four years of arguing about that while I knocked myself out both to work long hours and stroke his ego. When he ditched me to go back to his ex, I wasn't sorry. Just call me a bad picker of men."

"I have no idea about that. The point is, I know how you look when you really like someone. After all, I am your big sister."

"Only by a year," Starr said. "Height-wise, I'm a lot bigger, by a good six inches."

"Rub it in, why don't you?"

Dahlia held up a finger signaling she had something to add. "There's more to Sunshine's story. Word is, you and Brady were together at the Corner Café the other night, looking happy and very interested in each other."

Unbelievable. Starr gaped at her. "Who says?"

"Jake and I were there for lunch today and one of the waitresses mentioned it. She said you seemed happy with each other."

Starr rolled her eyes. "I'd forgotten how people in Miracle Falls talk. Some things never change. Happy, yes, but interested in each other, no. FYI, we met there to go over the rental agreement. I was thrilled, and that's it." Unable to hold back, she went on. "But the truth is, yes, I have a major crush on him. That doesn't mean I want to do anything about it. He doesn't, either. I'm here such a short time, and he's still carrying a torch for his ex-wife."

Sunshine studied her. "You talked about this?"

"No, and how can you even ask? He's my landlord. We don't know each other well enough to talk about anything much."

"How do you know about his ex?"

"From his cleaning lady Judy. He hired her to clean the guesthouse before I moved in."

"Judy Simon?" Sunshine's eyes widened. "She cleans my house, too. She's good at her job. Also pretty gossipy. I don't know anything about Brady's ex, but I get where you're coming from. There's no sense starting anything when you're leaving. Who wants to be the fallback girl?"

"Exactly. My focus is on getting healthy and sewing a fabulous wedding dress, two classy dresses for us and the matron of honor dress for Addie. Speaking of sewing, let's talk fabric. I see you yawning, Dahlia, and I should've shown you and Sunshine after you tried on the muslin dress, but we were all hungry. Before you go, let me bring out sketches and fabric swatches for you both to look at."

CHAPTER 9

*O*ver the next few days, Starr got quite a bit done. She revised parts of the pattern for Dahlia's gown and made the patterns for the bridesmaid dresses. Addie stopped by to approve the sketch of her dress and the fabric, which she really liked. Starr made a pattern for her, then bought fabric for them all. For the bridal party dresses, deep green soft velvet with bronze silk accents around the necklines and sleeve cuffs. Dahlia's dress would be the opposite—delicious bronze silk with pearl buttons and accents of deep green at the waist and along the hem. They were all going to be so pretty!

During the day she was too busy and engaged in her work to feel lonely, but evenings were dicey at best. After sewing up a storm Saturday, she took herself to a late afternoon movie, then came home, made herself a decent fire, streamed a show, and ate leftovers from the previous night. Not exactly fun and exciting, but a decent way to pass the time.

Sunday night, she read in front of the fire and enjoyed a long schmooze on the phone with Robin. They'd kept in touch through social media and periodic phone calls. Despite the different paths of their lives— Starr was married to her job, while Robin was divorced with an eleven-year-old son and worked at a retail store in the mall— they were as close as ever, like they'd never been apart. They scheduled lunch for Wednesday. Starr was eager to see her and hoped Savannah could make it, too. But she was busy with some project and unable to get away. They discussed another get-together some evening.

The entire time, she pointedly did not think about Brady. Or tried not to.

That worked out about as well as digging a trench with a sewing machine. In other words, she thought about him a lot. Several times she went outside, glanced through a tiny gap near the gate of the privacy fence and caught glimpses of his house. The lights through his windows looked cheerful and inviting. Where was his studio? Did it face the fence or was it on a side of the house she couldn't see?

Monday morning, in need of groceries, she drove past it. He was at work, of course. She would've peeked through the windows if Judy's car hadn't been there.

One thing was for sure— her wood supply was running low. Brady had a huge pile of it, but she wasn't about to take any or ask if she could. Wasn't going to ask him where to get her own supply, either. Not gonna bother him again, no way. Finding a good source of wood shouldn't be difficult. It was on her to-do list.

After a productive day Tuesday, she made another fire and set about searching online for places to buy firewood. No sooner had she started than her cell rang. When she saw Wes was calling, she almost didn't answer. He knew she was here to take a much-needed break, so what did he want?

But he was her boss, and she answered. "Hi, Wes," she said without an ounce of enthusiasm.

"Hey, Starr. Things aren't the same without you. Can you come back early?"

"Sorry, I can't. This is my first real vacation since I started working for you. I need the time off to refresh myself." And get calm and love her job the joyful way she once had. "I'm staying through my sister's wedding, remember?"

"I need you."

Words that in the past had made her feel valued and spurred her on to work longer hours and get more done faster. Now, though… Her mouth went dry, her jaw clenched, and she thought she might throw up.

Breathe, she told herself and touched her thumb ring which was often a source of calm and comfort. Not so much where Wes was involved, but she clung to the habit. "Bianca and Erica are talented," she said. "They've worked under me for three years now and know what you like. They'll make anything you want."

"What I want is for you to come back immediately," he demanded in the domineering voice that sent panic through her. "Don't worry, you'll be able to fly back to Miracle Falls in time for the wedding."

The thumb ring failed to help. She started to hyperventilate. "That's not possible, Wes. I have to go."

Before he could say another word, she disconnected. And went into a full-fledged panic attack.

* * *

Brady had noticed smoke from the guesthouse chimney almost every night since he'd taught Starr about making a fire. She was likely running out of wood. He loaded a pile into the back of his hatchback, too much to carry over, and drove it to her place. He didn't plan to see her, meant to pile it on the porch, then split. With luck, she wouldn't know he was there.

She'd left the living room drapes open. Something made him pause and look inside. She was seated in the armchair with an agonized expression on her face and her hands clasped midway below her chin and her breasts. Alarmed, he forgot about not making his presence known. He tried the door— unlocked— and went in.

"What's wrong?" he asked as he entered the living room.

"Panic. Attack."

Oh, man, way out of his realm. He knew nothing about that. She was pale and clearly struggling to breathe. "I'm calling 9-1-1," he said, and whipped out his phone.

"No need. Just—" she paused and wheezed in a breath— "Give me— a minute."

He sat down on the ottoman in front of the chair. Her difficulty breathing was tough to watch, and he couldn't help but draw in his own deep breath and blow it out. In through the nose, out through the mouth, a breathing technique he'd learned somewhere.

Starr's attention swiveled toward him. Linking her gaze to his, she copied him. He repeated himself and so did she. A few more repetitions later, she seemed better. She was also tearing up.

"You're crying."

"No, I'm not," she said, swiping her eyes with her fingers.

"You're not the first woman to cry in front of me."

"I'm not crying. It's just—" she paused for a few deep breaths— "you're the only person who's ever seen me this way, and it's embarrassing. What are you doing here, anyway? I didn't call and ask you to come over."

"If you had, I'd have been here sooner." She smelled good, like woman and something vaguely familiar but unidentifiable. He wanted to rub her back. "Is it okay if we trade seats and I touch your back?"

She didn't answer for a moment. Then looking away and sniffling, she nodded and switched places with him.

As soon as she shifted her hair off her back, he kneaded his way from shoulder to shoulder and then repeated the massage.

Her muscles were tight, so tight. "You're really tense."

"Think I don't" —pause, deep breath— "know that?"

She sounded almost angry, but with her face turned away he couldn't be sure. "If I'm out of line, I'll stop right now."

"Keep going. It's soothing."

As he went through the same motions again, he filled in the silence with talk. "To answer your question of why I'm here, I figured your woodpile was getting low, and I brought you more wood. I have a ton of it. The trunk of my car is packed with logs. You built a beautiful fire. I'm awful glad I stopped by."

"Thanks for bringing more wood. You don't have to do that. I'm quite capable of taking care of myself. But I'm glad you're here. You're making me feel better. You're also pretty good at massage. How did you learn?"

He paused before answering. "My ex-wife." Starr glanced over her shoulder at him and gave a knowing nod he didn't understand. "She liked massages." His and the likely other men she'd cheated on him with. Not wanting to talk or think about that, he shut his mouth. "I don't know much about panic attacks."

"Neither did I till I had one. They're scary. Until tonight, I hadn't had a single episode since I left LA. And here, I thought I was doing well. Wes called a few minutes before you showed up." She all but shuddered. "And it happened again." She pulled in another breath before adding, "Can we talk about something less stressful?"

"Sure." Brady made himself sound calm, but his jaw clenched hard. He wanted to know what the rock star had done to her in the past and why a call from him had set her off but decided not to ask. No sense upsetting her further. This was totally out of his range of knowledge. All he had to go on were his own instincts. "How are the dresses for the wedding coming along?"

"Not bad. I've been working hard. You can stop the massage now." She pivoted toward him. To his relief, her breathing was normal. "How did you know my wood pile was low?"

"Common sense. When you have a fire almost every night, you're bound to use up what you have."

"How would you know how many fires I've had?"

She wouldn't be happy with the answer. He felt like a moose caught in the headlights. "You said you were going to."

"For all you know, that was idle talk."

"I don't think so. When I step outside to get some air at night, I smell smoke from the direction of the guesthouse. Sometimes, if I squint, I can see it coming out of your chimney."

"So you're spying on me? Or maybe you're watching the

house that closely because you're afraid I'll wreck it in some way."

She wasn't wearing a teasing smile and likely didn't think much of him. "That's not it at all." How to explain what he didn't understand himself? "You want the truth? It's quiet out here in the country. You already know I like that. But sometimes, knowing you're just across the field and enjoying a nightly fire is a way of connecting." That sounded lame but was true. "Understand, it doesn't mean anything in particular. It's just how I feel. Don't you think you should go to the hospital and get yourself checked?"

"Been there, done that. I don't need to anymore." She gave him a sheepish look. "Since you confessed, I may as well do the same. When I'm on the porch getting wood some nights, I make my way to the privacy fence and peer through a slit near the gate. I can't see much of your house, but I see the light from the windows. Knowing you're there makes me feel, I don't know, like there's someone else nearby."

"You get it." She needed the connection, too. In that way, they were kindred spirits. He wanted to pull her into a hug and tighten that link.

He wanted more than that.

When she was barely out of a panic attack? What a douche he was. He ought to go home. "I'm going to stack that firewood on the porch now," he said and stood.

"Do you want help?"

"Sit and relax. I'll let you know when I finish."

Some minutes later, he returned to the guesthouse. "All done."

"Thanks. Do you need to get home right away? It's cold out

there and you're welcome to warm yourself in front of the fire. I'll make popcorn. Unless you'd rather not."

This was the second time she'd offered. He took a good long look at her. Her skin was back to its normal color, and she'd lost the tense vibe. She seemed to have recovered well, which meant he could leave without worrying about her.

But her eyes were bright and hopeful like she wanted him to stay. He couldn't deny her or himself again. They were both lonely. A friendly hour together couldn't hurt— as long as he behaved himself. "Sure, I'll stay for a while. Popcorn sounds great."

CHAPTER 10

*S*itting on the couch with Brady and munching popcorn in front of the fire was exactly what Starr needed tonight. Not only had he seen her in full-mode panic attack, he'd also helped her through it. She was grateful to him. And yes, more attracted to him than before. No need for him to know about that. He wouldn't notice anyway, as he was still in love with his ex. When he'd mentioned the woman earlier, Starr had heard the hesitation in his voice that masked his sorrow over losing her. Which of course, she already knew thanks to Judy. This evening was about neighborly companionship.

"I rarely relax in front of the fire, and I don't eat popcorn except at the movies," he said when the bowl was empty. "I've forgotten how pretty the flames are when they flicker and dance."

What a nice way to describe a fire. "You're so poetic," she said.

"That's a new one. Tell me about making clothes. Is it hard?"

"It has its challenges. But I'm having fun with the dresses for the wedding, more than I've had in years." Why had she brought that up? The thought of the hectic pace Wes insisted on from all his employees made her tense up again.

"So turning the smaller bedroom into your workroom is working for you." Instant deflation of tension, and bless Brady for that. "Any chance of me seeing it?"

Not sure how she felt about that, she hesitated. "Um…"

"Hey, it's your space. You're not obligated to show it to me."

Again a reply that took all the pressure off. Such a great guy. "I don't have a problem with that," she explained. "My issue is that I'm not ready to share my works-in-process just yet. When they're further along, maybe. Except for the wedding dress. Dahlia doesn't want anyone but her and Starr to see it till the wedding. That's the way I work."

"I get it. I feel the same way about my art."

Another thing they had in common. "If you don't mind waiting a few minutes while I cover up what I'm working on, I'll show you the room."

"Not at all."

"I'll show you mine if you show me yours," she teased.

What had possessed her to say that?

His lips twitched. "Are you flirting with me?"

Starr knew her face was red. "Please— I wouldn't know how."

"Could've fooled me."

Desperate to change the subject, she compressed her lips. "Do I get to see your workshop or not?"

"Any time. Let me know when."

"I will. Why don't you wait here while I get the room ready." Needing a moment alone, she fled. And admitted to herself that despite not knowing how to flirt, she'd definitely been doing it. It was a good thing he was still in love with his ex. Otherwise, if he made a move on her... She wasn't sure she'd stop him.

Never mind, he wouldn't. After carefully placing the patterns, adjustable dress forms and the partly stitched wedding dress in the closet, she decided to leave some of the sketches and fabric swatches out to show him. Moments later, she returned to the living room. "I'm ready now."

Fully prepared to maintain a safe distance for her own good, she pulled the fire curtain across the hearth. They headed down the small hallway, which was wide enough for the two of them but a little too close for comfort. She had to be careful not to brush her hand or arm against him.

His odd expression brought her to a standstill between the sewing room and her bedroom. "You have a funny look on your face."

"Ha ha funny?"

"More like you're confused about something." Which she hoped had nothing to do with her flirty behavior. It'd come out of nowhere and meant nothing.

"You're right. I'm trying to figure out what perfume you're wearing. It's familiar, but I can't place why."

He must be into scents, which was different.

"I wouldn't call it a perfume per se. It's a mixture of two essential oils I bought at Sunshine's spa the other day—orange and lemon. I especially like them mixed together. Early this morning, I put a dab behind my ears and on my wrists. I can't really smell it anymore and thought sure it'd worn off by now." She sniffed her own wrist. "It's faint, but still there. I can't believe it's lasted so long or that you have such a good nose."

"With nostrils that flare when I'm irritated." His mouth quirked. "You're good at pointing out things about me that I didn't know. Would you mind if I take a whiff? Maybe it'll help me remember why it's familiar."

"Go ahead." She held out her arm. He grasped her hand in his, lifted her wrist and inhaled. His fingers wrapped around hers, his face so close to her wrist that she felt his warm breath on her skin, right where her pulse beat. A flurry of feelings fluttered through her, and set off a fine hum in certain female body parts. She snatched her hand back. "Did that help?" she asked, knowing her voice wasn't quite steady.

"Surprisingly, yes." He stared into the distance, then broke into a grin that charmed her. "A girl who babysat me when I was eight or nine smelled just as fresh and citrussy. Julie Nichols," he said and shook his head. "She was an 'older woman,' about sixteen, and cute. My first case of puppy love. When I found out she had a boyfriend, I was devastated." The grin turned into a chuckle. "It smells better on you."

"Does it? Different body chemicals, I guess."

"I imagine so."

The heat blazing from his eyes was so potent, she almost forgot that she didn't want to get involved with him. She hurried into the sewing room. With Brady sharing the same space, the little room seemed even smaller. "Anyway, this is where I work. Don't worry, before I leave I'll put it back exactly the way I found it," she said to remind them both that she wouldn't be here long.

"I'm not at all worried— I like what you've done here." He squinted toward the top of the dresser. "Are those sketches?"

She nodded. "Only for the matron-of-honor and brides-maids dresses. For the wedding gown, even the sketch is top secret."

She let him look at the others and the color swatches. He seemed truly interested and asked numerous questions. Happy to talk shop and push her feelings for him away, she answered them all.

"When you come see my studio, I'll show you some of my art sketches."

"I'll look forward to it."

He checked his watch. "Speaking of the studio, it's late and I need to get some work done before I turn in."

Perfect— she needed him to go. Her unwanted feelings for him were out-of-bounds. She walked him to the door and opened it. "Thanks for coming over. You made the bad situation I was in better. I appreciate the wood, too."

Standing in the threshold, she kissed his cheek— or meant to. But he turned his head so that his lips were a hair's breadth from hers and changed everything. "Why don't you kiss me on the mouth instead," he said.

She wanted to say no, that it was a bad idea and remind him about the ex he still loved, but his mesmerizing eyes wiped all that from her mind. "What are we doing, Brady?" she said in a last-ditch effort to stop them both before they started.

"Something we shouldn't. But we're doing it anyway." He tucked her hair behind her ears with his big hands and let his fingers linger on her cheeks. She rose up to meet him.

* * *

THERE WERE SO many reasons he shouldn't kiss Starr, Brady told himself, but at the moment he couldn't think of a single one. Not with the dreamy look in her eyes and her lush lips slightly open in kiss-me mode. Pulling away wasn't possible. One little kiss couldn't hurt. Playing it safe, he brushed his mouth lightly over hers. Only nothing about that brief taste was safe.

Instead of moving away from him, she threaded her fingers through his hair and guided him again to her lips, this time with her mouth eager and welcoming. Killing him. His hunger for her skyrocketed and all he could think of was more. As if reading his mind, she tangled her tongue with his and shifted closer. As thin as she was, she felt soft in his arms.

"God, you taste good," he groaned, anchoring her hips more tightly to his.

The front door was still open and the night air frigid. Not that it mattered. He was burning up for her. And she seemed just as turned on.

What they were doing was dangerous. Too dangerous. With effort, he tore his mouth from hers. At the same moment, she pushed him away. Hard, onto the porch while she remained in the threshold.

They stared at each other, their breaths visible in the cold.

"I promised myself I wouldn't get involved with anyone while I'm here," she said. "Especially not you. Go home."

Genuinely confused, he frowned. "I will, after you explain that comment. What's wrong with me?"

"Two things. I barely know you, and you're still in love with your ex-wife."

Where had she gotten that idea? He was about to ask, but she took a step backward, which put her firmly in the entryway. "It's cold, Brady. Good night."

She shut the door. Puzzling over her words, he climbed into his car and drove home.

CHAPTER 11

*K*icking herself for kissing Brady the previous evening, Starr bent over the wedding gown and began to hand stitch nakpunar pearl buttons, the very best brand money could buy, onto the bodice. An arduous task that took a great deal of work. But oh, the payoff. The finished dress would be so gorgeous on Dahlia!

In a few hours, she'd meet Robin for lunch. Her bestie had taken the afternoon off to schmooze, laugh, and get caught up in person instead of through FaceTime or texts and emails. Until then, Starr intended to make decent headway on the hand stitching

That wasn't all. Tonight, Mama was coming over to see the guesthouse and enjoy a takeout meal, as Starr had little time or interest in cooking from scratch.

At the moment, she wanted to focus and do as much hand stitching as possible. Could she help it if her rebellious mind wanted a replay of the delicious details at the front door? If only she'd stuck to her plan to give Brady a light peck on the cheek as a friendly thank-you for steering her through the panic attack and keeping her company for a while.

But no, the turn of his head toward her had transformed the friendly thanks and good night into something far more potent and dangerous. The first gentle touch of his lips hadn't been enough. The deeper, hotter kisses that followed had pulsed through her veins, setting an aching need through certain long-neglected body parts that craved attention.

In short, he'd pretty much blown her mind. He must be quite the lover. Starr swallowed hard at the thought, but she'd never know. His heart belonged to someone else, and there was no changing that. Besides, she wasn't about to break the promise to herself to steer clear of sex until she met an available man who'd truly moved past any exes and wanted what she did, namely a healthy relationship with the hope of a future together.

Important things she'd all but forgotten after the first kiss.

Mad at herself, she smacked her forehead with the heel of her palm. The thimble popped off her index finger and landed somewhere on the floor. She spent a minute or two muttering and searching for it before she found it and slipped it back on. A waste of precious time and enough already! There was no point spending one more second reliving last night and worrying about what she couldn't go back and undo. "It won't happen again," she assured herself out loud.

For the next few hours, she concentrated solely on stitching. By the time the reminder alarm she'd set to keep her from being late to lunch rang, she'd made decent progress.

She met Robin at Geraldine's, a cute restaurant near the Miracle Falls Mall that hadn't existed when she'd last visited.

The two of them squealed and hugged each other like the teenage girls they'd once been, then headed for a table.

The server delivered menus and jotted down their orders. The food arrived soon after, and a good thing. Starr was starving.

"I'm jealous that you can eat anything you want," Robin admitted. "But then, you've always been like this. You look wonderful, not at all the way you described yourself. When you emailed that you'd dropped weight you couldn't afford to lose, I pictured a gaunt face and too-thin body."

"You should've seen me when I arrived." She'd told Robin about the panic attacks shortly after the doctor had identified the problem. "I'm still too thin but gaining back what I lost."

"Why do you think you're having panic attacks?"

"Because I haven't had a vacation in forever? That and a job that's been super stressful for several years now. I needed time away. Since I've been here, I've been doing much better. Not quite out of the woods yet," she added, remembering the previous night, "but getting there."

"That's a relief."

"I'm happy about it. You look great, too, all fit and toned."

"With dieting and all the working out I've been doing, I'd better. I've lost ten pounds. Five to go."

"Yay, you!" Nine or so months earlier, after years of focusing mostly on her son Merritt and her job and living in her parents' basement after the divorce, Robin had rented an apartment near his school. Now that he was in middle school and becoming more independent, she was on the hunt for a partner with husband potential.

"Fingers crossed that one of the dating apps comes

through for you and you meet the man of your dreams," Starr said.

"Let's hope. I haven't had much luck so far, but it's bound to happen eventually. In my heart, I know it will. It'll be nice to marry for love instead of because I got pregnant straight out of high school." She angled her head at Starr. "You don't happen to know of any eligible guys?"

Starr thought of Brady, but he wasn't eligible, not the way he felt about his former wife. "No, but I'm not looking at men like you are."

The talk moved to Dahlia and Jake's upcoming wedding.

"How's her dress coming along?" Robin asked.

"Slow but steady. She's going to look amazing."

"And she's marrying gorgeous Jake, lucky woman." Robin sighed. "I always liked him. I hear her engagement ring is amazing."

"It's special. The diamond is huge and came from the engagement ring Jake's grandma wore."

"Very cool. Who did the setting?"

"Brady Barton at Joseph Barton Fine Jewelry."

"I've met Brady. He's attractive. Hmm…"

Starr didn't care for the contemplative gleam in her friend's eyes. Only because he wasn't available, nothing more. After all, she had zero interest in him. "He's not bad," she said.

By the uptilt of Robin's eyebrows, she didn't buy that any more than Starr herself did. "He's hot and you like him."

Starr frowned. "What makes you say that?"

"I've known you since sixth grade, and I'm familiar with that narrowed-eyed, back-off my man face."

Dang. "Do you have any recent photos of Merritt?"

"Don't try to change the subject. You *do* like him."

Unable to fool her bestie, she gave in with a sigh. "It's true, I'm attracted to him. But after the wedding, I'll be going back to LA. Anyway, he's still in love with his ex-wife."

Robin grimaced. "Ugh."

"My sentiment exactly. I'm dying to know what Merritt looks like now. I've seen posts on Facebook but not lately. Do you have recent photos?"

"I sure do." Robin fished her phone out of her purse and located several cute pictures. "He's big into ultra frisbee. It's a huge sport here."

"Same in LA. He's getting tall. Cute, too."

"Some of the girls agree with you, but don't tell him that."

"Already? He's only eleven."

"He has female friends he pals around with, but that's about it as far as girls go. Today, at least. It's only a matter of time before that changes. Remember how we were at that age?"

Starr grinned. "I sure do. Totally—"

"Boy crazy," they chimed at the same time.

The laughter that followed felt really good. How long had it been since Starr had genuinely laughed?

"How do you like living in his guesthouse?' Robin said. "I'd love to see it."

"It's just the right size for me, and I really like it. I'll have you over sometime soon. I'd invite you tonight, but Mama J's coming over to see the place and have dinner."

"And I'm supposed to help Merritt with his science fair project. I'll come visit another day. How many times has Brady stopped by?"

She *would* ask. Starr told her about the minor fender bender the day they'd met, and then moved on to the smoky fire and how he'd taught her how to safely have one. She ignored the far more interesting parts of the story.

"No wonder you like him," Robin said as she finished her lunch.

While Starr did the same, she debated sharing the part she'd left out. She needed to confide in someone, and who better than her best friend? When she finished eating, she nudged the plate aside. "I want you to swear you won't tell anyone what I'm about to say. I haven't even told my sisters— I don't want them to know."

"I promise." Robin crossed her heart and leaned in closer. "Spill."

Starr started with the call from Wes, the stress and the ensuing panic attack. She explained about Brady stopping by with a fresh supply of wood in the middle of the panic thing and how he'd helped her calm down. From there, she moved on to eating popcorn in front of the fire, the way friends do. Then the goodnight kisses that'd changed everything. "That's it," she finished and bit her lip.

"Let me get this straight. You got physically turned on. With your landlord, who's still in love with his ex." Robin shook her head. "No wonder you want to keep your sisters in the dark. Wes must've scrambled your brain when he called. Because from where I sit, it looks like you've lost your marbles."

Starr winced. Her friend always had been honest with her opinions. "Maybe I have. Believe me, I never wanted anything like that with Brady. I don't think he did, either. It just happened. I won't let it again."

Robin's skeptical look echoed Starr's own self-doubts.

* * *

ON HIS LUNCH break that same afternoon, Brady was restless. What a shame he didn't have more time— he could use a good pick-up basketball game to clear his head. No reason he couldn't get outside, though. First, he texted Joe through WhatsApp to set up a Skype. He wanted to update his brother on the latest with Senior and get his take on Starr.

That done, he bundled up. With no ice or snow on the sidewalks and few people out in the cold, now was the perfect time for a brisk walk around the area. That should do the trick.

It didn't work. His mind messed with him, and he spent a good deal of time puzzling over the night before. A crazy evening that ended with both him and Starr getting hot and bothered. He hadn't intended for that to happen. But it had, a real turn-on that skyrocketed with each kiss. And there'd been a lot of them.

He felt like a man again, alive and aroused. Which wasn't smart when Starr was the woman he wanted, but damn, he'd enjoyed it.

What bothered him more was her parting comment as he exited the guesthouse. Why would she think he was still in love with Verity?

He didn't talk about his ex, didn't want to dredge up that painful part of his life. Sure, he'd mentioned her briefly when Starr had questioned him about the massage, but that was it. He regretted not opening up to her. If he had, she wouldn't have gotten the cockeyed idea that he still cared about Verity when he despised her.

Now, like it or not, the sleeping beast of his libido was

awake and very much alive. His need for Starr was strong. He considered letting her misguided belief about Verity stand. That might keep them from moving forward with what they'd started. Because getting any closer to her would be a disaster he didn't want to think about. He was in no shape to get involved with her. Or any woman, for that matter.

He wouldn't visit the guesthouse again.

Then why did he cross the meadow after work and head for the gate?

To set her straight. He didn't want her or anyone else to think he still cared about his ex. Verity had ruined his life for a while, but he'd put that behind him and moved on. Even so, he didn't want a relationship, not for a long time yet. Starr needed to know that.

It was the only reason he walked through the gate that night.

CHAPTER 12

Starr checked her watch for the third time in thirty minutes. Mama was late. Knowing how absent-minded she'd been lately, a call seemed in order. The phone rang a dozen times before voicemail came on. She left a message. "Hey, Mama, it's Starr. You're not here yet, but don't worry, our takeout is keeping warm in the oven. Where are you? I'll text you, too."

When that failed, she called Maureen, one of Mama's closest girlfriends. "Hello?" Maureen said. Conversation and clanking dishes sounded in the background.

"Hi, it's Starr. Sounds like you're at a party, so I won't keep you. I'm looking for Mama J. She was supposed to be at my place a while ago. Do you have any idea where she is?"

"Don't tell me she double-booked herself again. She's so busy going out with one friend group or another every night that she seems to be doing that a lot."

Maureen's words only deepened Starr's worry. "She didn't used to be so forgetful. Do you think she's okay?"

"I think she's way over-extended her social life, and that's the problem. Anyway, she's here with a bunch of us at Carol Ann's. It's a party of sorts, an impromptu potluck, and we're about to sit down to dinner. She probably turned off her phone. I'll let her know you're trying to reach her."

Moments later, Mama called. "What are you doing at Carol Ann's when we scheduled dinner here at my place?" Starr asked.

"Speak up, Starr. It's noisy in here, and I can't hear you. Never mind, wait while I move to a quieter room." A moment later, silence replaced the chatter and clang. "Now I can hear you," Mama said. "Is something wrong? Do you need me?"

"I'm okay, but you're supposed to be at the guesthouse having dinner with me."

"I am? I guess I forgot."

Starr was beginning to think the woman didn't want to visit. She stifled a sigh. "I thought you kept a calendar of your personal appointments."

"I do, and I'm all booked up."

So Maureen had said. "You were supposed to be booked up with me tonight. Didn't you write down our dinner together?"

"I don't know. I didn't check."

"Then what's the point of having a calendar? I'm starting to worry about you, Mama—"

"Well, stop. I don't have time to talk now. We're about to eat, and I want to get back to my friends."

"But—" Realizing she'd disconnected, Starr threw up her hands. She contacted her sisters on a three-way call.

"Mama was supposed to finally come over for dinner and see my place tonight," she said when they were both connected. I had to phone Maureen to find her. She was at what Maureen called 'an impromptu potluck.' She told Mama I was trying to reach her." Starr reviewed the conversation.

"Geez," Dahlia said. "Now you know what we've been going through."

Sunshine added, "Like Dahlia and I said before, she does tons of things with her friends, but nothing much with us. Except that first weekend you came home. That was nice."

"It was wonderful. I didn't realize how unusual it was until now. At first tonight, my feelings were hurt. I mean, she didn't react toward me with the apologies she gave both of you when she stood you up. Maureen explained that it isn't just the three of us Mama forgets. Apparently, she sometimes double books with friends, too."

"Dahlia and I hadn't heard about that. It's really weird."

Starr agreed, "How long would you say she's been like this?"

"Let me think," Dahlia said. "Since not long after her birthday, right, Sunshine?"

"That's about when it started. She's always had the quilt and the movie nights, but since she turned sixty, she's gone crazy. Parties and activities night after night on top of working forty hours a week. She's burning the candle at both ends and messing up plans by booking more than one social event at the same time. I don't know how she does it or why."

"I worry how much longer she can pull it off without collapsing," Dahlia said. "This is so unlike her."

"And super confusing," Starr said. "She's as sharp as they come on most everything else in her life so I doubt it's anything serious, but what if it is? She needs to see her doctor for a physical— if she can tear herself away from her friends for a little while."

Her sisters were of the same mind. Starr offered to set up the appointment and take her. "Do you know who her doctor is? Someone at the hospital, I'm guessing?"

"She doesn't see any of the physicians there," Dahlia said. "She doesn't want them knowing her health issues."

"Is there something wrong that she wants to hide from the people at work?" Starr wondered.

"I think it's more a matter of privacy."

"Where does she go and who does she see?"

"I don't know for sure," Sunshine said, "but I remember her talking about her doctor at the Women's Health Clinic. It's not far from Lolli's Other Place. I think the physician's name is Dr. Richards— if Mama still sees her."

"I'll give the clinic a call in the morning and see if I can make an appointment for her. I'll try to schedule something during her lunchbreak."

"I doubt they'll let you do that, but what do I know? If it's during lunch, I can meet you there," Sunshine said.

"I will, too," Dahlia said. "She won't like this at all."

"Too bad. She's going. I'll let you know if and when I book the appointment."

They disconnected.

Ravenous, Starr was pulling takeout from the oven to eat when footsteps thudded across the porch. She opened the door to find Brady there. Way too pleased to see him, she frowned. "What are you doing here?"

"I, um— gonna let me in? It's cold out here."

"Will this take long? I was about to sit down to dinner."

He eyed her warily. "You sound mad. I wouldn't want to put you out. I came over to talk to you. Never mind, I'll come back another time."

What did he want to talk about? At the moment, she was too hungry to care. "If you're fishing for a dinner invitation, you're in luck. I ordered way too much spaghetti with meatballs and garlic bread. Mama J was supposed to come to dinner, but she forgot. The table is set for two, so you may as well join me."

"It sure smells good. Sure, I'll join you." His eyebrows drew closer together. "How could she forget dinner with you?"

"Hold that question until we eat." Starr headed for the kitchen and he followed.

AT THE BEGINNING of the meal, Brady was silent. So was Starr, both of them chowing down. She seemed to have a voracious appetite that matched his and a great enjoyment of food. The companionable silence of two people eating with gusto was a nice change from sitting alone or dining with the parents while his mother tried to keep the peace between him and his father.

After some minutes, Starr slowed down. "You asked about Mama J. She double booked tonight and chose to be with her friends over me. Mainly because as I said, she forgot about this." She gestured at the food still on the table. "I'm hurt. This is a first for me, but it's happened with both Dahlia and Sunshine, and also Mama's friends. I wish I knew why. According to my sisters, she's been like this since around her birthday last November. She's forgetful and spends way more nights out with friends than she used to. She's head of Records at Miracle Falls Hospital, a demanding and challenging job. If I'm super busy, I forget things, too, but we're all concerned, which is why I'm going to call her doctor in the morning and make an appointment for a physical— if I have the right name of the doctor."

"Don't you think you should check with her first?"

Looking thoughtful, Starr picked up her fork and licked the tines clean. Which reminded Brady of their tongue play the previous night. This wasn't the time or place to get turned on, and he pulled his gaze to his near-empty plate.

"That's a good point," Starr said, "but no matter what she says, I'm not giving her a choice— I'm too worried."

He'd never met the woman but if she was anything like Starr... The clash of wills he imagined wasn't pretty. "I hope it works out. No fire tonight?"

"I'm not in the mood." She stared at him through slightly narrowed eyes. "Your turn. What did you want to talk to me about?"

He started with the foremost question on his mind. "Are you ticked at me for kissing you? Correction— at yourself for kissing me? You seem that way."

"When you're still in love with your ex? Yes."

Not from the kisses, then. He was pleased about that. Also puzzled. Where in the world had she gotten that crazy idea? He'd find out after he got answers to other questions. "Suppose you're mistaken about my feelings for her. Would you still be upset about a few kisses?" Killer kisses he wanted more of.

"But you do care about her. I repeat, I'm not mad, okay?"

"The way you glared at me when you answered the door tonight, you sure looked that way. Admit it, you enjoyed last night as much as I did. And don't say you didn't. You don't kiss a guy like that if you're not into it."

She didn't argue, just lifted one shoulder and let it fall. Her suddenly flushed cheeks belied the casual shrug. Time to set her straight. Brady set down his fork and wiped his mouth. "Here's what you need to know about Verity and me." At Starr's blank look, he clarified, "My ex-wife."

"You don't have to explain. My last boyfriend who supposedly loved me turned out to still have feelings for his ex, so I get it. Same thing happened in high school with another boyfriend. I refuse to play second fiddle to anyone's lost love, and I'm not about to get involved with you."

That explained a lot. "Heard. Now you need to listen to me. Without going into the gory details, I'll skip to the bottom line. We got married fast, within a few months after meeting. That turned out to be one of the worst mistakes of my life. A few weeks into our marriage, Verity suddenly changed. She made my life hell, spending money like crazy and sleeping around. How I missed that, I'll never know. Wait, I do know. I wanted someone to spend my life with and thought she was it." He let out a harsh laugh. "Looking back, I have no idea why she married me in the first place. The day our divorce was final, I celebrated. Yes, it hurt, but I was also relieved. I rarely think about her anymore, also a relief. Now you know."

Starr's eyes widened. "That's terrible. But I thought... Judy said..."

"Judy?" Brady scratched his head. "The woman who cleans my house?"

"That's right. She said something about how after your dog died, you really missed your ex. I thought you still cared about her."

"How would Judy know? I didn't even meet her till after I closed on this property. By then, I'd been divorced more than a year. She didn't know Verity, and I never mentioned her. I have no idea what put that crazy idea in her mind."

Starr shook her head. "All I know is what she said."

"She sure talks a lot." Brady was unhappy with the woman who spread fake news. "When you met her and said she was chatty, you didn't mention the part about Verity."

"I didn't think about that. Shouldn't you be working on the cat sculpture tonight?"

"I'm almost finished with it and plan to send it off Saturday morning. If you still want to see it and my studio, come over Friday night and I'll show it to you."

Starr nibbled the pad of her thumb. "I'll let you know. Maybe Judy heard something that made her think you still miss your ex."

Intriguing that she was still thinking about that. "I'll ask her next time I see her." And set her straight, too. "I'm glad we got that ironed out. Feel better about last night?"

"Not really. I promised myself... Let's just say that I don't think we should kiss again or anything else for two reasons. First, I'm not interested in a physical-only thing, which leads to the second, that I won't be around long enough to have a meaningful relationship."

Funny, with her, Brady wanted physical and nothing more. For now, the only way to live. A big change for him. "I understand. I'm steering clear of the love stuff until I really know the woman I'm with. Can I trust her, do we love each other and want the same things, like a long-term relationship and kids? We have to talk a lot and get through rough patches and down times." None of which had happened with Verity. He'd assumed they were like-minded when they weren't. "That stuff can't be rushed. I have no interest in getting involved like that now and may not for a long time. Which doesn't change the fact that I want you."

"I appreciate your honesty, but let's forget kissing at the door last night ever happened. From now on, you're my landlord, and I'm your tenant. We can be friends, though, if you're okay with that."

"I am. You're fun to hang around with." The urge to kiss her again just to see if the second time was as good as the first was strong, but he wouldn't act on it. If she changed her mind, she'd have to show him.

She looked tired, and her yawn confirmed it. He needed to work on that cat sculpture. "Thanks for dinner," he said. "I didn't expect that, but I sure appreciated it."

"You really helped me out by making a big dent in what would've been way too many leftovers."

He grinned. "Any time you want help with that, I'm your man."

She was laughing when she shut the door behind him. Still grinning, he headed home.

CHAPTER 13

Shortly after Brady got home from Starr's, Joe texted via WhatsApp that he could Skype first thing in the morning Brady's time. The following morning, Brady woke up early and initiated the call at seven a.m., which was afternoon a full day later for his brother.

"Hey," Joe said. He looked healthy and buff, no doubt from the hard physical labor he did on the ranch. "It's been too long. Good to see your face."

"Way too long. Thanks for taking off part of your afternoon for this."

"You wanted to talk, and I'm here for you. I don't have a lot of time, though."

"Then I'll get right to it." Brady unloaded about Senior. "He still doesn't trust me to run the store and is making me miserable. It's killing me, man."

"He's always been a hard nut."

"Not with you. You're the son he doted on."

"That didn't make him easy to deal with. Lately, I've been

thinking about how I walked away from the business and left you to take on the load."

"I think about that, too," Brady admitted.

"I'm sorry I didn't warn you before it happened. I should've apologized years ago."

"I'm over it now. Why are you bringing it up after all this time?"

"It's been eating at me and I wanted to get it off my chest. On Skype, not through a WhatsApp message. Wish I was there to talk in person. I miss you, Brady."

"Miss you, too. Apology accepted, so forget it and let's move on."

"Done. Sounds like nothing's changed with Senior, so why the call in the middle of the week?"

Time to talk about the other night with Starr. "You've read my texts about renting the guesthouse out for a few months."

"To a woman named Starr. Is this about her?"

Joe seemed eager to find out, and Brady jumped in. "Yeah. When I was over there a couple nights ago, things got…" He paused. "This is between us, okay?" His brother nodded, and he went on. "She had a panic attack, and I helped her."

"No kidding? Did you cause it?"

"Not funny. Hell, no. She, uh…" Not about to go into detail about Starr's boss and all that, Brady said, "It had to do with something personal in her life. I happened to show up when she was in the middle of it. I wanted to take her to the ER, but she wouldn't go."

"What'd you do?"

"Trusted my gut— took a few slow, deep breaths with her, stuff like that. It worked."

"Good for you, trusting yourself."

"Yeah, it turned out pretty well. She was grateful and asked me to stay for a while. We ate popcorn and talked. When it was time to go, she— " Not sure how to explain the sizzling heat that was still with him, he broke off.

"You kissed her, huh?" Joe grinned.

"How did you guess?"

"What else could it have been? Also, you're my brother, and I know you well. I'm glad to hear it. About damn time."

Brady agreed, but... "There's a problem. She's looking for a man to commit. That's not me."

"It definitely is you. You're loyal with a true blue heart. It's part of who you are."

"Not when it comes to women," Brady corrected. "I've only been in love once and suffered for it. No way, not now, and not this fast. Fool me once and all that."

"The divorce sure did a number on you. Did you tell her you're not into serious?"

"Sure did."

"But you want to take things further, have sex with her."

Bingo. "She wants more than that."

"You could try a relationship again."

"I'm a long way from anything serious."

"You can't help who you want, right? That's a tough one." Joe glanced at his watch. "The timer just went off. Much as I want to keep talking about this intriguing turn in your life, I have to go back to work."

"And I need to get ready to leave for the store."

"Nice talking, brother. I hope things work out with Starr."

Then he was gone.

* * *

THAT SAME MORNING at the guesthouse, Starr phoned Mama bright and early, before she headed for the hospital.

"Good morning, Starr," she said, and yawned. Loudly. "My, you're up early. Is everything okay?"

"I'm fine." But was Mama? "You're not easy to get hold of, and I wanted to touch base before you leave for work. You sound tired. I hope I didn't wake you."

"You know me better than that. The party last night ran a bit late. I could've come home before it ended, but I didn't want to miss anything."

What could she possibly miss? She'd been hanging out with the same friends forever. "You're always at work on time or early, plus you're the boss of the records department. I'm sure no one would mind if you went back to sleep for an hour or two."

"I'm not one to do that, and you know it. Besides, I have to go in extra early today. Don't worry, I'll manage— I work tired all the time."

Way to up the worry factor. "That can't be healthy. When was your last physical?"

"About a year ago. Why do you ask?"

"If you're always tired, maybe it's time for another one. Have you made an appointment for this year?"

"Is that why you called? You've never asked before. You know perfectly well that I'm quite able to take care of myself."

"I do, but..." Starr pulled in a breath, then plunged on. "You're so busy all day and every night, and you seem so scatter-brained."

"Because I forgot to come over last night? I should've checked my calendar. I'll get over there soon, I promise."

"This is about more than forgetting me, Mama. I don't like seeing you this frazzled."

The same way Starr got when Wes was on her case. Dang, she was as bad as Mama, only without the fun of hanging out with friends.

"Then you'll be happy to know that reason I'm going in so early this morning is because I'm leaving early for my annual checkup."

Relief washed over Starr. "I'm glad. Hey, why don't I come with you? Then we'll have dinner at my house." Maybe she'd find out why Mama spent night after night with friends instead of relaxing at home and getting the rest she needed. And why Starr and her sisters seemed to be after-thoughts, if that. "I'll pick you up at the hospital and drop you off at your car. Then you can follow me to the guesthouse."

"That'd be nice, but don't you need to work on the dresses for the wedding?"

"I have been, and things are going well, but I could use a break. When you come over, I'll show you what I'm working on. Except for Dahlia's gown, which is top secret." Mama was silent. Crossing her fingers, Starr added, "I'd really like to spend time with you and promise not to keep you out late. How about it?"

"I guess I could do that."

Did she have to sound so grudging? Refusing to let that get in the way, Starr put a smile in her voice. "Great. What time should I pick you up for the appointment?"

"Three-thirty."

As soon as they disconnected, she texted her sisters with the news. On such short notice, neither of them could get away. She promised to update them.

CHAPTER 14

*M*ama wouldn't let Starr see the doctor with her, which was fine. She sat in the third floor waiting room of the Women's Health Clinic along with a fair amount of women and a handful of men. In need of something to read, she picked up a *People* magazine that was several months old. Thanks to a subscription at home, she'd read it, but she thumbed through it anyway.

She couldn't help comparing Brady with some of the male celebrities in the magazine. He was as good-looking as any of them. Funny how she hadn't thought so that first day.

Her opinion had changed. Every time she thought of him, which was way too often, her heart lifted and certain body parts... Well, they got excited. She caught herself in a breathy sigh and frowned. They'd kissed more than a few times, nothing else. But the damage had been done. She half-wished he *was* still in love with his former wife, which would make it easier to resist him.

As if. Even when she'd thought he still loved his ex, she'd wanted him. No matter how many times she reminded herself of the promise she'd made not to jump into bed with him or any man who wasn't interested in a relationship and the possibility of a future together.

It would be so easy to give in and— *No, no, no.* She'd come to Miracle Falls to make dresses for the wedding and help the family get ready for the big event. Also of course, to recover fully from the panic attacks and get herself in shape to return home after the wedding. And it was working. She was healing, a big relief.

Though at the moment, the very thought of going back to work for Wes and all the stress around the job made her tense.

And there came Mama, returning to the waiting room. Hard to tell from her expression what the doctor had said. She certainly didn't have the wonderful twinkle that had once gleamed in her eyes, but then she hadn't since that first weekend Starr had come home. Another sign of running herself ragged.

She grabbed Mama's coat from the chair beside her, jumped up and forced a smile. "How was the appointment?" she asked and attempted to help the woman into her coat.

"Give me that," Mama said and hung it over her arm to carry it. "I need to stop at the lab on the first floor for blood tests," she said as they took the elevator down. "It's a good thing I don't have to go back to work. I'm exhausted."

With circles under her eyes and a weary expression, that was obvious. "What kinds of tests to you need?" Starr asked as the elevator descended.

"Dr. Richard wants blood tests for anemia, thyroid levels, and I don't know what all else, to see if anything is out of whack, et cetera."

Wise idea. "She sounds like a good doctor. What else did she say?"

"That my cognitive function is good, which I already knew. She gave me a verbal test a kindergartner could have passed. She also suggested cutting back on my social life." Mama made a *pfft* sound.

They reached the ground floor and headed down the hall toward the lab.

"You don't need to come in with me," she said and handed the coat back to Starr. "Wait out here."

Starr sat in one of the chairs placed outside the lab. While she waited, she ordered their dinner for later.

"When will you get the results?" she asked after she and Mama had bundled up and headed for the Civic.

"Probably Monday. Dr. Richards will contact me then. I'm hungry. What are we having for dinner?"

"Pot pies from Marsden's." Another new-to-her restaurant Robin raved about.

"I love that place," Mama enthused with a hint of the gusto she used to have.

"That's what I hear, and I can't wait to try the food. Dinner should arrive in less than an hour. After I drop you at your car and you follow me to the guesthouse, I'll show you around."

While Starr waited for Mama to get her car, she updated her sisters. Some twenty minutes later, she pulled into the driveway at the guesthouse and Mama pulled up behind her.

"This is adorable," Mama said after she stepped inside and glanced around. "Tucked away in the woods. How did you find it?"

"I lucked into it. Let me hang up your coat and show you the house."

She started the tour. Having stowed Dahlia's dress away earlier, she gestured Mama into the sewing room and showed her the dresses she was making for her, Starr and Addie.

"I like your workspace, Starr. It feels comfortable in here. And those dresses! They'll be perfect. It's going to be such a beautiful wedding. Can I please get a peek at Dahlia's dress?"

"I can't, Mama. I promised to keep it secret. You'll see it on her wedding day."

"All right." Mama leaned in and lowered her voice. "I hear you know how to build a mean fire, thanks to Brady."

"Who told you?"

"Your sisters." Mama smiled. "I like him."

Starr felt her face warm. "He's a good landlord." Not wanting to deal with any prying comments, she gestured at the hearth. "As you can see, we're ready for a fire. Yes or no?"

"By all means."

Not long after the logs crackled and the fire flared in the hearth, dinner arrived. "The guesthouse came with TV trays," Starr said. "I'll set them up in the living room so we can eat in front of the hearth."

As they sipped wine, ate and enjoyed the fire, Starr steered the conversation to Mama's health. "About what the doctor said. How do you feel about slowing down on the socializing and taking a few nights off a week, like you used to?"

"Are you kidding? I like my life just the way it is. I'll sleep in on weekends. That should take care of the problem."

She'd always been on the stubborn side, so this wasn't surprising. Didn't mean Starr liked the decision. Her sisters wouldn't, either, when she filled them in after Mama left.

"Although I doubt I'll sleep in much this Sunday," Mama

said. "Dahlia's brunch shower is going to be so much fun. What time will you be there to help Sunshine and me?"

"Early, I promise." They discussed the details.

"Now, let's talk about you," Mama said. "Every time I see you, you seem healthier. Living in Miracle Falls seems to suit you."

Starr agreed that she felt much better. "Remember, I'm not planning to stay."

"I know— you have to follow your heart. I have a question for you that I haven't wanted to ask till now. What happened between you and Wes? "

Even thinking about the man and her job in LA made Starr uneasy. She shifted in her seat. "What do you mean, Mama?"

"Does he have anything to do with the panic attacks?"

Everyone asked that question, and Starr gave her the same answer she gave them all. "I'm pretty sure they happened because I worked without a vacation for too long."

"That's not legal, is it?"

"No, but Wes has a hectic schedule and depends on me. I love my work and didn't want to leave him in the lurch when he needed me to sew. I'm going to change that now, though." Starr hoped he wouldn't have fits when she took an annual vacation from now on.

"Good for you. Now I want to talk about Brady. He'd make a wonderful boyfriend."

Starr gaped at her. "No, Mama, just no. He's my landlord. We're friends— that's it." Sorta kinda, if you didn't count their strong physical attraction for each other. Which Starr was doing her best to ignore. She checked her watch. "I've enjoyed spending time with you tonight, but it's getting late and you need a decent night's sleep. Text me when you get home, okay?" She walked Mama to her car.

* * *

SHORTLY AFTER HIS lunch break Friday afternoon, Brady got a phone call he'd long dreamed of and couldn't ignore. "I need to take this," he told Toni, who'd come in late and would be closing that night.

He stepped into the room that served as his father's office and would be his someday— if the man ever handed him the reins for real. "This is Brady," he said, masking his curiosity and excitement level as best he could.

"Hi, Brady. It's Alfonse Strang from Strang Gallery. I opened the gallery in town about two years ago. Have you heard of us?"

"I have," Brady said. "You support up-and-coming artists. I stopped in last summer and was impressed with your taste in art. I left my card with one of your employees." He'd meant to check back but it'd been a busy Christmas season and he never had.

"That would be Jonathan. He stuck it in a drawer. I didn't find it till late December. I've heard good things about your sculptures and started following you on Instagram. I'd like to take a closer look at your work and possibly feature you at a show here at the gallery. If you're interested."

Interested? Hell, yeah. "You bet I am." Although right now, he didn't have much art to show the gallery owner. "You should know that at the moment, I have limited work ready for sale, but if you want to stop by sometime this weekend, I'm happy to show you what I have on hand. I also have

ANN ROTH

photos of the pieces I've sold and sketches I've made for future works."

Strang sounded enthusiastic enough. He offered to stop by before the gallery opened the following morning, which suited Brady's schedule well. Good thing he didn't work Saturdays.

He kept the news to himself— no sense talking about it unless Strang offered him a show. Which, as he asked to see Brady's work, he might. Or might not, he cautioned himself. Regardless, he was stoked. Somehow, he made it through the rest of the day. He headed home in high spirits.

Starr would be here tonight to see the studio, and he debated whether to tell her. If he did, she'd be pleased for him. Maybe she'd pull him into a hug and show him just how happy she was.

But no, she didn't want any more fooling around with him.

Never mind. Tonight, nothing could dampen his good mood. He looked forward to showing her his work space and some of his sculptures. Even better with food and drink. With that in mind, he segued to Beekman's Grocery on his way home and picked up snacks and a bottle of Moët. Because even the possibility was worth celebrating.

Later, purchases done and champagne chilling in a bucket of ice, he sent her a text. *Come over anytime.*

She replied with a thumbs up. He flipped on the lights in the back to help her navigate the field in the dark, changed into jeans and a sweatshirt, and headed for the living room. There, he lit a match to the kindling in the fireplace— knowing she was coming tonight, he'd set it up early this morning— and built up the fire. Shortly after he finished, Starr knocked at the door.

"I've been cooped up inside, working all day," she said, her breath clouding in the cold and making no move to come inside. "It's so good to get out in the fresh air, even if it is cold enough to make my teeth chatter. Guess what?" she said. "I took Mama to the doctor yesterday, and—"

Not about to stand in the open door and shiver, he interrupted. "Hold that thought, come on in and get warm. Then tell me everything."

"Why didn't I think of that?" She stepped into the entry. As soon as he shut the door behind her, he took her parka and hung it in the coat closet while she got rid of her boots. Her socks were surprising. "Kermit the Frog," he said and grinned. "Is that coffee he's drinking?"

"Tea, I think," she said, matching his grin. From the entry, she glanced around. "Your living room is big, and so is that fireplace. I love it, and I love the beautiful fire!"

He'd never seen her this enthusiastic, liked her all the more for it. "I figured you would. Is all this excitement because you get to see me, or is there something else that's put you in such a great mood?"

"You'll do, but it's your studio that I really want to see," she teased with an impish smile. "Plus, I got a ton done today, and like I said, it's good to be out of the house." She nodded at the couch. "As eager as I am to see where you make those sculptures, I wouldn't mind warming up for a while in front of the fire and enjoying the pop and crackle. Are you going to invite me to sit down?"

"I was about to do that. Please sit, warm up and relax."

"I will. What's with the big grin you've had since you answered the door?" she said.

He was getting to know her expressions. Her forehead

wrinkled slightly and her head angled the way it did when she was puzzled. "I'm glad you asked. I have great news— or it could be nothing much. I'll share it after you tell me about Mama J."

"You should go first. After that comment, I'm dying of curiosity."

He blew out an exaggerated breath. "Like I said, after you."

"I never knew you were so stubborn. All right, I give. Mama J's appointment went well. Her doctor says there's nothing wrong with her mind, and that aside from exhaustion, she's good physically, too. Still, wanting to be on the safe side, she sent Mama J to the lab for various blood tests. When the results come in Monday she'll be in touch. Meantime, she suggested Mama J slow down with the nightly socializing and catch up on sleep."

"Seems like sound advice to me. How did she take the news?"

"Being stubborn, she pooh-pooh'd it an said she's having too much fun to do that. But she did agree to start sleeping in on weekends. We'll see how that goes. This Sunday she's hosting a wedding shower for Dahlia, and it's doubtful she'll sleep in then. Sunshine and I will be helping out and we hope to do most of the work. That's my news. Tell me yours, and then show me the studio."

"I will, but first, we need champagne and snacks."

Her eyes widened. "You didn't mention champagne. It must be really great news. Let me guess, your father is finally retiring and you're taking over."

The last person Brady wanted to think about now was his father. "This isn't about him or the jewelry business. I could use your help bringing everything to the living room. Come with me."

She stayed quiet as they headed down the hall. When they reached the kitchen, she glanced around with the same awed expression he'd noted in the living room.

"Wow, there's lots of space in here. And it's so clean."

He agreed. "Judy may have a big mouth, but she's great at keeping the house neat."

"I especially like the colorful tiles above the counters. And look at the fancy appliances. The truth is, I don't know what some of them are."

"Same here. According to my realtor, the previous owners custom-built the kitchen. They left me a bunch of owner's manuals. I don't cook much, but I like being in here. It's one of my favorite rooms in the house."

"I haven't seen your entire place, but this room is special. As big as it is, it feels comfortable and welcoming. So does the living room." She zeroed in on a bowl sitting on a counter. "What kind of popcorn is that?"

"Something I picked up at Beekman's. It's made with truffle oil and butter. There's a tray of assorted olives, too."

"My mouth is already watering. I'll bring the treats to the living room. You take care of the champagne."

As soon as they set everything on the coffee table in front of the couch, they both sat down. "I'll open the bottle after I explain why I bought it," Brady said.

"You'd better, or I'll wither away from waiting." The smile he so liked bloomed on her face.

"Can't have that. Ever heard of Strang Gallery?" he asked, and she shook her head. "It's a fairly new art gallery about four miles west of Miracle Falls Park."

"That's why I don't recognize the name. I haven't been home in years. So many new stores and restaurants to try. I've missed the fabulous waterfall our town is named after. As soon as I get more of this sewing out of the way, I'm going to take the time to revisit the park."

"You should. Even in winter, it's amazing." Curiosity made him ask, "Ever been up there with a guy?"

"Yes, the one I mentioned from high school. We stopped there before our senior prom. I thought sure he was in love with me and wanted us to be together forever, and like the folklore says, we went there to share our love with a kiss to seal our future. But no, instead of kissing me, he broke things off. He still loved his ex-girlfriend and was going back to her. We went on to the prom, but after an hour I called Sunshine to come get me. What a way to break up, huh?"

"Ouch."

"Looking back, I should've known better. We were only seventeen, too young for that kind of commitment. Also, he was sad a good deal of the time. Silly me thought I could cheer him up, but I never could. I realized later that he missed his former girlfriend. Who, by prom time was pregnant with their baby. You?"

"What a jerk." Brady shook his head. "I thought about going up there with my ex before the marriage fell apart, but it never happened." He wasn't interested in talking further about the past.

"Okay. I'm waiting, waiting, waiting to hear your news."

"Almost news," he corrected. "I'm ready to tell you. Alfonse Strang, the owner of the gallery, has a thing for up-and-coming artists. He likes to support them— by that I mean me and the rest of us. I stopped at the gallery last summer to look around and introduce myself, but he wasn't there. I left my card, but things got busy and I never followed up. He didn't either until he phoned this afternoon. He may want to do a show featuring yours truly." Starr opened her mouth, but he signaled that he wasn't finished. "Tomorrow morning, he's stopping by to take a look at what I have so he can see my work for real instead of on Instagram. Then—"

"Wait. Did you say Instagram?"

"Occasionally, I post pieces of my work there. I've made a few sales from it. And now—"

"That's amazing, Brady. I have faith that he'll love your work."

The warmth and happiness shining from her eyes were even better than he'd imagined and felt good. "You haven't seen my art yet. Even if Strang decides not to give me a show, the fact that he contacted me says a lot about my work. But man, I'd like to show it there. Cross your fingers, say a prayer, anything to make it come true."

"I don't need to— You're going to be famous all on your own!" She threw her arms around him, exactly as he'd fantasized earlier, only the real thing was sweeter than anything his mind conjured up.

"One can hope," he managed and returned the hug. She was warm and smelled good. She leaned her head back a fraction and beamed at him, her tempting mouth mere inches away. All he could think of was kissing her. But she didn't want that, and he didn't want to ruin the evening.

With reluctance, he let go of her and reached for the champagne. "Let's open this baby and dig into the snacks."

"All right!" With her cheeks flushed, she was even more attractive.

On the verge of getting into trouble with her, he stood up, popped the cork and filled the flutes before he sat down again, this time adding extra space between them. "To my almost good news," he said. And the willpower to control himself when he was with Starr.

She cleared her throat. "Forget 'almost.' To your success."

They clinked flutes and sipped. "OMG, this champagne is so good," she said.

"One of my favorites. Wait'll you try it with the popcorn."

Seconds later, having done exactly that, she moaned. "Heaven in the mouth."

Kissing her, and hearing a similar moan for reasons that had nothing to do with food, would be even better. He pulled himself together. "The olives also go well with champagne."

"I'll give them a try." After a few moments of sampling and sipping, she spoke. "You're right, that's good, too. I didn't know about the Insta account. You're full of surprises, Brady. Tell me the name of the account, and I'll follow you."

After giving her the information, he refilled the flutes. "Time for your studio tour. Let's take these with us and head for the basement."

CHAPTER 15

*B*rady's studio was at least twice the size of the room Starr had conscripted for her sewing room. Only one window, but light from the overhead fixture above a massive wood table in the center of the room more than compensated for that. Excellent heating, too. "When you said 'basement' I pictured a cold, gloomy place. This is anything but." She squinted at the rows of shelves and drawers along a nearby wall. "What's in those?"

"Materials I've stockpiled in case I need them. Take a look."

"I will." The contents of each drawer were labeled. "You're so organized," she marveled.

"Out of desperation. Otherwise, I'd never be able to find anything."

Starr smiled at that. "I'm the same way, although at the moment the sewing room is pretty messy. But as I said awhile back, it'll be nice and clean when I leave for LA." The thought of that all but obliterated the delicious aftertaste of the champagne. Surely by then she'd be fine and looking forward to working with her sewing team.

"I'm not at all worried. For me, messy is the name of the game when I'm creating. Right now, this place is reasonably tidy, but only because I knew you were coming and cleaned up last night. And a good thing I did. I don't want to spend another hour or two tonight making it look good for Strang."

He'd spent that much time straightening the studio up for her? "You didn't have to do that."

"Maybe I wanted to impress you." His lips flirted with a smile.

Such a charmer. She was so drawn to him. "I'm flattered." In one corner, she noticed the dog sculpture she'd hit with her car. "So that's where you're keeping Shep."

"For now. I'm going to fix him soon."

"Are you planning to put him back in the front yard of the guesthouse? Seems like you'd enjoy having him closer to this house so you could see him."

"I've been thinking about that. I might set him beside the front door."

His somber expression gave her pause. She still felt bad for what'd happened. "Wish I hadn't run into him. But then I wouldn't be living in the guesthouse." Or have met Brady.

"The way I see it, things have turned out pretty well." His eyes were warm and mesmerizing, making it clear he felt just as drawn to her.

Tempting and dangerous. All it would take were a few steps closer to each other… She turned away and wandered toward the whimsical fist-size cat on the table. "Is this the one you're making for your customer?"

"Uh-huh. There are a few things left to do." He pointed to a small metal bowl on the table with a pair of pretty little round green eyes in it. "I still need to add these to the face, plus whiskers and a few other things. I'll do that tonight. Tomorrow, after I show it and the rest of my finished work to Alfonse Strang, I'll package it up and send it to my customer."

"She's such a cute kitty, and once you add the eyes…. Does she have a name?"

"What makes you think it's a she?"

"Just a feeling. Why, is it a he?"

"Beats me. It's a whimsical cat."

"I see her as female, especially with those big green eyes. I'd name her Cleo."

Amused, or so it seemed, he smiled. "You would huh?"

She smiled back. "Yup. I wonder if the customer who ordered this will choose a name. I see why she ordered another cat. I absolutely love her. What else are you going to show Mr. Strang?"

"That's in the other room." He led her to a smaller space off the larger basement and pointed out a shelf of unsold merchandise: a porcupine, a horse reared up on its hind legs, a pair of ducks, a wolf, various fish, birds, and bunnies, among others. A few larger pieces sat on the table. "This is what I have now."

"More than I imagined," she murmured, awed by the details and whimsy of each. "You're incredibly talented, Brady. I really like your work." Really liked him, as well.

Too much, too soon. What a shame they wanted different things and lived so far apart. Although the way she felt about him, she was tempted to reconsider the sex thing.

Better not.

"Glad you do," he said. "I doubt it's enough for a show— I'm guessing I'll need to make more pieces in various sizes. I'll get a better idea of how many and what kind when I meet with Strang."

Despite his earlier words that he might not get the show, he seemed to be thinking positively. Starr crossed her fingers for him. "Any idea when he wants you to do it?"

"No, but I'm sure I'll find out."

"Keep me posted. I'll bet your parents are excited."

His expression blanked. "I haven't said anything to them or anyone except you."

"Just me?" She wondered about that. "Because it's not for sure?"

"Partly."

He didn't elaborate. It made sense that he wanted to nail down the show before spreading the news with his friends and family, in case it didn't happen. "I won't say a word to anyone," she promised.

"I'd appreciate it."

His sudden somber mood made her wonder. Maybe he wasn't as optimistic as she'd thought. Or she'd overstayed her welcome. It was getting late, and he wanted to finish the cat. "I so enjoyed this, Brady, but you have work to do, and I'm tired. I should go."

Silent now, he followed her up the stairs. After donning her parka and boots, she turned to him. "Thanks for the champagne and nibblies, and for sharing your momentous news with me."

"It's not momentous yet."

"Almost momentous," she corrected. "You'll let me know, right?"

"Definitely. This was fun. I'm glad you came."

The words and intent look on his face made her want to step into his arms. Instead, she zipped up her coat.

At the door, unable to stop herself, she reached up and touched his cheek. His eyelids drifted lower, just like when they'd kissed before. Way too tempted, she swallowed and stepped away. "I'll be in and out this weekend, but I'm around if you need to talk."

He nodded and stepped outside with her. "I'll watch you cross the meadow."

She didn't need that but didn't mind, either. As she headed through the fairy-like lights guiding the way, she felt his gaze on her.

By the time Alfonse Strang rang the doorbell Saturday morning, Brady had been up for hours. Too hyped to sleep much, he'd added a few last touches to Cleo— he agreed with Starr that the moniker fit the little cat. Then he'd rearranged the inventory of finished work on the shelves. He'd also brewed a fresh pot of coffee.

It was a gray day with storm clouds gathered overhead. Weather forecasters predicted the possibility of heavy snow in the afternoon. Nothing new there— such was January in Miracle Falls. As soon as Brady opened the door, the gallery owner wiped his feet on the mat and stepped inside. "It's freezing out there," he said, bringing some of the frigid air in with him.

Having never met the art dealer and only heard his voice, Brady had pictured a tall, lean male in his forties with dark hair. In reality, Strang was about five foot seven and heavyset, with a youthful face, a thick head of silver hair, and somber eyes under wire-rimmed glasses. Late forties, Brady guessed, and prematurely gray.

"Good to meet you, Mr. Strang." Brady extended his arm.

"Call me Alfonse," he said, his handshake firm. "You live in a pretty part of town."

In the living room, they made small talk and sipped coffee for a few minutes. Brady showed him photos of previous artwork he'd stored on his iPhone. Strang was a quiet man, asking questions here and there and nodding. When Brady showed him the photo of Shep he'd first placed in front of the guesthouse, Alfonse studied it carefully. "This is a remarkable piece of work. How much did you sell it for, and who bought it?"

"That isn't for sale." Brady explained why he'd crafted it.

"Even in the photo, that emotion comes through."

No one had ever commented about that. "I'm glad you noticed. It's an outdoor piece and helped me deal with the grief of losing my longtime companion. Recently, it had a little run-in with a car. Nothing too serious, though. I'm planning to make the repairs as soon as I have time."

"Can I see the piece?"

"Of course. I'm keeping it in the studio till I fix the dings." Strang's mug was empty. "More coffee?"

"No, thanks. I'm ready to see your studio and any sculptures you have."

Brady took him to the basement and showed him the homage to Shep, then led him into the room with the rest of the sculptures. Strang didn't say much while he took it all in. When he finished and they returned to the living room, Brady handed him the sketchbook to look through.

Astute questions showed he'd paid attention. It was obvious he missed nothing. Moments later, he shut the sketchbook and fell silent. Brady caught his breath and waited.

"My opinion hasn't changed," Strang said. "Seeing more of your work in the studio and those sketches has convinced me. Let's do a show sometime in late spring or early summer, when tourist season is in full force."

Later, after a discussion that included a contract to be reviewed and signed, Brady showed him out. Then he texted Starr. *You home?*

She answered seconds later. *Yes.*

Be right over.

CHAPTER 16

*W*ith heavy snow predicted later in the day, the Saturday night drinks and dinner Robin had orchestrated for Starr and their other bestie Savannah was postponed. Starr made a beeline to Beekman's and stocked up on groceries and decorations for the wedding shower brunch the following day. Surely by mid-morning tomorrow any snow would be cleared and the drive easy. Starr was counting on that. She looked forward to decorating Mama's house for the festivities and relaxing with the family.

Other shoppers had the same idea, and the store was crowded. While she waited in line to check out, she thought about tomorrow's festivities.

At home again, she was unpacking groceries and bopping out to a rockin' new Rihanna album when Brady texted. If he was on his way to the guesthouse now, he must have news. Excited to find out, she stowed the perishables and ignored the rest to put away later. Laundry and cleaning would have to wait, too. She'd barely managed to fit everything into the fridge— should've bought less —when his footsteps thudded across the porch.

"It's unlocked," she called out and started for the door.

He came in smelling like the fresh air and rubbing his gloved hands together. "It's way too cold out there."

"I know— I just got home from Beekman's. I wasn't planning to make a fire till later, but…"

"That's okay." His expression unreadable, he handed a folder to her. "Hold this for me."

While she itched to see the contents, he stuffed the gloves into the pockets of his parka and pulled his hat and scarf off. Did he have to be so quiet?

"Well?" she asked, unable to stand the suspense. "I'm guessing Mr. Strang has been and gone. What's the verdict? As if I didn't know." In the process of hanging his coat up, Brady raised his eyebrows, and she added, "You're too talented not to get a show."

"The vote of confidence is much appreciated." He started to reclaim the folder, then dropped his hands. "The way you're drumming your fingers on that thing, you're eager to see what's in there. Go ahead and open it."

She did and quickly skimmed the four-page document. "You have a contract, Brady!"

The grin she expected bloomed on his face. "I sure do. I haven't signed it yet. First, I want an attorney to go through it with me. So don't say anything to anyone yet."

"I won't. Smart man. But bottom line, he wants a show with you. That's freaking wonderful!" She set the folder on the tiny entry table, grabbed his hands and pulled him into the center of the living room for an impromptu circular jig.

Brady laughed, and so did she, until breathless, she pulled

ANN ROTH

him to a stop and let go of him. "That was unexpected," he said. "You're fun."

How long had it been since someone had said that— since she'd *been* fun? Coming home was definitely healing, like she was returning to the self she'd forgotten. Strange that she hadn't realized what she'd lost. Something to think about later when she was alone. "Fun is good," she said.

"You never fail to surprise me. And here, I expected a hug."

Hands on her hips, she arched her eyebrows. "Did you, now?"

"Well, yeah, like last night."

By his deadpan expression, he was teasing. How could she forget wrapping her arms around him, a man so fit and muscled, and the heaven of his arms urging her closer, then fighting with herself to let go? It was nothing to make light of. She clasped her thumb ring. "The way things are between us, it feels like we're on the verge of starting something I'm not ready for," she said for the sake of honesty. "And neither are you."

"Can't blame a guy for hoping. You know I'm attracted to you. I wouldn't mind exploring the chemistry we seem to have, but no worries— I know you don't want to. That's okay."

Oh, but she did, so much, and that was the trouble. Brady gave her a tender smile that melted her heart. "Thanks for understanding," she said, longing for him more than ever. She went back to the entry, picked up the folder and held it to her chest. As if the flimsy material would shield her from the hunger.

He nodded at the folder. "Can I pick your brain about that?" he asked.

On much safer ground now, she relaxed. "If you mean the contract, of course. How about coffee while we talk?"

"No, thanks. I had plenty with Alfonse."

"Alfonse, huh? Unlike you, I could use another cup. But I have to make it first. Okay if we sit in the kitchen?"

"Works for me."

Figuring he might change his mind, she measured enough water for two mugs and poured it into the coffeemaker. The beans were in the cupboard above. She reached for the container and brought it down. Sensing his eyes on her— how did she always know?— she turned toward him. "You're staring."

"Caught me," he said without a smidge of embarrassment. "I like watching you."

"Why?"

"Not many women are as tall and graceful. It's the next best thing to kissing you."

"Does that line work for you?"

"Line? I mean it, Starr."

Flattered but refusing to show it, she frowned and pushed the start button. While she waited for the machine to cycle through the brewing process and do its job, she sat down across from him. "You said you wanted to ask me something about your contract?"

"About contracts in general, if you know anything about them."

"As a matter of fact, when I was at Parsons I learned about business regulations and practices, including contracts."

"Do you have one with Wes?"

"Absolutely. From the start, I signed contracts with Wes and every other band I worked for."

"I didn't know you worked for other bands, too."

"Not anymore, but when I first graduated and started my career, I worked with several including The Wiglets. Each one stipulated the same thing, that my work for them included only the costumes we agreed on and things associated with that. The contracts covered a set period and included raises and laid out the steps for when or if either party wanted out, that kind of thing. Juggling the different bands kept me hopping, but I had a great time. Then Wes hired me to work exclusively for him. That was when he first got noticed by the media. Some of his albums went platinum and he started to sell out at the concerts he booked. He wanted to be a super-star and seemed to be heading in that direction. It was all so exciting."

The coffee was ready. She stood and filled her mug. Brady again turned down the offer for a cup.

"Tell me more," he said as she sat down again.

"I figured working with him was a great way to get my name out there and build my reputation. The money he offered was good, too, more than I'd ever made."

Having struggled financially throughout school, at first she'd gone a little crazy and had spent most of her paycheck as soon as the money landed in her bank account. But Mama hadn't raised her like that, and before long she'd changed her ways, upping the amount paid toward car payments and school loans so that she'd get out from under the debt faster. She'd also opened a savings account and deposited some of each paycheck there.

The first five years had been crazy busy but still enjoy-able. As Wes and the band grew in popularity, she'd hired help and the team had celebrated every award he and the band earned. The change in him had been gradual and barely noticeable until a few years ago, when he'd turned into a full-fledged prima donna. Demanding, pushing her and the rest of the costume design team to do more and do it faster, constantly riding his manager for one thing or another, and making everyone else in his entourage work harder. In private, they called him Mr. Impossible. Because he was.

"Something wrong with your coffee?" Brady asked.

Puzzled, she eyed him. "No. Why?"

"You look like you swallowed something nasty."

"Not from this coffee. It's Lolli's special brand. My sisters turned me on to it. I don't know how I'll survive in LA without it."

"I get that— I drink it, too. Take a bunch with you when you go back to LA. Better yet, ask them to ship to you. There has to be some reason for that face."

There was, of course. "And you're curious what it is."

"Not if you don't want to tell me," he said, leaning toward her as if finding out meant everything.

She'd already said too much and didn't like talking about the hellish pace Wes had pushed on her, and yet she wanted to confide in Brady, even if she couldn't. "I signed an NDA, remember?"

"Hey, I already know that even talking to the guy gives you a panic attack."

"How would you possibly know that?" She hadn't come out and said it, had she?

"It wasn't hard to figure out. I came over shortly after you ended a call with him and saw what talking to him did to you. You don't have to pour out the details, just paint me a brief picture of why you struggle with even mentioning him. I won't tell a soul— you have my word."

"The only thing I can say is common knowledge shared by everyone who works for him. Our boss is a tyrant. Please don't ask me to say anything else." She started to get the tight feeling that signaled an impending panic attack.

"I wouldn't want you getting another panic attack." Wondering how he knew, she scowled, and he added, "The suddenly rigid posture and tightly-compressed lips gave you away."

Already he knew her too well.

"Tyrants only have power when you give it to them," he said. "If you stand up to him, you might feel better."

The very idea caused her stomach to twist. Enough of that. She forced herself to relax. "Back to your contract."

"Right. Alfonse asked for an exclusive agreement."

"Did he spell out what that meant?"

"No, but I assume he doesn't want me working with other gallery owners. Do you see a problem with that?"

"Yes. You may not want to be exclusive with anyone. What if someone on Instagram wants to buy one of your sculptures? You shouldn't have to pay Alfonse a cut."

"Never thought of that. You sure are smart."

"I got good advice at school and also had a decent lawyer. He added clauses that protected me from getting into trouble."

"He wouldn't happen to live in town, would he?"

Starr shook her head. "He's in LA, though he might take you on if you ask. I'm happy to give you his contact info, but I'll bet you'll be able to find someone here in town. Dahlia and

Jake have worked with several lawyers and will have suggestions."

"Good idea." Brady glanced out the kitchen window. "Doesn't look like snow to me. The sun is out. But around here, you never know. The weather forecasters are predicting a big storm tonight. I should check in at the store."

"I thought you took weekends off."

"I do, but I still like to know what's going on. It's no trouble to make a call."

She nodded. "Congrats on your good news."

At the door, she started to reach up and touch his face again. As if they were together. Catching herself just in time, she grasped the doorknob instead.

They weren't involved that way and never would be. She knew it and so did Brady.

If only her body accepted that.

To Starr's relief, the storm that was predicted for Saturday night turned out to be a smattering of snow. Could've met her friends last night after all. Oh well, they'd get together next week. Sunday morning was cloudless and clear, perfect for the wedding shower brunch at Mama's.

The party was small— family, Addie, and a handful of Dahlia's close friends. In all, ten women plus Jake and Trevor. Looking forward to a great time as long as Mama didn't start with the find-yourself-a-man talk, which she probably wouldn't in front of company, Starr arrived with two pans of ready-to-bake cinnamon rolls, silly presents to hand out to winners of

the shower games and a boxful of decorations to create a cele-
bratory air. Mama had made a fruit salad and was putting a
large breakfast casserole together, and Sunshine had offered to
bring a cake and fixings for various cocktails and mocktails.

Once again, Mama pulled Starr into a warm hug. This
morning she seemed more like herself, even if she hadn't slept
in. Maybe she was simply excited. "You seem more rested
today," Starr said.

"I slept in yesterday and stayed home last night to clean
and get ready for this party. It meant missing dinner and
movie night, but the girls understood."

Cute how Mama referred to women in their late fifties and
early sixties as girls. "You knew they would. When you hear
from Dr. Richards tomorrow, let me know what she says."

"Of course." Mama cast a critical eye her way, and for a
tense moment Starr sensed she was poised to ask a question
about Brady. "You look rested, too," she commented instead.
"I'm glad I got to see that house. It's so cute. Sunshine texted
that she and Trevor will be along shortly. Dahlia, Jake and the
other guests should be here in about an hour. It's a good thing
Trevor doesn't have to work today."

"He works Sundays?"

"When he needs to. Sometimes he works seven or ten days
straight. So do you."

This was true. All too many times, she'd spent her weekends designing and sewing. Working a six- or seven-day week
was challenging and often brutal, at least for her. Trevor and
Sunshine probably didn't care for it, either.

But the subject hadn't come up during phone conversations, which tended to be sporadic, due to how busy they both

were. Living in LA, she'd missed so much. She needed to come home more often than once every six or seven years.

"I want to get these decorations up," she said.

Mama nodded. "And I need to finish getting the serving utensils, flatware and dishes ready. I'm preheating the oven to bake the casserole, but I won't put it in until everyone arrives. Don't worry, there'll be room in there for your cinnamon rolls."

Before long, Sunshine and Trevor arrived. "Good to see you again," Trevor said to Starr.

"You, too." He was as good-looking as Jake, but neither could compare to Brady. Not that Starr cared. She wasn't, was not, getting involved with him.

Shortly after they arrived, to everyone's surprise, Dahlia and Jake strolled in. Starr was glad to see them both, even if they were super early. Mama ordered them to relax and watch TV in her bedroom to get them out of the way.

Over the next hour, Sunshine, Trevor, Starr and Mama decorated the living room, set up a table for gifts, put the cocktail ingredients on the kitchen counter and otherwise bustled around. The casserole went into the oven to bake.

The other guests would arrive soon. When everything was ready, they let the soon-to-be-married couple know it was okay to come out of the bedroom. They sat in the living room to chat and wait for everyone else. Starr enjoyed that. It was obvious Jake and Dahlia were deeply in love, and Sunshine and Trevor weren't far behind. If they hadn't included her in the conversation, she would've felt like the lonely extra wheel. Someday, she, too, would find the right man and join the coupledom tribe. It wouldn't be Brady, and why had she even thought about him? She was here to enjoy her family and the shower.

The rest of the party showed up, and the good times began.

Trevor poured the cocktails, Mama slid the casserole into the oven, and everyone played a few shower games complete with the small prizes Starr had brought. Dahlia and Jake opened gifts to oohs and aahs. There was nothing from Starr — her gift was the wedding dress. Finally, brunch was served. They ate in the living room. When Dalia's friends left, Jake, Trevor and the rest of the family pitched in and cleaned up.

After that, they streamed into the kitchen and had seconds on cake. "What a great party," Dahlia said. "Thanks so much, you guys."

"It was our pleasure." Mama beamed at them all. "It's so nice to have the whole family at the same table. When Starr meets her special someone, I'll need a bigger one."

Here we go. "I'm in no rush, okay?" Under her breath she muttered, "And you'd better not start in about Brady."

Speculative looks all around. Apparently, her voice hadn't been as low as she'd thought. She didn't hide her irritation. "Mama's pushing the idea of Brady and me getting together, which is crazy," she explained. "I don't want that, and neither does he."

Starr's sisters shared a look. "You and Brady have discussed it?"

"Casually, in passing." Which wasn't quite true but would do.

Mama was quiet until she swallowed whatever was in her mouth. "I'm not pushing anything, Starr. I simply think he's a good man who happens to be single."

"Dahlia and I think a lot of him, too," Jake added. "I assume he's a decent landlord."

"A very good one. He—" Starr cut herself off. She'd been on the verge of telling them about the contract at Strang Gallery. But it wasn't signed yet, and she'd promised not to say anything. "Sunshine and Trevor, your cake is out of this world."

"Thanks," Sunshine said. "We made it together without tearing each other's heads off." She added a grin and Trevor shrugged.

"That's funny and sweet," Dahlia deadpanned. "Pun intended."

Everyone groaned except Mama. "You were saying something about Brady," she commented. "He what?"

When the woman got something in her head, she was relentless. It drove Starr and her sisters crazy. Today, she pretended it wasn't bothering her and moved on. "Before I forget, guess what I'm doing tomorrow evening? Having dinner and drinks with Robin and Savannah at Marsden's. That's where I got those pot pies for dinner when you came over the other night, remember, Mama? I saw Robin last week, and I'm really looking forward to spending time with both her and Savannah."

"The three of you back together, huh?" Sunshine smiled. "You used to have so much fun with each other."

Dahlia nodded. "I thought you were so cool. I always wished I was part of that group."

"You had a lot of good friends," Starr reminded her. "And you were pretty wrapped up with Jake." Since high school, if you didn't count the long breakup before they made up.

The lovers smiled at each other.

"What were you going to say about Brady?" Mama persisted.

Why wouldn't she let it go? Starr sighed. "That besides being a jewelry designer, he's also a talented artist."

"That's right, you damaged one of his sculptures." Mama gave her a knowing look. "That's how she and Brady met." Her gaze went around the table. "Did you know that?"

Enough was enough. Starr stood. "Excuse me." She headed for the bathroom and shut the door behind her.

Seconds later, someone knocked at the door. "Who is it?" she said, none too friendly.

"Your sisters," Sunshine answered in a whisper barely loud enough for Starr to make out. "Let us in."

"Oh, all right." After they crowded in and shut the door, Starr explained. "You know why I'm in here— I'm on the verge of losing it, and I don't want that kind of ending to this wonderful day. Mama made it sound like I orchestrated the collision in order to meet Brady, when it was an accident. The idea of me setting up a way to meet a man when I've never done that in my life is absurd. I'm not at all manipulative and never have been. She has to be blind not to notice how much she tees me off."

"We've all been there," Sunshine said. "We know what happened that day. The ground was slippery and you didn't have your snow tires yet."

"Thank you. Why does Mama say things like that?"

Dahlia shrugged. "The billion-dollar question. I don't think she means to back you into a corner. Once she starts, she can't seem to stop herself."

"It's how she's wired," Sunshine added. "I doubt she'll ever change. We love her, though, warts and all."

"So true," Starr agreed. "I just wish she'd forget about Brady and me."

"You have to admit, knowing you two talked about relationships does make the wheels turn." Dahlia tapped her forehead.

"I said 'casually,' remember?"

"That the subject came up at all makes me want to know more. You're seriously crushing on him, and I wonder if maybe he is, too."

"We like each other, yes, and we get along well. But besides the fact that I'm leaving after the wedding, we have different ideas about relationships."

"Such as?" Sunshine said.

Starr saw no reason to hold back. "He's interested in sex but otherwise doesn't want a relationship, I'm guessing because the divorce jaded him. That's not for me— I want more than sex. In other words, there's no possibility of us getting together." Dahlia opened her mouth, but Starr beat her to it. "Look, if we don't get back to the table, Mama will come in here with us. Thanks for talking me down from my hissy fit. It's good to have you both in my corner."

A quick hug followed, and they returned to the kitchen. Jake and Trevor were loading the dishwasher and otherwise setting the kitchen back to rights. "No wonder you guys snagged my sisters," Starr commented. "You clean up the mess. Where's Mama?"

"She took the garbage bag to the trash bin outside," Jake said. "I offered to do it, but she said she ate too much and needed to move."

Starr waited for her to come back in to thank her for hosting and say goodbye.

"I'm sorry I upset you," Mama said. "It's just… I want to see you happy."

"And I appreciate that. But you need to trust me when I tell you that I'm doing okay. I really am." She was tons better than when she'd first arrived. "Be sure to call or text when you get your test results."

"I will." Mama checked her watch. "Do you have to run off so soon? It's early yet."

"I need to finish a few things at home." The fun stuff—cleaning and laundry. Having put those chores off yesterday, she wasn't going to put them off again.

After one more hug with Mama and her sisters and a smile at their special guys, she left.

CHAPTER 17

onday morning, after getting into the rhythm of creating art through the weekend, Brady reluctantly upgraded his jeans and sweatshirt to the nicer clothes he wore at the store. He headed out shortly after breakfast. The sky wasn't as clear as it'd been Sunday, but the town had dodged the predicted weekend storm, which was both good and bad. Clear roads made for easy driving, but he could've used another day at home. Creating and turning what he envisioned into art was a slow process, and he wanted, *needed* to produce pieces or he wouldn't have enough for a show. He refused to let that happen.

The previous evening, he'd asked Jake about attorneys. Jake had suggested he get in touch with Trevor Holmes. Apparently, the private investigator knew quite a few of them. Trevor had given him the names of the attorneys he used.

Neither Jake nor Trevor had pressed him for details on why he suddenly needed legal help, and he didn't enlighten them. Once the contract was signed, he'd tell them and everyone else the news. Including the parents. Senior was bound to be impressed. Picturing the pleased expression on his face and the words he longed to hear, "I'm proud of you, son," Brady grinned.

As soon as he prepped the store for opening, he phoned the attorney Trevor had recommended as his top choice. A woman named Kelly Yarrow, who Sunshine had hired when she'd needed legal help. Kelly wasn't in, and he left a message with the person who answered the phone.

Like all Mondays in the dead of winter, this was a quiet day and he was by himself. Between the customers who came in and left, he was able to get some design work done. Toni showed up around lunchtime. By then, he was starving. He was barely out the door to get lunch when Kelly returned the call.

It was too cold to stand outside and talk, so he went back inside and muted his phone for a moment. "I'm going to take this call in the office," he said, then stepped into the room and shut the door. When the conversation ended some minutes later, he'd agreed to forward the attorney the contract, which he'd brought with him in case he needed it. He'd also set up a meeting with her for later that afternoon, two hours earlier than the time he usually left the store, as that was the only available slot she had that week. He decided to skip lunch, settling for a granola bar and a bag of trail mix instead while he scanned the contract and emailed it to her.

When he was about to take off that afternoon, his father stopped by. The man had impeccable timing. "You were here most of Friday," Brady said. "What brings you back today?"

Senior frowned, as if the question were insulting. "As you well know, I'm here several days a week. Not much going on today, is there?"

"Nothing we don't expect this time of year. If you're here to check on me, everything's okay."

"All right." In his usual terse way, the man said nothing more.

"I've had time to work on one of the jewelry pieces I'm designing— the bracelet. The customer is coming at the end of the week to look over the sketch and okay it. Would you like to see what I've done so far?"

"All I care about is that she likes it."

It had taken months to convince his father to let him design and create jewelry, and it was the one thing about Brady that pleased him. He hadn't even acknowledged Toni, who was finishing a call from a customer. Brady nodded at her. "Toni has done a lot of invoicing and made several sales this afternoon. She's doing a great job."

Her back straightened with pride, and she smiled. "Thanks, Brady. Hello, Mr. Barton."

A nod. "Hi, Toni. I gather you're locking up tonight."

"Yes, sir."

Brady checked his watch. He didn't want to be late for his meeting and had to leave. "I have an appointment and need to go."

He didn't expect his father to ask about that and the man didn't. "Two hours early." Senior shook his head.

"FYI, I skipped lunch today," Brady said, disliking his need to defend himself. "Can I help you with something before I leave?"

"I want to check on today's sales numbers." Which were available on the office desktop. "Oh, you ought to give your mother a call. I think she wants you to come to dinner next Sunday."

He couldn't make the invitation himself? Never mind, Brady was used to that. If all went well, by then the contract would be signed and he'd share the great news with them at dinner. "I'll call her tonight."

After Kelly Yarrow went through the contract with him while he made notations of what he needed to either change or clarify with Alfonse, some thirty minutes had passed and it was almost dark outside. Still, he was able to make out the ominous clouds packing the sky. The forecast called for the storm that'd been expected this past weekend. This time it seemed eminent.

Although he'd stocked up on groceries over the weekend and had skipped lunch, he was in no mood to cook. He stopped for takeout teriyaki with rice and vegetables and ate at home. He also texted Starr about the attorney.

He chuckled at her reply, an animated emoji of a man saying, "I'm so proud."

Then he phoned his mom about the dinner. "Is it snowing at your house?" she asked when the plans had been made. "It is here."

He peered out the window. "Coming down hard." When the call ended, he disconnected and headed for the basement to work.

AT DINNER MONDAY NIGHT, Starr had a great time with Robin and Savannah. In high school, they'd been known as the three amigas, a name they'd dubbed for themselves at a sleepover shortly before the jazz trio using the same name had formed. They spent awhile reminiscing and laughing a ton. Unlike

Robin, Savannah was married. She and Ian had two kids, both in grade school. Ian worked at one of the tech companies that'd opened recently in town. His job was to thwart hackers. An architect, Savannah loved what she was doing and was overall a very happy woman.

She was warm and as funny as ever. As much as Starr liked her, she couldn't help but envy her happy family. Robin did, too. Who wouldn't?

There was no talk about Wes at all, which was a relief. They talked about other men, though. Robin was in an unusually good mood. She'd met a guy named Harrison through one of her dating apps. A coffee date the past Saturday had worked out well enough for them to schedule dinner for the following weekend.

"That sounds promising," Starr said.

"So far, but who knows?" Robin shrugged as if she didn't care. "He could turn out to be a real jerk. I'm not getting my hopes up yet, and I'm not going to jump into bed with him just because he's cute and I haven't had sex in forever."

In that sense, she and Starr were alike. Savannah asked about Starr's love life. "Sex-wise, what Robin said," she answered. "But that's okay— I'm not ready to date, especially not here. I'll be leaving after the wedding and don't see the point."

Robin leaned in and lowered her voice. "What she means is, she likes Brady Barton. But his heart belongs to his ex-wife."

"Robin!" Starr scolded. "That was supposed to be confidential. But since you mentioned him, I found out that I was wrong about him and his ex. He doesn't like her at all. Which doesn't mean I want to get together with him."

"But you like him," Robin repeated.

"Yes, he's a great guy. Period." Starr glanced around the restaurant, then checked her watch. Eight o'clock already. "Looks like we're the last customers in here. How did it get to be closing time so soon?"

As they donned their coats, she silently thanked the universe for her longtime friendship with the two women. Her friends in LA were people she worked with or others who designed costumes for celebrities. Good people, but not as special as the two she was with.

She didn't realize it was snowing till they stepped outside. "Will you look at that? It's starting to stick and I have a good half-hour drive ahead. I'd better scoot. This was so fun! Let's do it again sometime soon."

Both friends seconded that. "Be safe," they said, and exchanged quick hugs.

Starr intended to be super careful and was grateful for the snow tires. The roads had last been salted a few days earlier, but tonight's snow had pretty much erased the benefits. She drove slowly and didn't get too close to the few cars also on the road. She didn't reach Woodlawn Road till after nine. Worried that she'd skid off the road like she had before, she inched toward the driveway. Thick snow there. Afraid of getting stuck, she stopped several feet short of it. Except for Judy's visit to clean house the day Starr had moved in, only Brady, her sisters, Addie, and Mama had driven up here. But what if someone did and hit the Civic?

There was only one solution: get the snow shovel and clear a path up the driveway, then pull up and park there. She thought about phoning Brady for help, but she hadn't seen him since he'd brought over the contract. He was likely hard at work on his art. Never mind, she could handle this.

Congratulating herself for keeping her snow boots on the floor of the passenger seat, she traded the leather ankle boots she'd worn to dinner for the other ones. She estimated the snowfall so far to be around four inches, only a few inches shy of the tops of her boots. And it was still coming down fast and furious. She made her way slowly to the porch steps. Brushing snow from the banister as she went up and nudging the snow on the risers to one side with her boot, she cleared a path of sorts to the porch and grabbed the snow shovel. Careful not to slip, she toted it down the steps and headed for the end of the driveway

Shoveling wasn't easy but kept her warm. She made slow, steady progress. Too bad the snow was coming down so hard. When her arms ached and she was ready to quit, she'd cleared enough of the driveway to keep the car safe— fingers crossed. Winded and proud of herself, she returned to it to drive it up to the point where she'd stopped shoveling.

Unfortunately, despite the snow tires, she couldn't get any traction. Stuck, darn it. If only there was someone to push the car forward while she gunned the engine. She phoned Brady.

CHAPTER 18

*B*rady was in his basement working on a bear and cub sculpture when his phone rang. Starr, huh? It'd been several days since they'd seen each other or otherwise been in contact. Smiling, he answered. "Some snow, huh?"

"More than I can handle. I'm sitting in my car unable to move it. I could use your help."

That didn't sound good, and he rubbed the back of his neck. "And here, I thought you were calling because you missed me."

"Very funny. Do you have time to give me a hand?"

"No problem. I have snow chains. It'll take a few minutes to put them on, then I'll come get you. Where are you?"

"You don't need to drive. My car is three or four feet shy of the driveway."

Confused, he frowned. "In weather like this, I figured you'd be home at this hour." The lights were on at the guest-house— he'd glimpsed them through gaps in the drapes when he'd looked out during his dinner. Since then, he'd been preoccupied with the bear sculpture and hadn't left the basement in several hours. He wondered if she'd hit a tree.

"I went out to dinner and didn't even know it was snowing till we left the restaurant. I made it all the way here, which was no picnic, but I managed to get up Woodlawn Road close to the driveway before the snow stopped me."

She went on, but Brady was stuck on what she'd said. Who had she been out with that she hadn't even noticed the snow? A stab of what felt like jealousy reared up. Ridiculous. She wasn't dating, or so she said. Regardless, it wasn't his business.

"Brady, are you still there?" she said, and he realized she'd stopped talking.

"Yep."

"Do you think you could give me a push up the driveway?"

"I'll be there in a few minutes."

The snow was deep and traversing the field was tricky, especially with the shovel he was carrying. Thanks to careful walking and his good boots, he made it in one piece.

She stood by the car, her cap and parka coated in white. Not all of her hair was protected, and the parts that hung to her shoulders glistened with melted snow. "Why aren't you sitting in the car?" he asked.

"I wanted to watch for you. You didn't need to bring your snow shovel. There's one here."

"I know. I brought another in case we both needed to shovel." He noted the extra snow piled on either side of the driveway. "Looks like you already have."

She nodded. "I thought if I cleared a few feet off, I'd be able to pull the car up and out of harm's way. In case another car happens to come up this road. I wouldn't want it to crash into mine. I've had enough of that."

Her lips quirked in an almost smile he appreciated. "You did good. Must've taken you awhile."

"I got quite a workout. On the plus side, it kept me warm." She shivered. "I'm not so warm anymore."

"Why don't you go inside while I clear more snow off the driveway and from around your tires. I'll text when I'm done and we'll see if we can get the car into the driveway."

"I'm not that tired," she said, "and I don't want to sit inside waiting while you do the work. As I said, shoveling is a great way to keep warm."

Fine with Brady. Working together, they cleared a larger patch of driveway.

"You're tough and a hard worker," he said, admiring her for hanging in there. "Get in the car and start it while I clear snow from around the back tires. Keep it in park with the brakes on. When I finish, I'll let you know. Then release the brakes and accelerate while I push."

"Okay."

"Accelerate," he called out when he was done.

At first, the stubborn wheels spun in place. Grunting, he threw his whole body behind the push. That worked, and she made it halfway up the driveway.

A moment later, she turned off the engine and exited the car beaming at him. "We did it! Thanks, Brady. You're the best." Still smiling, she shook her head. "I've said that so often, it's becoming a cliché."

Not minding at all, he shrugged. "I'd been working for several hours and needed the break. I met with a lawyer this afternoon."

"That's fast. Why don't you tell me about it inside. I, uh, really need to use the bathroom," she said, and started up the steps, again brushing the railing and moving with caution. "I should've used the one at Marsden's, but they were getting ready to close and I didn't realize it'd take me so long to get home." She unlocked the door, then quickly pulled her boots off. "Come on in. I'll be right back."

As she disappeared down the hall, he untied and stepped out of his boots, then his gloves, hat and parka. Even without a fire the guesthouse was homey and warm. He'd been here many times during winter months, but it had never felt so... He searched for the right word. Homey. What had changed? Starr returned, and he had the answer. For some reason he didn't understand, her presence made it feel that way.

Not something he wanted to think about.

She'd changed into jeans that hugged her long legs and a loose-fitting, long-sleeve sweatshirt. Her face was ruddy from the cold and much of her hair was wet. She was shivering. "You're cold," he said.

"Now that I traded my wet clothes for dry ones, I'll warm up."

"I can help with that." His offer caught him off-guard, as did his arms that had opened all on their own.

"I shouldn't, but I'm too cold and tempted to turn you down." She nestled in, and he wrapped her in a hug. "You're warmer than a comforter, exactly what I needed."

Some parts of him warmer than others, he thought with a wry smile. She hugged his waist, and he rubbed her back and her arms to get the circulation going.

She sighed. "Thanks to you, I'm beginning to thaw."

"You're not shivering as much. That's good." He inhaled her scent. "You smell like snow and fresh air."

She looked up at him with a slight frown. "Snow has a smell?"

"Sure does. On you, it's..." He paused, breathed in the scent again and thought about how to describe it. "Clean and fresh as a winter day, with a whiff of evergreen."

"Oh, I like that. Hmm."

She leaned in and sniffed the crook of his neck, her nose glancing his skin. It was ice cold, but her warm exhale touched him like a gentle caress and stirred his heat level to the edge of trouble.

"I don't smell that on you," she said, while he willed his body to behave. "You're more like soap and something I can't identify. Just you, I guess."

He was so turned on, he barely took in the words. "What are you doing?" he said, his low growl warning her to stop the torture. In vain. She continued to cling to him.

"The same thing you did with me— inhaling your scent."

"I didn't move in close like that or bury my nose in the crook of your neck. My nose isn't cold like yours, either. When you do that, you make me want things you don't."

"Oh." Her lips parted a little, as if she wanted exactly what he did. The long, heated look that passed between them confirmed it.

His last coherent thought was that he should pull away. Then she kissed him. Thoroughly and deeply and hotly, going back for more like she couldn't get enough. Right there with her, he cupped her hips and brought her firmly up against his body. Soft, sweet, driving him crazy with her passion. Her breathing deeper and faster, she wriggled against him, at the same time slanting her upper body back just enough to put his hands on her breasts. As he tested the heft and firmness, she moaned in pleasure.

Dimly, he realized that things were heating up way too fast. Any time now, he'd go up in flames and they'd end up doing things she might regret. With a great deal of restraint, he pulled away. "I thought you didn't want to do this," he said, his body aroused and aching, his breathing heavy.

This time her face was flushed from heat instead of the cold. "I didn't, only…" She broke off as if thinking, then went on. "Even if I want to, I made a promise to myself that I wouldn't. You know that. Anyway, how was I supposed to know sniffing your neck with my cold nose would get you all hot and bothered?"

"Hey, you kissed me first. And FYI, your nose isn't cold anymore. If you don't want to have sex, it won't happen," he pledged, no matter how much he wanted her. "But you can't play with me like that. I'm a man. I have needs."

"I didn't think about that."

"You should. It's obvious that I want you." He was still hard and ticked at himself for letting it happen. As if he could control his reaction. Ready to leave, he took his coat from the closet, then reached for his boots. Or started to.

Suddenly, the lights went out. Not counting the two of them breathing, the house was utterly silent. He swore under his breath. "The power is out."

"So I noticed," she muttered. "What do we do now?"

"First, get some light in here." He slid his cellphone from the back pocket of his jeans and turned on the flashlight.

"I left my phone in my coat pocket," she said. "Shine yours on the closet, will you?"

Seconds later, she had her phone in hand and its flashlight on. "That's better," she said. "Now what?"

"We're in luck— I happen to have a standby generator."

"I know what a generator is but haven't heard of a standby. What's is it?"

"A useful invention that works as a backup. It senses the outage and automatically turns the power on."

"No way." Her eyes widened. "How long does it last?"

"Until normal power is restored. Then it flips itself off."

"That's amazing. Why doesn't the guesthouse have one?"

"There's no need for it. If and when someone stays here and this happens, they bunk at my place until the power problem is fixed." He moved to the window and pointed out. "The field lights are on, see? So is the light at the house. Heat, too. Grab something to sleep in and a change of clothes for tomorrow just in case. Then bundle up, and we'll head over there."

"Maybe the power will come back on in a little while," she said, and bit her lip.

"With this storm, it's doubtful, but if a miracle happens and it does, then come straight back here." He pulled his boots on and bent over to lace them up.

Still, she hesitated. She really didn't trust him. Brady straightened. "You have my word that I won't touch you, all right? I'll be up for a while yet, working in the studio. It's gonna get cold in here real soon. Grab your stuff, and let's go."

She went to her bedroom and came back with a small suitcase. As soon as she put her boots on and donned her coat, hat and gloves, they left.

* * *

BRADY HAD EXPLAINED that he had heat and light, but Starr was amazed anyway. "I can't get over that you have power," she said as she put her jacket and hat in his coat closet. "That's so cool. Where should I put my things?"

"Upstairs, first door on your left. The bed isn't made up."

"I'll do that."

"I'll get the sheets and blankets while you stow your stuff up there."

The second story had several bedrooms and plenty of space. A lot for a single man not looking for a relationship. Judy had mentioned a family of five had lived there before he'd bought it. As Starr entered the room Brady had directed her to use, she flipped on the overhead light. Roomy with thick carpeting and off-white walls decorated with scenic paintings of a wild curtain of water cascading down the falls, snow-capped Cascade Mountains rimming the horizon and a meadow dotted with spring flowers.

A queen-size bed with lamps on both bedside tables and a flatscreen TV on the wall opposite the bed. In the time it took to take the spread off, Brady delivered the bedding. "Your bathroom's right across the hall," he said.

"Mine?"

"The master bedroom has its own."

Well, duh. Starr was relieved— sharing a bathroom with him would be way too intimate. "This is a beautiful room," she said.

She made her bed and returned to the living room, where he was building a fire. "What are you doing, Brady, when you'll be in the basement working? You won't get to enjoy it."

"This is for you. I haven't told you about the lawyer. Why not talk about it with a blazing fire to keep us company."

He'd made another fire for her? Her heart lifted in a sigh. She wanted to hear about the lawyer. First, though… "The whole time I was shoveling snow, I thought about cocoa. I was so looking forward to a hot, chocolatey mug. The power loss ruined that. You wouldn't happen to have any in the house? If so, I'll make some for us both."

"As a matter of fact, I do. Come into the kitchen while I find it."

"I don't picture you as a man who keeps cocoa in his pantry," she said as he pulled a large mason jar from a cabinet.

"You'd be right. This was a Christmas present from Judy. She made it herself from some recipe she likes."

"You exchange gifts with the woman who cleans your house? That's sweet."

"I give her extra cash and she gives me something in return. Candy or cookies, or a set of kitchen towels. She's a pretty good cook. She'll be glad I finally tried this stuff."

Such a considerate guy. The kitchen wasn't quite as tidy as when Starr had visited his studio a few days earlier. "She's due to clean on Friday," he said as if he somehow knew what she was thinking. He studied the label on the jar. And read, "'Add a heaping tablespoonful or two to a cup of hot water or milk.' I say we go the milk route."

"Definitely milk. I'll nuke two mugs of it."

When the steaming cocoas were ready, they carried them into the living room. The fire was blazing, and they sat down. Cozy. She wanted to scoot close and cuddle up. Better not if she meant to keep her promise to herself. Which less than an hour ago she'd almost broken. Thanks to Brady, she hadn't. So, no.

By some tacit agreement, she glued herself primly to one

end of the couch and he stayed at the opposite end. "This cocoa is great," she said. "Tell me about your meeting with the lawyer, and then forget about me and go work."

"Slavedriver, aren't you?" He flirted with a grin.

"What I mean is, I don't need entertaining. I don't want to keep you from working."

"You won't. I'll give you the two-minute version. The attorney, a woman named Kelly Yarrow, pointed out a bunch of stuff I didn't know that should be in the contract."

"It's a good thing you contacted her. Kelly Yarrow," Starr repeated, trying to place the woman. "Why do I know that name?"

"I believe Sunshine hired her when she had the trouble at her spa last year."

"That's it. How did you know?"

"Trevor told me when I asked him for the name of a good lawyer. With Kelly's help, I have a list of questions that need to be answered and statements that should be revised and/or added to the contract before I sign anything. I scheduled a face-to-face with Alfonse for tomorrow, but we'll have to wait and see."

"Unless the power is fixed and the road crews clear the streets first thing in the morning." Starr held up crossed fingers.

"The way it's coming down? I wouldn't get my hopes up, but we'll see. Your turn to answer my question," he said. "Who'd you have dinner with tonight?"

He didn't seem in any rush to start working, so she told him about Robin and Savannah. "We're as close as ever, and we had a really good time. So good, that we never glanced out the windows and closed Marsden's down. But then, they close at eight."

His expression was full of admiration or something similar and puzzled her. "Why are you looking at me that way?"

"What way?"

"Like I'm special." Her cheeks felt hot, a sure sign of blushing.

"You are," he said. "And you have the prettiest smile."

"Talking like that is what gets me into trouble."

"Yeah, well when you kiss me, then *I* get into trouble. We both need to tamp down our reactions."

"Like we are now," she said.

"Right." Brady drained his mug and stood. "Time to head downstairs. When you get tired of the fire, close the screen and let it run itself out. See you in the morning."

As soon as he was out of sight, Starr texted Mama and her sisters. *My power is out. Yours?*

All three replied that they were in the same boat. Like Brady, Mama had a generator. Several of her girlfriends who'd come to the house and didn't have one planned to sleep over. She was still busy partying.

How are you keeping warm? Mama texted.

What to say that wouldn't cause speculation and snarky comments. *Brady has a generator and several spare bedrooms. I'm using one of them. Don't judge me, okay? He's a great landlord.*

In no mood for the teasing replies sure to come, she set her phone to Do Not Disturb.

CHAPTER 19

*I*n the dead of night, Starr woke up. At first, she didn't know where she was. Then she remembered — the power had gone out, and she was at Brady's. What time was it? According to the clock on the bedside table, four-thirty a.m. Last night, wondering when he'd come up from the basement, she'd sat by the fire until almost midnight. When she'd finally hauled herself to bed, he was still down there. After working a full day at the store, then meeting with the attorney, he must be exhausted. In bed, she'd lain awake, listening for his footsteps, until at some point she'd fallen asleep.

Curious to know if the power had been restored at her house, she flipped on the table lamp and padded to the bedroom window. Despite the darkness outside, the bright snow was visible. She could also see stars twinkling in the sky. The storm had passed, but she heard the hum of the generator, which meant the normal source of power was still out both here and at the guesthouse.

A yawn hit so hard her eyes watered. Ready to fall back to

sleep, she returned to bed and turned the lamp off. The mattress was comfortable and a down comforter kept her warm, perfect conditions for sleeping. Yet she stayed awake awhile, her thoughts drifting.

Please let there be power in the morning, she silently pleaded to the weather gods. With a scant month before the wedding, she really needed to sew. Even without power, a fire in the living room ought to keep her warm enough. She hadn't finished the hand-stitching on Dahlia's dress and could work there as long as she was careful and the fabric didn't absorb the smell of smoke. Thanks to the efficient way the damper whisked it up the chimney, that wasn't likely.

Speaking of smells, Brady's incredible olfactory skill had almost gotten her in big trouble. What had happened in the guesthouse last night had been dangerous and potent. For a little while she'd forgotten everything but him. Holding her, kissing her, touching her...

She wanted him so much, when she knew better. Making love with him, a man who wanted sex without any future together, meant breaking a promise to herself and setting the stage for heartache. She must be out of her mind to be thinking about him that way.

Blame it on the self-inflicted celibacy. In dire need of physical connection, she yearned for him, missed sex more than she'd ever imagined. Right now, she half-wished he hadn't pulled away, that he might this very moment be lying here beside her. In the dark of night, that sounded pretty good.

They were in the same house. It wouldn't be too hard to find his room....

Frowning, she dismissed that bad idea and chalked up the

wayward thought to waking up in the middle of the night. She closed her eyes and took a few breaths meant to relax and soothe. It didn't help.

Alone in the dark, she clung to the extra bed pillow and tried to sleep.

* * *

THOUGH BRADY HAD WORKED until after midnight, something woke him up in the dead of night. Groggy, lying in the dark with the only sound the hum of the generator, he checked the clock on his bedside table. Four-thirty, way too early to get up. He shut his eyes and was almost asleep again when he remembered— the power was out at the guesthouse. Starr was sleeping at his place, in the bedroom just up the hall from his.

So close and yet so far.

Damn.

Hours earlier, knowing she was in the living room enjoying the fire while he spun his wheels in the basement in a fruitless effort to lose himself in work had been pure torture. He'd replayed everything that'd happened at her house shortly before the power had gone out. The feel of her soft body pressed hotly to his, the thrust of her breasts in his hungry hands, her low moan— all of it driving him crazy.

Good thing he'd pulled himself together and stopped what they were doing. For her, sex meant a committed relationship. Count him out.

If that wasn't enough on his mind, the pressure of creating what he needed for the gallery show bore down hard. Alfonse wanted it a mere few months from now. How was Brady supposed to pull that off and still work full time at the store?

Not possible, unless he could convince the man to postpone the show until fall. He'd bring it up at their meeting today, although if the idea was a dealbreaker, he'd agree to Alfonse's schedule. He wasn't about to lose this opportunity.

Forget sleep— he needed to get back to work. Rubbing his weary eyes, he got up. Not wanting to wake Starr, he stole quietly downstairs and into the kitchen to brew a pot of extra strong coffee. He drank two cups while browsing his laptop and checking out the power situation in the area. According to the outage map, a large chunk of Miracle Falls was still without it and no estimated repair time given. It didn't help matters that the temperature was in the low twenties.

He counted himself lucky to have bought the automatic backup system soon after moving into the house. He'd installed another at the store. A pricey business expenditure, but one of the rare purchases Senior had approved without objection.

Regardless, he wouldn't go in today. No one in their right mind would venture out. He could use the time to work on his art.

Things being what they were, Starr wouldn't be able to go home for a while. He didn't want the distraction of knowing she was here in the house. But with things the way they were, he saw no solution except to insist that she stay until the utility company restored the power.

Too bad he hadn't installed a generator at the guesthouse. Best to spend most of the day in the basement. With so much art to craft, he had little choice to do anything else— no time to shovel snow and clear the driveway until later in the day. If he had his way, he'd get wrapped up in the bear piece and forget about everything else. As he'd hoped would happen last night.

Distracting himself, he wondered if Strang had a generator. If so, they'd Facetime. Buzzing from the caffeine, he crept upstairs to his bedroom and crossed into the adjoining master bath to shave, shower and dress.

As he exited his room, he paused outside the closed door of the bedroom where Starr was and cocked an ear toward it. The only sound, a low-pitched hum, came from the generator. Good, she was still sleeping. He scrawled a note for her and left it on the kitchen counter, letting her know he was working and to help herself to anything in the cabinets and fridge. Ready to get to it, he descended the stairs to the basement.

CHAPTER 20

The next time Starr opened her eyes, gray early-morning light was creeping through the drapes. Her first thought was of the weather and the outage. She peered out the window. No heavy clouds that she could see had formed after she'd gone back to bed, which gave her hope. Growing up in Miracle Falls, she'd seen her share of snow but nothing like last night. The blizzard-like weather had transformed the bushes into soft mounds of white. Overburdened by the extra weight, snow-laden branches of several trees had snapped off. Others looked ready to do the same.

The hum of the generator meant the power was still off. She wouldn't be surprised if errant branches had caused the outage. After turning off Do Not Disturb on her phone, she checked for messages. And found the snark she'd anticipated.

*He sounds like a terrific landlord and a **very** special friend,* Dahlia had texted. *I'm sure he'll keep you warm.* She added a wink.

Sunshine and Mama hearted the comment.

They had no idea that Starr had ached for exactly that last

night. In the light of day, she was glad she and Brady had agreed to put on the breaks. She texted an eye-roll.

As soon as she showered and dressed, she headed down the hall, pausing briefly at the door to his bedroom. It was open a fraction. Unable to stop herself, she peeked inside.

Bed made, but the room was empty. Maybe he was in the kitchen. No sign of him there either, but she found a note. She wasn't surprised that he was in the basement working again and was both disappointed and relieved. Also ravenously hungry. The note said to help herself to breakfast. Who was she to turn down the offer?

The coffee maker had just enough liquid left for a jumbo mug full. Silently thanking him for that, she filled a mug and heated it. Then, following his suggestion, she opened the fridge and helped herself. An omelet and piece of buttered toast later, she gathered the dirty dishes and took them to the sink to rinse before loading them into the dishwasher. Suddenly she paused. The low humming sound from the generator had stopped. The lights flickered momentarily, then steadied.

The outage must be over. As soon as she washed the skillet and loaded the dishwasher, she returned to the guest bedroom, packed her things, and brought the overnight case to the main floor. She headed down the basement stairs to tell Brady she was leaving.

As she entered the basement the soft sounds of jazz floated through the air. She smelled something she didn't recognize. Not pleasant, not awful, just different.

Dressed in a faded t-shirt and jeans and wearing a heavy pair of gloves and safety goggles, Brady didn't seem to know she was there. "Hi," she called out over the music.

He jerked his head up and set down the tool he was using. The gloves came off next. He pushed the goggles to the top of his head and shut the music off. "You're awake."

"I was up for a while around four-thirty, then fell back to sleep till around seven. How about you?"

"I was up then, too."

Starr found that curious. "I wonder what woke both of us at the same time."

"Beats me. At least you went back to sleep."

"You didn't?"

He shook his head. "I had coffee and a breakfast sandwich and have been down here since."

"Goggles and gloves and the unfamiliar smell— are you soldering?"

"That's right." By his less-than-thrilled expression, he wasn't pleased with the interruption. "Do you need something?"

"The humming noise from the generator stopped around the time I finished breakfast. The regular power is on again." In full victory mode, she raised her arms over head à la *Rocky* and moved in a silly high-stepping circle.

She expected him to laugh, but no. He stared at her with hooded eyes that made her feel self-conscious. "I didn't mean to ruin your concentration," she said.

"It's okay. I'm surprised I didn't notice the generator had gone silent. The repair crews must've been out all night."

"Maybe that's what woke us, or maybe it was a branch that snapped off. You should see the broken branches scattered around the yard. I'll bet that's what caused the outage."

"All over town," he said, looking thoughtful. "Could be. I have to see that." He went to the back door of the basement and opened it, or tried to. "Snow must be piled against this side of the house. Guess I'll have to get outside and take care of it."

He didn't sound any happier about that than he was about her being there. "I'd be glad to do some of the shoveling. After you helped me with my car last night and let me sleep here, it's the least I can do."

"Thanks for the offer, but I'll do it myself. It'll be a good break for me."

"All right. I came down here to let you know that I'm going home, if I can get out the door."

"You shouldn't have a problem. The front door is on the opposite side of the house under a five-foot long overhang. The guesthouse will be awful cold."

"The furnace is electric, right? It'll warm things up. That is, if it went back on. I assume it did."

"If not, press the reset button on the side of the furnace. That should start it. Any problems, let me know."

Not if she could help it. He already had enough on his plate and wanted her gone. "You're not going to the store today, are you?" she asked

He shook his head. "I already let my father know. He agreed that we should stay closed today and reopen tomorrow."

"I can't believe you've been working down here since well before dawn when you went to bed so late."

"I don't have much choice. If I want to do this show, I need to make more art." He squinted at her. "How do you know when I turned in?"

Not about to admit she'd fallen asleep while she'd waited for the footsteps that hadn't come— not understanding that herself —she shrugged. "I sat by the fire till almost midnight, and I didn't hear you come upstairs when I turned out my bedroom light."

"You stayed in front of the fire for a long time. I would've, too, if I'd had the luxury. I needed— need to make more art." For the first time since she'd met him, he seemed uptight.

"I saw a fair number of wonderful pieces on your shelves," she said. "How many more do you need?"

"The show will last a full month, so at least double what I have. Alfonse likes the one of Shep, and mentioned wanting something that size, too."

No wonder he was on edge. "How long do you think it'll take to do all that?"

"Longer than I have. Remember, the final decision whether or not to have a show hasn't been made. First, Alfonse and I have details to iron out. But I can't afford to wait for everything to be resolved. My work isn't the kind that can be rushed. It takes time."

"All you can do is your best, right?"

"And that's not going well." He gestured at his sketchbook. "This thing is full of ideas, but I'm having a rough time figuring out which ones to make. Or if I want something else I haven't sketched out yet."

She'd been through similar situations too many times to count. "I totally understand. Stress can interfere with your creativity."

"You mean I'm not the only one?"

"It's fairly common. 'Hurry up and get it done, and it better be good,'" she mimicked in a bossy voice. "'Forget about lunch and your personal life.' That's been me for five years, since I went to work solely for Wes."

The way his brow wrinkled, Starr wasn't sure if he was impressed or thought she was crazy for living that way.

"How do you do that and maintain your sanity?" he asked.

"Good question. At first, I enjoyed the adrenaline rush and feeling of accomplishment when I met my deadlines. Now... I don't know anymore. Keep my head down and get it done, I guess." She wasn't looking forward to restarting the hamster-on-a-wheel routine and didn't want to think about it. "When is your meeting with Alfonse?"

Brady glanced at the clock on the wall. "In about an hour. I'd better text him about how he wants to meet. He may not have power yet." He pulled his phone from his pocket and worked on that. Minutes later, he finished. "We're going to Zoom— he never lost power."

"Lucky man. I hope the meeting goes well. Do you realize we're almost through January? If I want to get the dresses ready in time for the wedding, I really need to get home and sew. Where do I put the bed sheets?"

"There's a laundry chute in the master bathroom that goes straight to the laundry room." He nodded toward a small room at the far end of the basement, where she noticed the washer and dryer. "Drop them in there and they'll end up in the laundry bin down here. Don't worry about making up your bed. Judy will do that."

"A laundry chute. Classy. I've never seen one."

"I hadn't, either, till I bought this place. It's pretty cool. Did you have breakfast?"

"Eggs and toast and the last of the coffee. Thanks for letting me stay over, Brady. If you have time, let me know how the meeting goes."

On the second floor again, she pulled the sheets off the bed where she'd slept and remade it despite Brady telling her to leave the job to Judy. It was her mess and she'd tidy it herself. She scooped up her sheets and towels and took them to Brady's room. The master bath was on the far side of the room, meaning she had to walk through the bedroom.

The drapes were still drawn as they had been earlier. Her arms were full, and she used her elbow to flip on the light and look her fill. Being a master bedroom, it was bigger by half than hers and definitely masculine. A thick navy comforter served as the bedspread. King-size, she noted. One of the pillows had a slight indentation in it. Like her, he favored the side closest to the windows.

An impulse she couldn't resist made her drop the laundry on the floor and pick up the pillow. Burying her nose in it, she let the scent of him surround her senses. She really wanted him, even if he wasn't interested in a serious relationship, and she regretted not tiptoeing into his room the night before.

Don't.

Lips compressed, she dismissed the thought, fluffed the pillow and set it back in place. Arms full again, she headed into a bathroom about the size of the dining room in her Brentwood townhouse— wow. She stuffed the sheets and towels into the chute and watched them disappear. After making her way downstairs, she donned her boots, bundled up and called out a goodbye as she tromped into the snow and crossed the field.

* * *

BRADY WAS ABOUT to head upstairs to the den that doubled as his office and log into the Zoom meeting with Strang when he heard Starr call out, "Bye, Brady," as she left. Now that she was gone, surely he'd stop this relentless lust that distracted him and messed with his creativity every bit as much as stress.

When he reached the main floor and started toward the den, the silence and emptiness made him regret that she'd left. Just like at the guesthouse. No one else made the place seem so full of life. He wasn't happy when she was here or when she was gone. "You gotta be kidding me," he muttered in the silence. Great, now he was talking out loud to himself. No doubt about it, she'd messed him up big time.

The meeting started with the usual small talk. "I'm amazed you never lost power," Brady said.

Strang shrugged and they chatted about the storm before getting down to business. Brady went through the items Kelly had pointed out line by line, and the back and forth negotiations started. Strang was open to adding some things and editing others, but he was adamant about doing the show in the spring. With Brady's time restraints, he wasn't thrilled, but after some dickering they settled on the third week in May. Better than April.

Brady agreed to show the sculpture of Shep, which meant taking the time to repair it. Not to sell, of course. Strang wanted to use it to showcase his talent for crafting a larger piece with the hope of spurring orders to custom-make items of similar size. At least he didn't press Brady to make other large sculptures.

Brady wanted to discuss pricing and percentages with Kelly, and Strang was okay with that. Sometime later, satisfied, he forwarded the notes to amend the contract to the attorney. A conversation followed along with a few tweaks

Strang needed to approve. That done, the attorney sent copies of the amended contract to both him and Alfonse.

As soon as they both signed off, Brady texted the good news to Starr, the only person he'd told. Knowing she'd be excited for him, he smiled. He asked her to keep quiet about it till he shared the good news with his parents at dinner on Sunday. Then he went down to the basement, called up a Spotify playlist, and went back to work.

CHAPTER 21

*S*tarr read Brady's text. He and Alfonse had a signed contract! Thrilled for him, she let out a *whoop*, got up from the sewing machine, stretched her legs and back, and did a happy dance. It wasn't as much fun without him, but it'd do. She felt pretty good herself, too. The sky was blue and cloudless with no precipitation expected in the near future. Better still, the furnace in the guesthouse had restarted itself sometime before she walked through the door. The house had been chilly at first but now felt toasty warm.

Soon after she started attaching the sleeves to Dahlia's wedding dress, she forgot about everything except her work, including Brady. She made excellent progress and was enjoying herself when Wes phoned.

Again? Like before, her stomach turned over. She didn't want to answer but did anyway. "Hey, Wes," she said, standing up and putting a smile in her voice she didn't feel. "This is unexpected. Aren't you flying to Copenhagen today?" She had the information on her phone calendar. "Two nights there, then on to Stockholm, then Reykjavik, for one concert each."

"That's right. I leave tonight and plan to sleep on the plane." He had his own bedroom on the luxury jet and often used it during long flights. "I'll be home a week from Saturday. Jacky"— his agent— "booked us a month-long tour in Asia for May, and I'm going to need a lot of new outfits. I want you here and working on those when I get back."

He would start that again. All tensed up, Starr took a deep breath before replying. "That's not possible," she said, sounding eerily calm to her own ears, when inside she was a mass of nerves. "I'm up to my chin in wedding dresses."

"Still?"

"It takes time to make a full wedding gown and the dresses for two bridesmaids and the matron of honor. All by myself. I don't have anyone helping."

"I've seen how fast you work." He paused. "You're putting the wedding ahead of me."

Darn straight. Not about to make things worse, Starr bit her lip to keep quiet— so hard, it hurt. She left the sewing room and started walking around, down the hall to the kitchen and back.

"I'm your boss, and I don't like playing second fiddle to someone else."

Intimidating much? She attempted to explain. "They're my family, Wes."

"Then they should understand. I *need* you."

Brady's comment awhile back popped into her mind. *Tyrants only have power when you give it to them. If you stand up to Wes, you might feel better.*

As scary as the thought was, she was determined to try it. She straightened her spine and raised her head, although her hands shook. "You saw the awful shape I was in when I left," she reminded her boss. "I needed a break and a long-deserved vacation. You gave me the time off, and I'm not going to short myself. I'll do any work you need when I'm back in LA. In the meantime, I'd appreciate it if you stopped asking."

Brady was right, getting it out did feel better. She caught her breath.

Wes was ominously quiet, a sure sign of mounting anger. "If I were you, I'd think carefully about that," he warned.

Click.

He'd hung up on her? He'd never done that to her before, but then he'd never had reason to. She'd witnessed it happening to others countless times, a childish and hostile move that caused wincing all around.

No longer feeling so good about standing up for herself, she chewed on a nail, a bad habit she thought she'd quit. What if he fired her? He might. Instant stress. Fighting the urge to vomit, she put her head in her suddenly cold hands and rocked herself. She wanted badly to phone Brady and talk about what had happened.

Refusing to bother him when he had enough on his mind, she phoned Erica instead, one of the women she'd hired to work with her on Wes's clothing.

"Hi," the seamstress answered, almost whispering.

Uh-oh. "Is Wes in the room?"

"That's right."

"He just hung up on me."

"Yes, I do need to talk to you," she said sounding all business. "If you could hold for a minute… I need to take this call, Wes."

"Who is it?"

Even the sound of his voice in the background rattled Starr.

"One of our vendors. We have to order the rhinestones you want added to the magenta jeans."

"Go ahead, but keep it short. I need you."

He emphasized "need." Starr waited a few minutes, then Erica expelled an audible breath. "He's gone," she said in a low voice. "I can't believe he hung up on you."

"It felt awful. He says he needs me and wants me to come back early. I can't do that, Erica, I can't. I told him the same thing when he phoned last week. This time, I stood up to him and told him to please stop asking."

"I admire that," Erica said. "He talks about you all the time, but he doesn't need you. Bianca and I are doing fine."

"I know— I hired you because you're the best. Who's going with him on this trip?"

"I am, and I'm not looking forward to it."

Starr didn't envy her. "It'll be hectic, but you'll do fine." She paused and voiced her deepest fear. "What if he fires me?"

She prayed he didn't. It was true that around the time she'd come home to Miracle Falls, she'd considered walking away from the job, but she really didn't want that. As difficult as Wes was to work for, she wanted to continue. Designing and sewing for a rock star at the top of his game was a prestigious job, and she liked her standing among other costume designers in the field. And really did enjoy what she did. She was sure that by the time she left Miracle Falls for LA she'd be back to normal, and wished she hadn't blurted out her fear.

"He'd never fire you," Erica said. "You're too valuable."

Starr crossed her fingers. "I appreciate that. If you need to talk or have questions while you're traveling, contact me anytime. Call me anyway when you're back and let me know how it goes."

"I will. And Starr, don't worry. When he calms down, he'll get over it. He always does."

Knowing she couldn't afford to waste energy worrying when there was too much to do before the wedding, Starr managed to push Wes's tantrum from her mind.

It wasn't until she quit sewing hours later that she realized she'd made it through Wes's call without having a panic attack.

"WHAT'S THAT FOR?" Brady's mom asked when he arrived at his parents' house Sunday with a bottle of the same brand of champagne he'd shared with Starr. He intended to celebrate his good news with bubbly as he had with her.

"I didn't want to come empty-handed." His mother looked like she was ready to ask a question. Not wanting to share his exciting news until both parents heard it at the same time, he glanced around. No sign of Senior. "No questions, Mom. I'll tell you later. Where's Dad?"

"In the den, working on who knows what. He'll be along soon. I think we should chill this. There's an ice bucket in the kitchen."

"Great idea." Brady followed her there and waited while she found the bucket.

"You look tired," she commented as he arranged ice around the bottle.

"I've been working a lot in the studio." Delicious smells

made him salivate. "Are you cooking what I think you are— chicken and rice casserole?" One of his favorites, and he licked his lips.

"I agree it smells good, but if I didn't know what it was I couldn't guess. There's no fooling you, though— you've always had a great sense of smell."

Same thing Starr said. She was on his mind all the time, but they were both busy. They hadn't connected since she'd left his place when the power had been restored five long days ago, and he missed her. With so much on his plate and hers, that couldn't be helped. Later, after he told his parents about his gallery show and before he fell into a dead sleep, he intended to get in touch with her.

"If working in the studio makes you happy, I'm happy," his mother said. "Just please, take care of yourself. It wouldn't hurt you to relax now and then. You know what they say about all work and no play…"

"I'm planning to turn in early tonight," Brady assured her. He was too tired to work anymore today. Cheered by the 'if it makes you happy' comment, he smiled. "I'll go get Dad. There's something I want to share with you both."

She studied his face, then broke into a knowing smile. "Let me guess— you met someone. It's about time you moved on after the divorce. Why didn't you invite her to join us tonight?"

He'd moved on some time ago, and his parents knew that. He couldn't help but think of Starr again, but he wasn't even close to ready for what she wanted. "This has nothing to do with dating, okay? It's about— I'll wait to tell you and Dad at the same time."

"You can do that over dinner, which conveniently happens

to be ready now. I'll let your father know it's time to eat, and you take the casserole out of the oven and put it and the salad bowl on the table. We'll have the champagne instead of wine."

Some minutes later, they sat down to eat. After helping themselves to the food, Brady picked up the champagne and stood to fill the flutes. His father eyed the bottle in his hand. "What's this mysterious announcement that rates champagne? Have you met someone?"

Brady was surprised both parents wondered about that and ignored the question. "This is delicious, Mom."

"Thanks, but I don't think that's what you want to tell us."

"Well?" Senior said around a mouthful.

Eager to share the news, Brady sat back down. "I've been asked to show my art at Strang Gallery. It's a fairly new gallery about four miles west of Miracle Falls Park."

"How exciting!" His mother clasped her hands over her chest and shone a bright smile his way. "I've heard about the Strang. The art there is supposed to be really good. So they offered you a show there? How did they find out about you?"

"I left my card when I visited last year but never heard back. Then a few weeks ago, Alfonse Strang found the card and phoned me. He saw some of my work on Instagram and wanted to take a look at the studio. I invited him over and showed him the pieces I have on hand and sketches of ideas for future work. He liked what he saw."

"That's wonderful. I can't wait to see your work on display. When will that be?"

"The show opens the twenty-second of May and will run for a month. Mr. Strang wants what I showed him and more. I have a lot to do to get ready."

"No wonder you've been working in your studio so much.

I'm glad you brought champagne with you. "Let's toast to your success." She raised her glass and waited for Brady and his father to do the same.

Senior's reaction was subdued. "I know Alfonse— we met when he bought a watch from me. He's also a savvy business-man. You must be pleased. I have to admit I'm surprised he appreciates your art enough to want to sell it. But should you be spending your valuable time working on that? Your future is in the jewelry business, and that's where your priorities should be."

Not much in the way of praise or even the hint of a smile. Refusing to let that dampen the evening, Brady raised his glass. "I'm extremely pleased, sir. You already know that creating something new and unique with my own hands gives me a great deal of satisfaction, and that I bring that good feeling with me to the store. It shows, too. Sales are up, and we have more repeat business than ever, thanks to my hard work and the help of Toni and our part-timers. How about a toast to my gallery show and to all I've done at the store and will continue to do?"

Brady tipped his flute toward each parent, and was relieved when his father joined in with a hearty taste.

He added, "I see nothing wrong with having a second priority, as long as it doesn't interfere with the jewelry company."

Senior's jaw tightened, and Brady's mother shifted in her seat. "Why don't we put the judgments away and enjoy this meal?"

They ate in silence for a few minutes before his father shook his head and set his fork down. "This is why I haven't turned the business over to you. In dividing your loyalties, you're telling me you're not ready."

Between fatigue and years of attempting to earn a modicum of praise for his success at the store that never came, Brady's temper flared. "I *am* ready, sir, and aware that Joe is the son you chose and groomed. You only turned to me when he resigned and left the country, and you never let me forget I'm a poor second. You reject most of my suggestions to boost business, and God forbid you give Toni a much-deserved promotion." Before he said something he might regret, he silenced himself.

Senior opened his mouth to speak, but Brady's mom shushed him with a look and laid her hand atop his. "It's my turn to speak," she said. "Brady has worked hard and deserves credit for what he's done with the business. We haven't seen any indication that his art gets in the way of that. I don't know anyone who focuses on work all the time. Having outside interests is important. You could benefit from finding a few for yourself."

Brady was grateful for the support. By his father's forbidding frown, he was far from convinced. In no mood to put up with anymore lecturing tonight, he stood. "I should get home. Thanks for a terrific meal, Mom. I'm sorry I didn't eat more of it." He nodded at his father, whose expression didn't change. "Sir."

He drove home fuming, yet also relieved that he'd spoken up for himself. He'd planned to relax at the house, touch base with Starr, and turn in early. But when he parked the car at home, he was still too angry to contact her. He prowled the house restlessly, then took himself outside for the fresh air.

Somehow, he ended up striding across the field between his place and the guesthouse. No smoke rose from the chimney, but the lights were on, and her car was in the driveway. He needed to vent and she was the perfect person to listen. He headed toward the light.

CHAPTER 22

By Sunday evening, a full day after the Wiglets' most recent tour had ended, Starr had yet to hear from Erica. But then, the poor woman had never traveled with Wes before, and he'd no doubt run her ragged. Jetlag and exhaustion from trying to meet his demands had likely turned her into a zombie incapable of holding a conversation. Having been there many times herself, Starr understood. She was also beyond curious to hear about the trip. Taking a short break from sewing, she texted the woman and asked about the tour.

When she heard nothing back, anxiety got the best of her and fear took over. Was she about to get fired? A sewing marathon helped keep her mind off her troubles, but the apprehension stayed with her, hovering in the background and rising to the forefront when she paused to stretch. Any appetite for food faded, and she wondered if she'd be able to eat tonight.

She needed to be with people who cared and would take the edge off her raw nerves. Like Brady. But as much as she missed him, she didn't want to take him away from his work. Besides, he was probably at his parents' sharing his good news. He must be doing that now. Picturing their pleased reactions made her smile and helped calm her some.

She was thinking about calling Sunshine and Dahlia when Mama invited the three of them to an impromptu Sunday dinner, which brought a smile to Starr's face. She jumped on the invitation.

The visit started just as she'd hoped, with everyone in good moods during the meal. Mama seemed more rested than she'd been since Starr had first arrived in town, a promising sign that she was sleeping in on weekends. Dahlia was full of excitement for the upcoming wedding and the honeymoon plans she and Jake had made, and could hardly wait for her fitting at Starr's the following afternoon. Sunshine was happy with Trevor and the spa, which was busier than ever and growing.

Not wanting to energize the anxiety gods, Starr kept quiet about her personal concerns and talked instead about the progress she was making with the dresses.

So far, so good, until Dahlia threw a wrench into the conversation. "How's Brady? Had any more overnights?" she said, grinning.

Praying the subject didn't set Mama off, Starr kept her voice matter-of-fact and her expression neutral. "I don't know how he is. We're both super busy and haven't talked lately." She wanted to tell them about the gallery show but not until he gave her the okay.

Sunshine pulled a sad face. "Then you really aren't seeing each other? He lives across the field from the guesthouse."

"That's true, and of course I see him, but not lately." The

sudden gleam in Mama's eyes was a sure sign she had ideas about that, and Starr set her straight. "Don't go getting excited about things that aren't going to happen. Can we talk about Wes now?"

She hadn't intended to bring up her boss, but the subject turned their attention from her and Brady.

They all seemed surprised. They knew about the panic attacks but not the latest. She filled them in on Wes's recent phone call and her fear of losing her job.

"Why would you want to work for a man like that?" Mama grumbled. "He's rude and a narcissist."

"Probably," Starr agreed. "It doesn't help that his successful career and a ton of adoring fans constantly stroke his ego. I've never done that, and neither do the women who sew for me. We keep our heads down. I do what I'm good at— designing clothes for him. It's a great job, and I don't want to lose it." As much as she dreaded going back to work, she meant that.

"I'm no expert on the subject, but if he fires you without cause, contact a lawyer," Dahlia suggested.

Sunshine weighed in. "He actually can fire you pretty much at will, so unless you think there's discrimination or something behind it, you're powerless. You learn that kind of thing when you run your own business and hire and fire employees."

"I wouldn't call what you do a great job," Mama said. "Not the way your health has been affected."

Like you with your over-socializing, Mama? With sudden insight, Starr realized she was a lot like the woman, blindly plunging on to the detriment of her health. "He does run me ragged, but that comes with the territory. I happen to like the work and the money, but I really needed this break. Getting away and coming home has helped."

The family sympathized and did their best to reassure her that things would work out, which was sweet, but what did they know?

"There's something I've been meaning to ask you, Mama," she went on.

"Oh?"

"You're burning the candle at both ends to the point of exhaustion, and I wonder why socializing is so important to you."

Sunshine and Dahlia nodded that they wanted to know, too.

"I'm happy to explain. For so many years, I worked all day and came home, worked and came home. Except when Ben was sick with leukemia when I was twenty-eight. I took time off then to be with him." Her husband had died only ten years after their wedding. She'd been single ever since.

"After he passed, I went back to my regular work routine. Yes, there were monthly quilting nights and bridge and movie and dinner get-togethers, but I wanted more. I started at the hospital as a clerk when I was twenty and I love being head of medical records, but counting the jobs I had in high school, I've worked for forty-five years— four in high school and forty-one at the hospital."

"That's a long time," Dahlia said. "Is there a chance you could retire early?"

"Draw a smaller pension? No way. I'll retire at sixty-five. In the meantime, there's no reason why I can't kick up my heels at night and make up for lost time."

"Lost time?" Starr echoed, confused.

"Ah, you girls don't know what I'm talking about. You never met my Aunt Hilda. Like me, she worked her whole life, starting in high school. She set her social life aside to focus on work. You should've heard her talk about the fun she planned to have once she retired. That kept her going. Then, when she was sixty-two, she had a heart attack and died."

Starr bit her lip, and Sunshine spoke for the three of them. "We're so sorry, Mama."

"It was sad. Aunt Hilda never got to have the after-retirement fun she dreamed about. I don't want the same thing to happen to me."

Did Mama have heart problems she'd kept to herself? Worried sick, Starr opened her mouth. Closed it until she felt calmer. "Is there any reason you'd think it would?" she asked, proud of her mildly curious tone.

"You know I'm healthy. Not a heart issue in sight. But nothing in life is guaranteed, and I want to pack in as much fun as I can."

No wonder Mama was so busy. Starr exchanged glances with her sister. "It's hard to have fun when you're exhausted," she said. "Trust me, I know."

"You're right. Maybe I'll cut down a bit."

Heartened by that, Starr came home in better spirits than when she'd arrived. She ought to do the same when she got back to LA— if she still had a job. Doubt and anxiety ate at her. She wanted to share her fears with Brady, but he was at his parents'. If she knew him as well as she thought, he'd worked in the studio all day. After so many days apart, there was much to talk about. She was searching for her phone to contact him when the footsteps that had become familiar over the past weeks pounded across the front porch.

Brady was here. "Hi!" she greeted at the door, smiling. It was so good to see him. "I was just thinking about you."

"I've been thinking about you, too," he said, his breath clouding in the cold.

He had? Aww. "Come in. I got home a few minutes ago and was about to call you."

"Is that right?" The broad grin that reached his eyes warmed her.

He unlaced his boots and toed out of them, leaving them beside the door. "Did you have dinner out tonight?"

She nodded. "Mama J invited me and my sisters over. I was glad to get out of the house."

He shrugged out of his coat and hung it in the closet. The navy pullover turtleneck brought out the blue in his eyes, and the gray flannels fit him perfectly. So handsome, she thought as she admired his broad shoulders and fit body. Not much extra padding on him, just enough to make him buff and gorgeous. How did he stay in such good shape when he spent so much time working?

He must've come straight over after talking with his parents. "We both got out tonight," she said. "Hooray for us for taking time off."

"I needed it. I worked at the studio every night last week and the entire weekend. How's the sewing?"

"Going well. I worked all day, too." She was eager to ask about his parents' reaction to his news and also ready to share her fear about losing her job.

"We have—"

"I need—"

They said at the same time. Brady gestured for her to speak first.

"You always let me go first. It's your turn. Why don't we sit in the living room and pretend there's a fire. Or, as you can see, I'm all set up for one." Getting the newspaper and kindling ready had become a habit. "All I have to do is strike a match."

"Save that for another time, when I'm not too beat to enjoy it."

For the first time since he'd arrived, she noted the circles under his eyes. He looked totally spent. They sat down together on the couch, but not within touching distance, which could be dangerous.

By his haggard expression, more than fatigue bothered him. Something bad must've happened. Forgetting her own problems and that she shouldn't touch him, she scooted closer and placed her hand on his forearm. "You had dinner with your parents tonight, or so you mentioned the last time we talked. Is someone sick?" she asked, catching her breath.

"They're both fine," he said, and she exhaled and reclaimed her hand. "I told them about my gallery show. My mother was full of excitement and praise." A fleeting smile brushed his lips. "Senior, though..." He drew his brows together in a frown. "I expected— make that hoped for— at least a congratulations from him. Should've known better."

That didn't sound good. "You call him Senior?"

"That's right. He's let me know countless times that he doesn't support my passion for my art, and that my focus should be solely on the store. Never mind that business has been better than ever since I took over for my brother Joe after he decided he didn't want to run the business and moved to New Zealand. Sales are up and the number of repeat customers is growing, as is my reputation as a jewelry designer.

"I don't get recognition for any of that. Instead of congratulating me and at least pretending to be pleased about the gallery thing, he lectured me. In his mind, I've never measured up. It stings. Usually, I let his negativity roll off, but this art show means a lot to me. I'd finally had enough. I lost it, said things I shouldn't have."

Brady shoved his hand through his hair. "Damn, I sound like a whiner. And you're the lucky listener."

Starr didn't mind. She was filled with warmth and compassion for this man who trusted her enough to air his feelings. "You're not whining, you're unloading. With good reason. Your father insulted you. Surely he approves of what you do at the store. If he didn't, you wouldn't be managing the business."

"Managing in name only. He still makes most of the decisions. He's been crabby and disappointed since Joe left. I'm stuck running the business, like it or not. Right now, I don't." His voice had risen, but he seemed to catch himself. "I'm through dumping on you." He laced his fingers through hers and softened his tone. "I don't expect you to say anything, just needed to vent with my friend. Thanks for listening."

She was stuck on the "friend" word. Which they definitely were and had talked about. Yet she felt so much more for him. Not very smart, but she couldn't help it. From the warmth shining in his ice-blue eyes whenever he looked at her and the way he kissed and held her like he cared, he must have similar feelings. Or maybe that was wishful thinking and she'd misread him. Face it, he'd told her from the start he didn't want a deeper involvement. She ought to be grateful for the reminder. Was. It'd keep her from making a mistake and getting hurt.

Too late— she was falling for him.

He still had hold of her hand. She extracted her fingers and folded both hands in her lap. "I never knew about your father."

"I don't talk about our relationship. I've told Shane some of it, but you're the only person besides my mom and brother who really knows."

"This is the first time you've mentioned your brother. You're not close?" Starr was sorry about that. She couldn't imagine being distant with her sisters. No matter how busy they were, they found time to catch up.

"We are, but we don't touch base as often as we should."

"That happens when I'm in LA."

"Like that, with a big time difference. Joe runs a cattle ranch, which keeps him busy. He's also married and raising two kids. It's been too long since we connected. He'll want to hear about the art show. I'll set up a Skype meeting with him and tell him about Senior's reaction then."

"That's a good idea." Starr thought a moment. "If you're unhappy at the store couldn't your father put someone else in charge?"

"Nope. It's a family business that started in 1915. There aren't any other siblings, and our cousins and relatives have their own professions and don't live in town. I get that. If he'd trust me and back off, I know I could be happy both there and doing my art. For now, I'll go on the way I have been. Talking about it with you makes me feel better. Your turn."

She shouldn't hold his hand but reached for it anyway, just

as he had, and told him about the previous week's phone call from Wes and the conversation that had followed with Erica.

"I took your advice about standing up to a tyrant. I reminded him that I wasn't coming back till the date we'd both agreed to and asked him to please let me have the rest of my time away in peace."

He gave a thumbs-up. "I'll bet that felt good."

"It did, until he warned me to rethink that and hung up on me." Starr glanced down at their hands. Brady's fingers were callused from working on the art that meant so much to him. She fought an urge to kiss each and every one. "The band and Erica got back yesterday. She said she'd call, but I haven't heard a thing. My common sense tells me she has jetlag and is probably too exhausted to talk, but you know me. I can't help worrying about her silence. I wouldn't be surprised if Wes fires me." She chewed her index finger, then made herself stop.

"Maybe you should end the suspense and call her."

"I will. I don't want to lose this job, Brady."

He frowned. "Hold on there. That doesn't track with what I know. The man gives you panic attacks, remember? I watched you suffer after he called you." He put his arm around her shoulders and with his free hand, rubbed his thumb over hers like they were a couple. She thought about pulling away but didn't.

"How could I forget? I hate that you saw that part of me, but I'm also not sorry you did. You helped me calm down. Mama J and my sisters also question me for still wanting to work there. The truth is, besides the money I like the prestige of designing costumes for a mega rockstar. Jobs like mine don't come around every day.

"Anyway, now that I'm away from him, I'm much better. I've put on weight, I'm sleeping well, and best of all I didn't have a panic attack when he called the other day." She was proud of that. "Until now, I haven't had time away for more than a day here and there in a good five years. I was worn out, and I think my body was trying to tell me I needed a break. That played a big part in the panic attacks."

"Could be. He'd be nuts to fire you."

"I agree, but the decision isn't up to me. I can't shake the feeling that in the very near future I'll be without a job."

"Funny— I half wish my father would fire me. We're in opposite boats." He shook his head. "Fine pair we are."

A pair. She preferred that way more than the friends comment, which should've bothered her but didn't, thanks to her powerful feelings for him. "Look at you, coaxing a smile out of me. I'm so glad you're here. I've really missed talking to you."

"It's been hard for me, too. Let's make a deal to touch base more often." He let out a loud yawn.

"Poor guy, you're exhausted," she murmured, smoothing the hair from his forehead.

"Mmm, that feels nice." He leaned his head back against the wall, closed his eyes and sighed. "I really like you, Starr."

Sweet talk that made her go soft inside. "I feel the same about you."

Eyes still shut, he yawned again. "What should we do about it?"

She considered the question and was torn. Her feelings for him were way deeper than she wanted them to be. If that wasn't bad enough, they kept growing. A longing she couldn't fight filled her, to be with him tonight regardless of the consequences. To fall asleep in his arms.

Go back on the promise to herself? Wanting to cave when she knew Brady's feelings weren't as strong as hers was reckless, a set-up for heartache. All she knew right now was that she wanted him. Even more than the night she'd stayed at his place.

"I think I'm falling in love with you," she dared to admit, speaking so softly, she wasn't sure he heard her. Or what his reaction would be if he did.

He didn't move. A little nervous, she glanced at him from out of the corners of her eyes. His head still lolled against the wall, and his breathing was deep and slow. "Brady?" she prodded a little louder.

No reply. He was asleep, sound asleep. Too peacefully to disturb. Thank goodness there was no room on the couch, or she'd climb in beside him. Better not to give in to her longing and decide what she wanted overnight. She carefully extracted herself from under his arm and tiptoed toward the bedroom. Minutes later, she returned with the spare pillow from her bed and the extra blanket from the top shelf of the bedroom closet. Then, grunting a little with effort, she gently maneuvered him onto his back on the couch. She put the pillow under his head and covered him with the blanket. He was longer by a foot than the couch, but that couldn't be helped.

He didn't stir. She dropped a kiss on his mouth, then shut off the light and headed for bed herself.

* * *

BRADY WAS SLEEPING SOUNDLY when something woke him. His foot had fallen asleep and was ice cold and prickly. He rolled over to find a better position— and fell out of bed.

"What the eff?" he said and opened his eyes.

The room was dark, but the light in the hallway was enough to make out where he was. On the floor near the couch at Starr's.

What was he doing here at— he squinted at his watch— five a.m.? Groggy, he stumbled up. Or tried. His foot hurt like hell. Well, crap. He hoisted himself onto the couch and sat down.

The last thing he remembered was the gentle touch of her hand smoothing his forehead. She might have kissed him, too — he wasn't sure. He wiggled his foot around. That seemed to help and eased some of the tingling. He appreciated the pillow and blanket, but why hadn't she waked him up and sent him home?

The foot was warmer now and a good thing. In need of the bathroom, he stood without a problem and flipped on the table lamp. After he did his thing in the bathroom, he splashed water on his face. He had a bad taste in his mouth and opened the cabinet to find the toothpaste.

He couldn't help looking at what else she kept in there. Deodorant, makeup, aspirin, comb and brush. Also birth control pills. So she was on the pill. Always smart to be prepared, even if she didn't want to have sex, at least not with him. That didn't mean he wasn't interested. He was, more than ever. Frowning, he put that out of his mind and gave up the hunt for a spare toothbrush.

Winging it, he squeezed toothpaste on his index finger and did his best on his teeth. Much better. He exited the bathroom in bad need of coffee but would make it at home. He was in the living room folding the blanket and getting ready to leave when she shuffled toward him. She looked sleepy. Cute, too, in bunny slippers and a fuzzy pink robe. Her long, thick hair was every which way, like she'd had a restless night. That or great sex.

What a jerk he was to go there. "I didn't mean to wake you," he said. "Go on back to bed. I'll let myself out."

"Don't worry about that. I've been up for a while, thinking. Excuse me for a minute."

She disappeared into the bathroom. "I can't believe you're awake," she said when she returned. "You were so tired last night."

"I don't even remember drifting off. Thanks for the pillow and blanket. If my foot hadn't fallen asleep and waked me up, I'd probably still be in dreamland."

"I was worried about you not being able to stretch out. That couch is too short for either of us tall people to nap on."

"It's the perfect size for the living room. Why didn't you wake me?"

"I couldn't bear to. You were sleeping so peacefully."

Had he dropped off that fast? Apparently. "You said you were already awake this morning thinking. Something bothering you?"

"Lots of things." She fiddled with the sash of her robe. "You were sleeping so hard that you didn't even move when I steered you onto your back and laid you down."

"That must've been something. I'm no lightweight."

"I did my share of grunting to get you there." She smiled. "So you didn't hear anything after you closed your eyes?"

"Not a thing." He swore she looked relieved. "What'd I miss?"

"Nothing, really. I was talking and at first didn't realize you'd dozed off."

"The way you're blushing? I don't think it was nothing. What did you say while I was out? Did it have anything to do with the thinking you mentioned, or was it worry about your job?"

Her cheeks grew redder still. "I'd rather not say."

From somewhere, a hazy memory floated into his mind. "Did you kiss me goodnight, or did I dream that?"

She lowered her head, framed her face with her hands and groaned. "You *were* awake."

"Guess I was." He wasn't sorry she'd kissed him. "Too bad I wasn't alert enough to participate."

"I probably shouldn't have. I just… I wanted to. I—" she bit her lip. "Never mind."

"Uh-uh, you don't get to say that and blush, too. You have to explain." He raised his eyebrows.

"If you'd been awake, you'd know. Anyway, it's too early in the morning to talk. We haven't even had coffee. Where are my manners?" She started for the kitchen. "I'll brew a pot now."

"You don't have to do that." He caught hold of her wrist and stopped her. "Tell me what's on your mind, then I'll go home and get ready for the day job. I'm not looking forward to seeing my father."

She didn't appear to have heard and didn't pull her hand away. "You're doing that thing again."

Confused, he squinted at her. "What thing?"

"Rubbing your thumb over mine. You did it last night, too."

He hadn't been aware either time. "You don't like it," he said and let go of her.

"I so do— a lot."

She was quiet a moment, lifting the hair off her shoulders and letting it fall again while a host of expressions flitted across her face. A frown, compressed lips, then a weary sigh and something he couldn't make out. Like she was in a silent battle with herself.

Finally, she nodded. "All right, I'll tell you what I've been thinking about on and off for days now. I want to make love with you."

He couldn't have been more stunned if a wild animal had crashed through the window. "But you made that promise to yourself," he said. "Also, you're leaving in under a month, and I can't commit."

With a snort, she put her hands on her hips. "Are you trying to talk me out of having sex with you?"

"Not at all. I think about it day and night, even when I'm working. He touched her soft cheek. "But I don't want to hurt you, Starr."

"I appreciate that. It's one of the main things I thought about last night and this morning. I don't care if you can't commit, Brady, okay? All I know is what I want more than anything— you."

Her big brown eyes held him. "When?" he said.

"As soon as you can afford to take a break from the studio."

"How about tonight?"

"But you have a ton to do before the show. You need to work."

"It won't hurt me to take an evening off."

"If you're sure."

He was primed and ready right now. "Hell yeah. Why don't you come over for dinner. I'll order something. What sounds good to you?"

"Anything."

Words that made him want to take her to bed now. He would've if he hadn't needed to open the store. He put on his boots and laced them, shrugged into his coat. Then gave her a long, deep kiss that left him way too hot and bothered. "Tonight," he said.

CHAPTER 23

*S*omehow Starr managed to work most of the day. She almost finished Dahlia's dress and texted her to set up a final fitting. Once the adjustments were made, she'd finish Addie's and then do her last fitting along with Sunshine's and her own. She also made plans to have lunch with Robin later in the week. She didn't mention Brady to either of them. Too personal.

Erica finally called. In a hushed tone, she explained that the tour had been crazy and that Wes had kept her working like a madwoman during the trip and ever since. "I sympathize," Starr said, relieved she hadn't been drawn into the frenzy and that she had three weeks left in Miracle Falls. "Has he said anything about me?"

"Not a word."

Good to know. Maybe he really had forgotten about his threat to watch herself. The call ended and she laid her worries to rest for the time being. There were other things on her mind, namely the night ahead.

Since Brady had offered to take care of dinner, she

decided to bring the dessert. She knew just the place: Champagne, a restaurant with delicious gourmet food. She bought a dark chocolate mousse cake, which seemed perfect for romance. Then it was time to get ready for the evening ahead.

After a shower, she dabbed a mixture of jasmine and orange sweet essential oils, which smelled amazing, in strategic places. Even if Brady didn't care what scent she wore, she wanted tonight to be perfect. Love— she'd passed from falling for him to actually being there —wouldn't enter into it at all. Nope, that feeling would stay locked up tight.

She put on a sexy pair of sheer leopard thigh highs and shimmied into the sassy red dress she'd designed and made for herself months ago but had yet to wear. Makeup followed. She wanted to wear her black heels, also sexy, but crossing the field in them wouldn't do. For that, she wore boots and added the heels to a tote bag containing the carefully boxed cake. No overnight bag with clean underwear and a change of clothes, as she had no idea whether she'd stay all night. She made her way safely across the field, and after one last pat to smooth her hair, both excited and nervous, she knocked at Brady's door.

He opened right away. "You're all dressed up."

"Wait'll I take off my coat and put on my shoes."

Desire lit his eyes "Please, come in and show me." He nodded at the tote. "What's in there?"

"My shoes and dessert."

"I thought you were the dessert."

"Maybe I will be, but I also wanted something for my sweet tooth and yours."

"I'm in." He licked his lips. "Is it chocolate?"

"You have to ask?" She traded her boots for the heels, then undid her coat.

Brady helped her out of it and whistled.

"You like it." She smiled to herself.

His eyes were slightly hooded. "I more than like it. With your high cheekbones and those long legs, you could be a famous model."

Feeling flirty, she twirled around. "I made it a few months ago."

"Talented and beautiful— you're something special."

Her pulse rate hiked up. "When you look at me like that, I feel that way."

"Yeah? Just you wait." He pulled her into a kiss that left her breathless. "Dinner will be here soon," he said when he released her.

At the moment, food was the last thing on her mind. "What are we having?"

"Duck a l'orange from Champagne and a good Pinot Noir to go with it."

"Yum. Funny, I bought our dessert at Champagne."

"Great minds—" they chimed in together and laughed.

"We may as well open the wine now," he said.

They sat on the couch in the living room, this time close to each other. "Another good fire," she said. "I love it."

"Figured you would. I started it as soon as I got home. Before I forget, an invitation to Dahlia and Jake's wedding arrived today. Dahlia added a note that I designed the rings, and she and Jake wanted me there. I'm looking forward to it and seeing you up there with them."

"I've never been part of a bridal party. Should be fun."

"There's a first time for everything, including tonight.

Here's to that." He tipped his glass her way. When they both tasted their wine, he set both glasses aside. His arm around her shoulders, he nuzzled her neck, setting off a kaleidoscope of delicious heat in her body. "You smell fantastic. "

"Thank you." Pleased that she'd chosen the right mix of scents, she tilted her head to give him better access.

"Maybe we should go upstairs now. I'll leave a note at the door for the delivery person."

She was about to give in when the doorbell chimed. "I guess we'll have to wait."

Moments later, they sat down in Brady's dining room and helped themselves.

"I'm glad you ordered this," she said. "It's really good and goes nicely with the wine."

"Sharing with you makes it even better."

"Laying it on a little heavy, aren't you?"

He gave her a dopey smile. "Yeah, that was pretty sappy. Now and then, it happens."

"I like you anyway. How did it go, working with your father today?"

Brady's smile slipped. "He didn't show."

"Doesn't he usually come in Mondays?"

"Not always. He likes to switch things up. Sometimes he's at the store before I get there, and I usually arrive before nine. Other times he waits till after lunch. It was a relief not to see him."

"You'll have to face him at some point."

"I know. I'm going to call my brother soon and fill him in. Did you contact Erica?"

"She phoned this afternoon. We didn't talk long because

she's completely exhausted. According to her, my name hasn't come up."

"Is that good?"

"I think so. Wes does this sometimes— gets mad and then forgets all about it."

"I don't know how you put up with him."

"There's no sense hashing over that when we've already discussed it, " she reminded him. She'd finished the meal. "Are you ready for cake?"

"Maybe later. Let's go upstairs." He pulled her to her feet and clasped her hand.

Eager to be with him, she didn't argue. They were moving through the living room when he wrapped his arms around her. "As much as I like you in that dress, I want you out of it."

A searing kiss wiped out her thoughts. She was aware only of sensation, his lips devouring hers, the tug of the zipper on the back of the dress. She pulled away and wriggled out of it. It fell to the floor and pooled at her feet. She stepped out of it and laid it on the couch. Brady's gaze traveled to her leopard thigh highs and up to her crotch. "You're not wearing panties."

"A first for me. I've never owned or worn hose like these, either. Do you approve?"

In the time it took her to ask, he shed his sweater and the tee underneath. Such a gorgeous torso. She kicked off the heels and removed her bra.

"Your breasts are beautiful," he murmured, touching her there with hands that shook slightly.

Pleasure, oh the pleasure of his fingers, his lips on her nipples. Wanting him more than she'd ever wanted anyone, she hooked her knee around his thigh, bringing him up nice and close, her breasts against his bare chest.

Groaning, he thrust against her. "Forget the bedroom. I want you now."

"I'm ready. I've never had sex in front of a roaring fire."

"You'll like it. I'm clean. You?"

She nodded. "I'm clean and on the pill."

"I know."

How? She wanted to ask, but he grabbed the throw from the back of the couch and quickly spread it out a on the carpet several feet from the hearth, and she forgot the question.

"Those stockings are smokin' hot, but I don't want anything in the way." He knelt and peeled them down her legs slowly, his warm hands close but not close enough to her most sensitive body part. Turning her on even more.

Wanting him naked, she pulled away. "No fair— you're still wearing pants."

In a blink, she got her wish. They lay down and went back to kissing and exploring each other. Everywhere, with fingers and lips and tongue, sharing what they liked with yesses and moans.

"I love touching you," he murmured, his breath hot on her stomach.

"Me, too. Head south, please."

He let out a low laugh and reached the part of her that most craved his attention. Before long, she arched up closer to his mouth. "I'm about to climax."

"Let go."

"Don't you want to be inside me?"

"Oh, I will be. Next time." He went on working his magic.

An earth-shaking orgasm blanked out everything else. When it ended, she was spent and utterly relaxed. "Thank you."

"My pleasure." He came up beside her and wrapped his arms around her.

They lay in silence for a while. Then, wanting to satisfy him as well, she propped herself up on her elbow and blatantly licked her lips. "Your turn."

"I'm all yours."

She started at his chest, licking his nipples. He didn't have much patience, kept groaning and urging her on. Suddenly, he stopped her. "As much as I'm enjoying this, I need to be inside you. Now."

He flipped her over. It didn't take long before they climaxed together. This second orgasm was even better.

When it was over, he pulled her close. "That was great."

"Yes," she said, barely capable of speech. Her body was thoroughly sated and her heart... Never mind, she wouldn't think about the love filling her. He may not feel as deeply about her, but he'd loved her body with attentiveness and passion as no one ever had. "You're an amazing lover. Really amazing."

"I'm thinking the same thing about you. We're good together— we should do this again." He kissed her, then rose, scooped his clothes up off the floor, and disappeared up the stairs.

So much for cuddling. None of the guys she'd been with had been big on that. A pitfall of making love with a man who wanted sex and not much more.

She'd assumed Brady would be different, that even if he didn't love her, he cared enough to want to linger awhile with her.

So much for that. The neglected fire had fizzled and would soon die out. Feeling dismissed and wishing she'd brought something to change into after all, she retrieved the dress and hose she'd arrived in and went into the powder room to clean up.

* * *

UPSTAIRS IN THE MASTER BATHROOM, changing into a tee and loose jeans, Brady felt vaguely uneasy. He had no complaints about the sex, which had been off-the-chart spectacular. Starr's passion was something else, and her body... Even thinking about it revved him up all over again. He wanted more. At the same time, he questioned the wisdom of that.

Say what? Frowning, he studied himself in the mirror. It took a minute before he figured it out. He was worried she was falling for him. Her sweet smile and tender expression when she looked at him pretty much gave her away. That had to be it. Well, crap, and after they'd talked about it several times.

Best discuss the matter again and make it clear that when it came to falling in love, he wasn't that guy.

He padded down the stairs to the living room. The fire was on its last legs. Starr was dressed and wearing the snow boots she'd arrived in. Her heels poked out of the tote she'd brought. The throw had been folded and returned to the couch, and she'd taken her coat from the closet.

Hadn't expected that. "You're leaving?" he said, disappointed.

"I think I should. You have to go to work in the morning. So do I."

She seemed as ill-at-ease as he was. Also unexpected. He'd left her content and relaxed. What had changed? Must've misread her. Seemed she wasn't falling for him after all. Wouldn't be the first time he'd misread a woman— look at his rotten marriage.

Still, he knew enough to sense when something was wrong. He needed answers. "What about dessert? I was looking forward to sharing that cake with you. Also, I think we should talk."

She hesitated. "About what?"

"What we did in here."

"We had sex, really good sex."

"Absolutely, but there's something you're not saying. I think you should stay and talk while we try the cake. It's chocolate, remember?"

"I admit, I do want some." She eyed him. "I'm not sure about talking, though. There's really no reason to."

He didn't believe her. "Let's get our dessert first. Then we'll get into that."

CHAPTER 24

*J*nstead of restoking the fire and eating cake there, which would've been romantic, Starr helped Brady transfer the dinner remains from the dining room table to the kitchen. "What's the rush cleaning up?" he asked. "There aren't many dishes to do, and they'll keep."

Starr didn't like a messy table. "Maybe dirty dishes don't bother you, but they do me. I was raised to clean up sooner rather than later. "I contributed to that—" she gestured at the plates stacked on one of the countertops— "and I want to take care of it." Also, she needed a minute to think. What was so important that Brady wanted to talk about it now?

The job went quickly—too quickly for her to figure out anything.

When they finished, she brushed her hands together. "Everything is tidy and back to normal. Doesn't that feel better?"

It was a rhetorical question, of course, and he didn't answer. He cut a generous wedge of cake for each of them and handed her a plate.

She wanted to leave, wasn't at all in the mood to talk, let alone eat, but the smell of chocolate was irresistible. In the dining room, she managed a taste, then another. "I'm so glad I bought this," she said. "It's delicious." Brady hadn't touched his, seemed lost in thought. "Let me guess what you want to say. You liked the sex but what happened is physical only, with no strings of any kind. It's what you said you wanted weeks ago."

"Yes, and I'm relieved you heard me. I'm confused, though. We had a great time in front of the fireplace. When I left to go upstairs, you were relaxed and content. When I came back, things had changed. You were tense, dressed and ready to leave." He scratched the back of his neck. "Either you had a change of heart about the sex or I did something that upset you. I can't fix it unless I know. I'm asking you to be honest with me. In return, I'll be honest with you."

She hadn't wanted to talk about this, but... "All right, here's my honest answer. I don't regret what we did, Brady. I meant what I said— you're a wonderful lover. When we finished, I wanted to be held for a little while. I've always thought that if two people shared the kind of loving we did, it meant something. But like most of the guys I've been with, you left without a word."

He didn't look any less confused, in fact his frown deepened. "You're telling me that your partners in the past skipped out on you immediately after sex? Sounds like hookups to me."

"Unfortunately, you're right." She let out a sigh. "My last real relationship ended about two years into my job in LA, just before Wes hired me to work exclusively for him. Since then my, let's call them liaisons, have consisted of brief, meaningless flings that left me feeling empty and bad about myself. That's why I decided not to settle for that anymore. I want and deserve better."

He shook his head as if trying to clear it. "Let me make sure I heard correctly. You were into casual sex but now you're not."

"That's right."

His nostrils flared and his expression hardened in a way she didn't recognize. Now *she* was confused. "Is there a problem with that? Don't tell me you're judging me for my past. I don't care about yours, and you shouldn't care about mine."

"I don't, okay? I'm surprised, that's all."

"From my view you're more upset than surprised."

"I'm not upset."

"Tell that to your nostrils. I haven't been with a man in a long time, haven't wanted to. Then I met you."

He was silent, and suddenly she understood. He was worried that she was in love with him.

Admitting it would send him running and she couldn't bear that. Seeking to reassure him, she added, "You know why I had sex with you, Brady? Like I told you, the attraction between us is so powerful that I thought about it all the time. The more I got to know you, the more I wanted tonight to happen. I don't regret a single second of what we did. The sex was beautiful, better than I ever imagined it could be. I finally understand why it's called making love. Don't worry, though, I'm not in love with you."

It was a good thing she wasn't Pinocchio, or her nose would be a foot long.

"That's a relief."

She'd expected as much even if it did sting. The sudden disgust on his face shocked her. "Why are you looking at me that way?"

"What way?"

"Like I'm the worst person in the world. This is the twenty-first century. Men and women have sex with whoever they want."

"I'm aware of that. My feelings have nothing to do with you." He reached across the table, surprising her, laid his hand over hers and gave a gentle squeeze. Right away, she felt better.

"Thank you," she said.

"For what?"

"For reassuring me. Why did you make that face?"

"My turn to be honest. I was thinking about the first time I caught Verity cheating on me."

"You mentioned she did that." Starr hadn't thought much about it but did now. She bit her lip. "It must've been awful."

He nodded and blew out a loud breath. "It hurt."

"I can't even imagine, and I'm sorry it happened to you. I've made my share of mistakes, but I never cheated on anyone." After another uncomfortable pause, she glanced at him. "Did something I said remind you of that?"

"I— it doesn't matter."

She sensed the opposite. "It obviously matters a great deal to you, Brady, and I want to hear the rest of what's bothering you."

"Okay. You asked why I went upstairs after we had sex," he said, totally skirting the issue, whatever it was. "There's only one bathroom on the first floor. I figured you'd want to get in there, so I used the one in my bedroom. I should've said something."

At least she had the answer to that. There was no use trying to get him to talk about the things he clearly didn't want to share. In the interest of civility, she dropped the matter. "That was considerate of you, Brady. You're right, you should've let me know." And saved her some grief. "No problem, I'm over it now." Eager to devour the cake and end the evening on a light note, she picked up her fork. "We can't neglect this yummy dessert one more second. We have our cake, Let's eat it, too."

They dug in, and for the most part the tension faded and the conversation was easy. But not as natural as during dinner. He seemed somehow absent and distracted, as if he'd closed off a part of himself. The part he wouldn't talk about.

By the time their plates were empty, she was ready to leave. She stood. "I'm going to head to the guesthouse and let you work on your art."

He nodded. They collected the plates and he put them in the dishwasher. "No more mess," he said with a fleeting smile.

"You get a gold star. Thanks for dinner," she said after bundling up. "And for tonight." Meaning that, she tugged him down for a warm goodnight kiss. But his lips barely brushed hers, as if she were more friend than lover. No eye contact, either.

If only he'd open up and talk to her. Wanting that more than anything, she shot him a questioning look. He didn't seem to notice. The studio was calling to him, and he wanted her gone.

He switched the outdoor lights on. As she headed across the field, she realized she didn't know him that well after all.

* * *

AFTER STARR LEFT, Brady spent an unproductive few hours in the studio. Finally, he gave up and headed to bed, but a fitful night made sleeping difficult. The evening had started better than he'd ever fantasized. Then Starr had told him about the casual sex she used to have. For some reason her words had dredged up old pain and anger from the time before his divorce, stuff he'd thought he put behind him. Starr was nothing like his ex, and Brady agreed with her— what had happened in her past was none of his business.

He wasn't clear why what she'd said galled him so much, or why he felt like a damn fool for opening himself up to a woman he'd known less than a few months in ways he'd never intended to. What the heck was wrong with him? Starr hadn't lied to him, hadn't hurt him. She hadn't done anything wrong except drive him crazy. Her body, the way she kissed him with passion and hunger and looked at him with those expressive eyes that said he mattered. How they went soft and hot with desire when she wanted him.

After he'd steered clear of women for so long, she'd made him feel good. He wasn't sorry about any of it. It was a good thing she wasn't falling for him. Good thing he hadn't fallen for her, either.

Tired and mad as hell at himself and the world for no reason he understood, he arrived at the store the next morning in a sour mood.

Senior, the last person he wanted to see, had beat him there. No hello, no apology for his negativity about the art show, nothing but a narrow-eyed look at Brady. "You look like you got in a fight and lost."

Brady felt exactly like that, only his fight was with himself and he had no clue what it was about. If his father said one negative word about the gallery show, he'd explode. He needed time to calm down and get right in his head. "I had a rough night," he said, and shrugged out of his coat.

"Why don't you go home, then."

Was this a test of some kind, a challenge? He blinked at his father, who'd never said anything like that. He believed that "a man does what he has to," especially at work. Brady knew that game, knew Senior expected him to tough it out. After thinking about it for a moment, he decided that for once he wouldn't play. "You're right, I'm in no shape to be here today. Anyway, I have a lot to do yet to get ready for the gallery show." Senior's disapproving scowl had no effect on him. "Toni has the day off, but I know she'll fill in for me. I'll do the same for her another time."

His father opened his mouth, no doubt to nix that idea. Silencing him, Brady held his hands up, palms out, and shook his head in warning. Turning away, he phoned the woman. After a brief conversation, he disconnected. "She'll be here in about thirty minutes, shortly before we open."

Without another word or backward glance, he donned his coat again and headed out.

Once home, he contacted Joe through WhatsApp. *Really screwed myself last night.*

Within minutes, his brother phoned him. "You don't send a message like that and leave out the deets. Were you in an accident?"

"Nothing like that."

"Well, something must've happened. Are you at the store?"

"I was, but I was in no shape to be there. Senior said I

should go home. I surprised him by agreeing and said I had work to do at the studio to get ready for my gallery show."

"He said that?"

"I was as shocked as you. We both know he figured I'd man up and stay."

"But you didn't. You took his words literally. I'll bet that pissed him off."

"I expect so, but I didn't stick around to find out."

"You stood up to him. I'm proud of you, brother."

Brady hadn't thought of it that way, had simply wanted to go home, but Joe was right. He felt better, was even impressed with himself. Surprised, too, that he'd taken the same advice he'd given Starr about tyrants. In a sense, his father was exactly that. "Thanks."

"You could've texted that."

"I called for a different reason." Too antsy to sit, he roamed around the main floor, went upstairs, and then down again while he told his brother about the night that had started out so well and ended so badly. "For some reason, crap I thought I'd put behind me got all stirred up inside," he finished. "It's a good thing I'm not in love."

"But you like her a lot." No need to reply to the obvious. Joe added, "What kind of crap?"

"I can't really explain." Brady scratched his head and tried to gather his thoughts. "All I know is, we were having a conversation and suddenly things got weird."

"Let me see if I have this right. Something's bothering you, but you don't know what it is."

"Yup."

"Maybe if you two talk about it, you'll figure it out."

The thought made Brady uncomfortable. "Uh…"

"You're giving her the silent treatment, aren't you." Joe barked a laugh. "News flash— that doesn't work. Trust me, I know. When something comes between Jessica and me, we talk it through."

"I'm not you," Brady grumbled. "I don't do that."

"You will if you want a relationship that works. Some things are hard to bring up, but it's good to get them out. If you don't, they have a way of festering inside you. Nothing good comes of that."

"I don't even know why I'm so effing pissed off."

"Maybe you're scared."

"Me?" Brady hooted. "Not at all. There's nothing to be afraid of."

"Sure about that? Listen, we're about to inseminate the cows and heifers, and I need to get out there and help. Let's touch base again soon."

CHAPTER 25

uesday morning, aka the morning after the most beautiful night of Starr's life with the most baffling, unhappy ending, she woke up feeling terrible. Falling in love with Brady was bad enough. Worse, she had no idea why he'd pulled away. Stubborn man wouldn't tell her. The final blow had been his aloof kiss when she left. Their first ever kiss had been warmer.

Frustrated and sad, she wanted to pound her fists and cry, but any time now Dahlia would be here for her fitting. This was not the time for a pity party. A complete mess, she was in no mood to work, but too bad.

Dahlia arrived on time, smelling like fresh air and radiant with excitement. "I'm getting married in three weeks! Well, technically in twenty-three days. I brought the shoes I bought for the wedding to try on with the dress like you asked me to." After dropping her coat and purse on the couch, she opened a shopping bag with the shoe box in it and pulled them out. "Don't you love the rhinestones up the heels and back?"

Starr looked at the gorgeous things and burst into tears.

"Not the reaction I expected," Dahlia said, frowning. "I thought sure you'd love these shoes."

"They're beautiful." Starr blinked furiously and wiped away the tears. "Sorry, I didn't sleep well last night."

Dahlia's exuberance evaporated. "Tell me you're not getting sick."

"No way. I wouldn't do that to you." Unless sick-at-heart qualified.

"Why don't I make us tea and we'll talk."

While the tea steeped, they sat down at the kitchen table. The story poured out of Starr. "He pulled away because of something I said or did. He wouldn't tell me what it was, and it's driving me nuts."

"Hmm."

"That's all you got?" She blew out a heavy breath. "Maybe sex was all he wanted."

"Come on. We both know he's not that kind of guy."

"What if he is? From the beginning, he made it clear that he wasn't interested in a serious relationship. Otherwise, it doesn't make sense. Not to me."

Dahlia tapped her lip with her finger and looked thought-ful. "This is a tough one."

Starr's eyes filled again. "At least I hid my true feelings from him. I assured him that I'm not in love with him, only I am."

"Ah, this is beginning to make more sense. When did you know?"

"It happened little by little. The more time we spent together, the more I liked him. I never wanted to fall for him."

Starr groaned. "It figures that when I'm finally ready for a man I can see a future with, the guy I give my heart to doesn't want it. Too bad I won't have much time for a romance in LA. No, I'm going to change that. Somehow. With my career it won't be easy."

Dahlia fiddled with the mug. "Speaking of LA, have you heard from Wes lately?"

"No, and as I said at dinner the other night, I'm pretty sure that any day now he's going to fire me. That'd fix my lack of time for any personal life issues. I guess I could quit while I'm ahead and hand in my resignation." Starr hugged her waist. "But to be honest, the thought terrifies me. Designing clothes is my life. It's who am." Lowering her voice, she admitted her deepest fear. "Without it, I don't know what I'd do."

"Believe me, I get that. I agree that it's better to quit than get fired. That's exactly what I did, remember? Okay, I had a job, but I'd been demoted. I was seriously unhappy and knew it was only a matter of time before they let me go. And look what happened— Jake and I formed a partnership and went into the PR business. We're the best public relations company around. If for some reason you can't find a more satisfying job, we'll help you. It might not be till after the honeymoon, but we're here if you need us."

"I appreciate that so much, but I need to think about it more." Feeling better, Starr managed a smile. "Ready for your final fitting? I can't wait to show you how your wedding dress turned out."

* * *

AFTER TALKING TO JOE, Brady spent the day in the studio. The idea was to focus on work and not think about anything else. He started with the sculpture of Shep. Repairing the damage didn't take long and reminded him of the first time he'd met Starr. A lot had happened since that day, things he'd never imagined.

He was so freaking screwed up about her. Yet, for some reason working on the memorial to his longtime companion eased his angst from the night before. Go figure. When the sculpture was good as new, he was able to push her from his thoughts and move on to new work.

By the time he finally quit for the day, he'd accomplished quite a bit and was pleased with himself. As long as he didn't think about Starr or the comment Joe had left him with. Scared? Of what?

The only thing he knew for sure was that he and Starr needed a break so he could figure stuff out.

The evening loomed ahead. Having worked through lunch, he was starving. Plus, he needed to get out. He was thinking about what to eat and where to grab dinner when Shane phoned.

"Wanna meet at Chet's for burgers and a pitcher?"

"You bet."

"You look tired," Shane commented while they sipped beer and took the edge off their appetites with a plate of Jalapeño poppers.

"I didn't get much sleep last night. I walked into the store this morning, then turned around and went back home. I worked in the studio all day and got a lot done. I'm feelin' good." For now, anyway.

"Are you working on something for a customer?"

Brady hadn't mentioned the show at the gallery yet. "Even better than that." He shared his good news.

His buddy smiled broadly. "Congrats, man. That's really something. Text me the dates and I'll be there. What'd your father say about that?"

"The usual— I should be focused on the jewelry business and forget the art."

Shane shook his head. "Man, that's tough. It's hard when your parents don't support your goals. I lucked out with mine. But then, I'm a software engineer with a job that pays real well." He winked. "The ladies like that, too."

"Do we have to talk about women tonight?"

Shane eyed him. "Something happen that I don't know about?"

"Maybe."

"Let me guess— it involves the tall, beautiful Starr." Brady shrugged, and Shane frowned. "What's up with her?"

"Like I said, I'm not in the mood to talk about women tonight. But I'm okay if you want to update me on the latest with Aurelene— if you two are still seeing each other."

"We sure are. Unlike you, I don't have a problem talking about my love life. We spent the weekend together."

Brady didn't want to hear the guy brag about that, but he managed a smile. "That's good news."

"You seem kinda down." Shane eyed him. "So you bombed out with Starr."

"Butt out."

His friend assessed him for a minute, then raised his eyebrows. "You didn't bomb out." He grinned. "About damn time you got back on that horse. You're having a thing with her. Why aren't you celebrating?"

How to answer that without going into detail? "It's complicated."

"So it's like that. I've been there myself. Women are hard to understand."

Starr seemed easy enough to read. The problem was with himself. Once again, he thought about Joe's comment that he was scared. As if. "What do you like most about Aurelene?"

"Well…" Shane stroked his chin. "We always have fun together. I feel good when I'm with her."

"How so?" Brady asked, figuring the reply might help him understand himself.

"You sound like a therapist."

"I really want to know."

"Okay. She makes me laugh. I make her laugh. I really like her."

Sounded a lot like how Brady felt. "Does that scare you?"

"No. Why would it?"

"I'm curious, is all. I talked to Joe this morning and he says I'm scared. I can't figure out what he meant."

"Your brother the philosopher."

"He's a rancher, remember?"

"Yeah, but he always says stuff that makes you think. At least he did when we were in high school and college. I haven't seen him in years."

Neither had Brady. "He's a good guy, all right. I guess I'm asking, besides making you laugh, how does she make you feel?"

"Good. Happy. Relaxed. Hot— red hot. We've been together almost three months, and things are good. She's special." Shane paused. "Wow, listen to me. I sound like I'm falling for her. Shoot me now."

Brady drove home thinking about their conversation. And wondered if his friend would feel the same way months from now, or when his feelings— or Aurelene's— faded. Because sooner or later, they would.

CHAPTER 26

*S*tay or resign? Over the next ten days, Starr drove herself crazy trying to decide. Wouldn't you know, Wes called two days in a row. When she didn't answer, he left the same message both times, demanding she return to LA immediately. Almost as if he'd forgotten about the break she was taking— or didn't care.

The calls jangled her nerves and ruined her appetite. She was tempted to phone him back and remind him that she wasn't finished with her vacation and was busy getting ready for a wedding. Instead, she reflected on Brady's comments, echoed by her family: Why did she still work for Wes, when he was so hard on her? True, she liked the prestige and the paycheck, but the rest...

The more she thought about it, the more she tended to agree with them. All of a sudden, he stopped bothering her, almost as if he knew what she was thinking. Or maybe he'd finally gotten the message to let her finish her break in peace. Wouldn't that be nice. A person could hope, right? If he'd agree to her taking an annual vacation in the future and bringing Erica with him to concerts instead of her, things just might work out.

Unless the silence meant he'd made up his mind to fire her.

Talk about stress. If she hadn't had so much sewing to finish before the wedding, she'd have been a complete basket case. She missed Brady something terrible and longed to get in touch with him but quickly talked herself out of that idea. Like her boss, the man she'd foolishly given her heart to had been silent. If that wasn't a clear message to leave him alone... Besides, if she knew Brady, he was up late every night, crafting wonderful art pieces. He wouldn't want to be bothered.

She was at the mall one afternoon just to get away and think, when a deep male voice called her name. She turned her head and saw Keith Jamison, a guy she'd dated briefly in high school. They ended up having coffee together at the mall and caught each other up. Divorced with a son, he worked in finance at the bank. She told him about her job, but refrained from mentioning Wes or the Wiglets, which felt surprisingly freeing.

Keith was tall and good-looking, but there was no attraction on her part and didn't seem to be any on his. He handed her his card and she gave him hers. She doubted she'd hear from him and didn't plan to stay in touch. But talking for a while had been a brief, needed escape.

On a Friday, Erica, who kept her apprised via texts and the occasional call, let her know that Wes hadn't mentioned her in days. Starr took that as a bad sign and decided to give her notice before he axed her. That afternoon, alternating between sadness and a whole lot of fear about what she'd do now— aside from a few short gigs after graduating from Parsons, this was the only job she'd had— she put on her big girl panties and crafted a letter of resignation.

That evening, after swearing Robin, Savannah, her sisters and Mama to secrecy, she forwarded the letter and asked them for feedback ASAP. Taking their comments to heart, she tweaked the letter. Then let it sit for a while. It would have been nice to get Brady's input but she left him alone.

A few nights later, she met Robin and Savannah for cocktails.

"I hear you and Keith Jamison got together the other day for an intimate conversation," Robin said. "I thought you liked Brady."

"What?" Starr gaped at her friend. "Whoever told you that is way off. Keith and I ran into each other at the mall. We had coffee and caught up. There was nothing intimate about the conversation, so please set the person spreading that story straight. You asked about Brady." She let her friends know they weren't getting along. "It feels like he's ghosting me."

"You don't know that," Savannah said.

Robin nodded. "What she said. He doesn't strike me as someone who'd do that. Guys need space. Give him time."

At dinner another night, she shared the same information with Sunshine and Mama (Dahlia already knew). Other than Mama's surprise that they'd been seeing each other without her knowledge, they were sympathetic. Like her friends, they suggested Brady needed time to think things through. Whatever that meant.

The following Monday, Starr screwed up her courage and called Wes. Erica answered and summoned him to the phone.

He picked up with a terse, "Yes?"

Not a friendly start. She swallowed. "Hi, Wes. I'm calling to let you know that after much thought, I'm resigning." Hoping he wouldn't yell, she caught her breath.

"I'm not surprised," he said without raising his voice at all.

Phew. "I didn't decide till recently. How did you know?"

"You took so much time off."

Showing a little resentment there, Wes? He knew good and well that every bit of that time was owed her and essential to her physical and mental health. She did a slow burn, but wasn't about to show it. "I enjoyed working with you," she said, proud of her civil tone. "And I learned a great deal."

"We both did. I don't know how I'll manage without you."

Starr had the solution to that ready. "Erica would make a great replacement for me. She's terrific."

"That's what I've been thinking. What's next for you? Going to work for another band?"

The billion-dollar question that kept her up at night. "I don't think so." Working for one superstar had been more than enough. "I'm not sure yet what I'll do, except that it'll involve designing clothes."

"Best of luck in your next endeavor, and remember the NDA."

"Always. I'll be sending my letter of resignation today. I know you're too busy to write a recommendation for me, but if I write one instead, will you sign it and send it back to me?"

Wes said he would as soon as he got it. Doubting he'd read anything but the last paragraph, she'd already written a two-page recommendation, saying wonderful things about herself on the first page and ending with the standard closing on page two.

After heaving a relieved breath that the conversation had

ended well, she immediately sent Wes her resignation letter and the recommendation she'd crafted. And promptly decided to treat herself by taking the weekend off. With the wedding still two weeks away, she could afford to. She still had to finish the matron of honor and bridesmaid dresses. Then she'd pitch in to help with the wedding wherever she was needed. The experts at the Miracle Falls Wedding Pavilion were doing most of the work, but there were always errands to be run and countless other little things that needed to be done.

Then she texted her family and friends.

She had to text Brady, too, couldn't not. Even if he'd ghosted her, some of the credit for her decision was due to him. Soon, but not until she worked to strike the right tone, newsworthy but impersonal. After several trials, she had it. *Hi. I took your advice and resigned today. Big shock— Wes was civil. He even agreed to sign a letter of recommendation written by me. OMG, right? Hope you're well.*

She didn't expect to hear from him. What mattered was that she'd resigned and he knew.

Replies from family and her two besties came immediately. *"You did it!" "So proud of you!" "Yay, you!"* She rolled her eyes at Mama's comment, *"Good girl. You're going to move back to Miracle Falls, I assume."*

Starr had thought about where to live and was torn. Jobs for designers were far and few between even in LA, although there were some. Too bad she no longer wanted to live there. After all the years away, Miracle Falls still felt like home, and the thought of being in close proximity to her family and friends made her happy. She wasn't ready to make any decisions yet, but should soon.

Regardless, she needed a job. She'd be okay unless she couldn't get work and her savings ran out.

Anxiety dimmed some of her newfound relief, but she wasn't going to go to the dark place right now. She pushed her misgivings away. She spent the rest of the day putting the finishing touches on the matron of honor dress.

That night, for the first time in more than a week, she slept soundly.

SINCE BRADY'S about-face at the store some week and a half ago, life there had changed for the better. He refused to take any crap from his father and ignored demeaning comments. As manager and co-owner of the business he didn't need Senior's permission to put new ideas in place. He called in an expert for a long overdue update of the computer system, promoted Toni to assistant manager with a much-deserved raise, and hired an additional salesperson with a background in jewelry and metal design to help with the growing design part of the business. His father seemed surprised, but grudgingly went along with most suggestions.

For the first time, Brady enjoyed working there. Between the jewelry business and making art, he was busy. He would've been happy if not for the big hole in his chest.

He missed Starr something awful. It'd been some ten days since they'd last been in touch, and God above, he wanted to see her. But he needed distance and space to figure things out. Trouble was, he seemed to have a brain block about anything related to his confusion. So he ignored the whole situation. Which didn't solve anything. Driving himself at a grueling clip at both the store and the studio was supposed to keep his mind off her.

That hadn't worked, either. She was in his head no matter what, and he was no more clear about their relationship, if they even had one, than he'd been before. It'd help if he could figure out what was holding him back. No luck as yet.

The only thing he knew for sure was that life without her seemed colorless and empty.

He was on his lunch break Friday when he received a text from her. So she'd resigned. He was proud of her, and felt good that she'd taken his advice.

For now, keeping his distance seemed the best route. But the message deserved a reply. He sat on that, waiting until after he'd finished up in the studio late that night. *Got your text. Great news!* Then, because that seemed abrupt and he also had much to share, he added a few lines. *I'm getting a lot done at the studio and should have what I need in time for the gallery show. Work at the store is better too. I let my father know that I'm in charge and it seems to be working.*

He signed off without expecting a reply.

Some minutes later, a text from Joe arrived, almost as if he sensed that something was up.

Talked to Starr yet?

Nope. Except for today's texts, the silence between them went both ways. *Still trying to figure stuff out.*

Cut to the chase or you risk losing her.

Not what Brady needed to hear right now. He slept badly.

CHAPTER 27

*S*aturday morning, Starr woke up ravenous. Unfortunately, there was little to eat in the house. Again. She ought to get into the habit of buying groceries on a regular basis. For now, she cut up the last of the cheese and sprinkled it on a heel of bread, all that was left of the loaf. By the time she polished that off, she'd made a grocery list.

While she sipped a second cup of coffee, she checked her phone. Brady had texted her back! Her friends and family had been right, he wasn't ghosting her after all. He was simply super busy. Why couldn't he just say that in the first place?

She read his message several times. There was nothing in it to make her sigh or cause her heart to thud harder, but those were her reactions. They were borne out of love.

The changes he'd made at the store sounded momentous, and she really wanted to see him and find out more. But she couldn't decide whether to initiate a get-together.

She toyed with phoning him. As long as she kept her true feelings hidden, that could work.

If only he loved her, too… She clasped her thumb ring and

once again asked for what she wanted. "Please help Brady and me get back together."

A silly thing to do and a useless daydream. His feelings for her were nothing like hers for him. She focused on the message instead. He sounded good, and she barely restrained herself from immediately replying. He'd waited hours to reply to her. So as not to appear too eager, she'd wait, too. After a shower, she dressed. Not long after she started a load of laundry, she slid into the Civic and headed for Beekman's.

The store was crowded, but Saturdays were like that. She was hungry again. Beekman's sold ready-to-eat food and tasty treats of all kinds. She bought a lox and bagel sandwich and a yummy-looking cookie, ordered a decaf tea, and sat down at a little café table in the small eating area. To her surprise, Robin and her son Merritt walked by on their way to the checkout area.

Starr jumped to her feet. "Hey, you two," she called out.

Robin lit up and they shared a quick hug. "You remember Merritt."

Starr was amazed at the changes in the boy. "Last time I saw you, you were in preschool. You're eleven now, right? You've gotten so big." His face turned red, reminding her of how awkward that age was. "I'm about to eat before I shop. Do you want to join me?"

She hadn't spoken with Robin in a week, and wanted to ask about Harrison, the man she was dating, and talk about the text from Brady. Better not in front of her son.

"I wish, but Merritt has plans to go snowboarding, and we need to get home. Let's catch up soon."

With the rest of her day open, Starr had no plans. She enjoyed the lox and bagel, sipped her tea, and scrolled through her phone. Several hours had passed since she'd opened Brady's text, a long enough wait. Before she left the table, she composed a simple message and sent it. That done, she grabbed a cart and started shopping.

* * *

As BRADY HEADED toward Beekman's midmorning Saturday, a text from Shane beeped through his Bluetooth. *Word is, Starr met up with Keith Jamison for a coffee that lasted awhile.*

Say what? He knew Jamison, had commiserated with the guy shortly after their mutual divorces. What were he and Starr doing together?

Never mind that she was leaving soon. What if Joe was right, and he lost her?

Panicky now, he muttered a few choice words and looked for a parking place. As he drove around, he heard from Starr. *Thanks for texting me back. You sound good. Emoji smiling face.*

Trust Bluetooth to explain the emoji. Hearing from her was a big relief. He shook his head and considered texting a reply, but a written message fell short of what he had in mind. He finally realized that Joe had nailed it— he was scared. His strong feelings for Starr spooked him.

Or had. He snickered at himself. Unbelievable his thick head was only now realizing that.

He wanted to see her and make things right. Had to. Never mind he had no idea what to say. The longing haunting him was so powerful, he considered turning around and heading for the guesthouse. Would've if he hadn't spotted a parking slot, which wasn't easy to find on a Saturday morning. He was here and may as well pick up the food he needed.

On a mission to get the job done and get home, he wheeled the cart through the various departments. Meat, dairy, fruit and veggies, junk food. He turned into the crowded produce aisle. There his gaze, like scrap metal drawn to a magnet, homed in on her. Starr. Model-tall and beautiful, wearing her wool cap, she was chatting with one of the produce people. A male who seemed as captivated by her as Brady was, and likely Keith, too. Jealousy stabbed him, and he rolled his cart toward her.

As if sensing his laser focus, she glanced at him. Her eyes widened, and the employee gestured at the multi-colored potatoes in one of the bins and went back to whatever he'd been doing.

"Brady," she said as he reached her. "I just sent you a text."

"Got it. Thanks. I didn't expect to run into you here." His hungry eyes roved over her. "It's good to see you."

"Really." She didn't smile or look directly at him, which made him wary. Well, hell. While he shifted his weight and wondered what to say, she adjusted her cap, moved things in her almost full cart, reached for a bag of the potatoes and added it to the cart. "Have you tried these fingerlings? Scott, the man I was talking to, says they're good. Popular, too."

It wasn't the conversation he wanted, but at least she was friendly. "I haven't, but I'll give them a try." He added a similar bag to his cart. "You're buying a lot today."

"I don't have a choice. Once again, my cupboards are bare. That has to change."

"Right there with you." Awkward silence filled the air between them before he cleared his throat. "Do you want to get together later and talk?"

She shrugged. "I suppose I could."

Like she didn't care one way or the other. But she hadn't told him to get lost. Good enough for now. "When and where should we meet?"

"Let me think." She tapped a finger to her lips, leaving him dangling for a few painful seconds. "Why don't you come over when you finish at the studio."

He doubted he'd be able to focus until they talked. "How about after lunch?"

They parted ways, and Starr moved on to a different grocery department. Feeling much better than when he'd entered the store, Brady whistled and continued shopping.

CHAPTER 28

While Starr unloaded the groceries, she phoned Robin. "It was fun running into you this morning. Do you have time to talk?"

"I'm meeting Harrison for lunch in an hour, but now's good."

"You two must be really hitting it off."

"Yeah, it's nice. We've been seeing quite a bit of each other."

Starr smiled, although Robin couldn't see it. "That's great. So after you left, I ran into Brady. He... Let me back up. I should explain about the texts." She filled her friend in.

"He wasn't ghosting you after all. I knew it! Tell me everything."

"There isn't much to say. He wants to talk."

"When?"

"Today, after lunch. I have no idea what to do. Tell him I miss him so much that I can't stand it? Or pretend I haven't been losing my mind and everything is fine?"

"I don't blame you for stressing out about this. If it were

me, I'd wait to hear what he has to say, then go from there. If there's one thing I've learned from this latest round of dating, though, it's to be yourself."

"Myself wants to strangle him for disappearing without a word."

"You're angry." Robin sounded surprised.

"Furious. I didn't realize how much till today. I still have no idea why he's been giving me the silent treatment."

"He's a guy and may not have realized what he was doing. Ahem… As I recall, Savannah and I told you he probably needed space. What do you want from him?"

Starr didn't have to think long about that. "To let my anger out, then grab onto him and never let go." She huffed scornfully. "We both know he doesn't want that."

"Don't assume when you don't know. He's had time to think about you and what he wants. If he wasn't interested in you, I doubt he'd ask to talk. Quit driving yourself crazy, take a deep breath and relax."

Determined to follow her friend's advice and calm down, Starr stopped worrying about what might happen and stayed in the present by focusing on the usual Saturday chores— finishing the laundry, vacuuming and dusting, and otherwise tidying up. After lunch, she considered making an afternoon fire, but decided against it. Brady didn't deserve a fire.

She brushed her teeth, just in case, and combed her hair. Then, unable to stop herself, she went outside and peeked through the tiny gap in the fence. He was headed her way. She dashed back inside, took her shoes off, picked up a magazine, then set it down again. And made up her mind to be herself.

* * *

A FEW HOURS after leaving Beekman's, Brady knocked at Starr's door. He was nervous but ready to talk about the things he'd skipped over before.

She opened the door, cool and distant, as if he were a stranger. "Come in," she said, without an ounce of warmth.

Uh-oh. On high-alert, he took his boots off. He felt uncomfortable about hanging up his jacket. "Where do you want me to put this?"

"The closet is fine."

Okay, then. He took care of that. Silence. "I think we should sit down," he ventured, shoving his hands in the pockets of his jeans. "Living room or kitchen?"

"Kitchen."

She hadn't made coffee and didn't offer him anything to eat or drink. As leery as he was, he had things to say. But his mouth had gone dry. "Mind if I get myself a glass of water?"

"Go ahead." She sat down and folded her hands on the table top.

Sitting across from her, he glugged half the water, then wiped his mouth with the back of his hand. "I miss you," he said with all the feeling he could muster.

No comment from her. At last, she met his gaze, but she narrowed her eyes a fraction like she didn't trust him. She wasn't making this easy.

He drank more water. "How's the sewing?" he asked, stalling for time.

"Going well, but that's not why you're here. The last time you said you wanted to talk, you walled yourself off instead and disappeared from my life without a word."

She really knew how to lay on the guilt. Brady scrubbed

his hand over his face. "I was mixed up and needed to do some thinking."

Her eyes flashed anger, which he'd never seen. "And you never thought to tell me? If you had, you'd have spared me a lot of hurt and confusion."

Two thoughts passed through is mind— that Joe was right about talking things through, and that Starr was beautiful when she was mad. "I was in the wrong, and I apologize."

She arched her eyebrows and pursed her lips with disapproval.

Couldn't she cut him a break? "This morning, I finally understood what's been going on with me."

"Huh."

Damn, she was hard on him, but he was determined to finish what he'd come to say. "I wouldn't call myself happy before I met you, but I was doing all right. Then you came along, rocking my world from day one, and I started to change. I didn't know how empty I was inside till I pulled back from…" He stuttered to a halt.

The fire in her eyes turned into curiosity and she tilted toward him a fraction. "From what?"

Nothing to do but go for broke and bare his soul. He took a fortifying breath and confessed. "From us and how close we were getting. You'd become an important part of my life. After the incredible sex we had that night, I didn't know how to deal with my feelings. When you said casual sex made you feel bad and that you changed your ways, dark memories from my marriage, stuff I thought I'd put behind me, churned up. They had nothing to do with you, and I couldn't talk about them, so I distanced myself."

"That explains the disgusted look on your face that night."

He nodded. The next part was harder to put into words. His mouth was uncomfortably dry again, and he paused to drain the last of the water from his glass. "I understand now that I was scared of getting hurt. That's why I stayed away."

"In other words, you may be over your ex, but you're not over the heartbreak she caused. Do I have that right?"

"Yeah, and it really messed with me. My reaction sucked and I'm sorry. Will you forgive me?"

"I already have," she admitted with the warmth he'd missed.

He was relieved and had more to say. "You know my feelings about long-term commitment." He waited for her nod, a very somber one, before he went on. "I want to be with you, Starr. Unless you're involved with Keith now."

She gaped at him. "You, too? I wish I knew who was spreading that lie. We ran into each other and had coffee, then we parted ways. End of story."

"Okay." Relieved, Brady went on. "We know a lot about each other, and I want to know more. For now, that's what I'm comfortable with." Would it be enough for her? He bit the inside of his cheek.

A full-out smile bloomed on her face. "I want that, too."

Thank God. He could breathe again. One hurdle cleared. "You're only here for another two weeks."

"Actually, fifteen days."

It wasn't nearly long enough. "Are you planning to stay in LA?" If so, the distance would be hard on them both.

"I'm not sure, and I won't decide till I'm back there again. It depends on the job possibilities. I've never looked before."

She chewed a nail, signaling her anxiety about that. "You know my opinion— you're extremely talented and won't have

ANN ROTH

any trouble finding work." He really didn't want her to live in LA. "I'll bet you can get something similar here."

"Neither of us knows for sure." She played with a lock of her hair. "I've never been in a long-distance relationship. Have you?"

He shook his head. "If you stay in California, we'll figure it out."

Needing to touch her, he stood and moved toward her. Grasping hold of her hands, he brought her to her feet and wrapped his arms around her. She hugged him back. *Home.*

"This is one of the things I missed, being held by you," she said. Minutes later, still holding on, she pulled away a fraction. "You mentioned making updates at the store. I want to hear about that."

He told her about standing up to his father and becoming the manager and co-owner he was supposed to be.

"You're amazing, Brady. I'm proud of you."

"I feel good about it, too. I'm just as proud of you for leaving your job with Wes."

"That wasn't nearly as hard as I thought. He was surprisingly nice about it. I haven't told you about the recommendation letter. I knew he'd never get around to writing one, so I offered to write it myself and send it to him to sign. He took me up on that." Her lips twitched. "Figuring he'd never read it, I made it two pages, the first one singing my praises and the second one with the usual sign-off. I got lucky— he signed and sent it back to me right away."

"Clever woman."

"That I am. Here we are, both feeling good about what we've accomplished." Her eyes twinkling, she threw him an impish look. "I know how to feel even better." She crooked her finger at him. "Follow me to the bedroom."

Later, sated and happy, Brady put one arm around her and cupped her hip with the other hand. Her contented sigh was music to his ears.

"Now I know why people say make-up sex is so great," she said.

"Sex with you is great, period."

He felt fantastic now, but what would happen when she headed back to LA after the wedding?

He kissed her shoulder, loving the corresponding quiver of desire in her body, and pushed the future from his mind. "Hey, Valentine's Day is this coming Wednesday. I want to take you out to dinner."

"A real date?" He nodded and she smiled. "I'd love to."

"Great, I'll make reserve—" He broke off as she wrapped her thigh around his hip and urged him closer. He kissed her and lost his train of thought. For a long time after that, no more words were spoken.

CHAPTER 29

$\mathcal{T}$he next few days flew by. Brady saw Starr whenever possible, sometimes for a walk, a quick meal out, or hot sex before putting in long hours at the studio. He touched base with Joe to let him know that he and Starr were together.

On Valentine's Day he took her to Giatti, a fancy Italian place with great food. She was decked out in another red-hot dress, this one royal blue and snug fitting with a slitted, ruffly thing on one side that swished when she walked. Black hose with a seam up the back and the same heels she'd worn the night they'd first had sex. "You look amazing," he said, then murmured in her ear. "Did you leave your panties at home?"

She gave him a wicked grin. "You'll find out later."

He was so turned on, he seriously considered skipping the meal and getting out of there.

Oblivious to his thoughts, she chattered away. "I haven't been here since I don't know when. I've always loved the look of the place. Linen tablecloths are so classy, and the crystal vases with red and white roses on every table are a perfect romantic touch for Valentine's Day. I remember how good the food is."

"Lots of garlic," he warned.

"Which we're both going to eat, so no worries."

The hostess seated them at a table on the far side of the room, where other couples were chatting and eating. He couldn't help but notice a number of guys checking Starr out and didn't blame them. *She's mine,* he silently warned through narrowed eyes.

They'd ordered drinks and were talking about the dinners they each wanted when an attractive woman who looked to be in her twenties approached. "I saw you when you came in," she told Starr, "and have to tell you how much I like that dress. Where did you get it, and who's the designer?"

Starr beamed. "I'm the designer, and I made it."

The woman's eyes widened. "That's so cool. Do you have a shop in town or an Instagram account?"

Starr shook her head. "No, and no website, either— I'm between jobs. I do have a card, though."

"I want one. Do you take orders?"

"Not at the moment."

"What a shame. If you ever do, please contact me. Thanks for your card. Here's mine."

Brady was impressed. "Look at you, already in demand."

"One person isn't what I'd call 'in demand.'"

"Believe me, you will be."

"Hmm." Starr tweaked an earring and looked thoughtful.

Brady hoped it happened and that she moved to Miracle Falls for good. They were sipping cocktails when of all people, his parents stopped at the table. "What are you doing here?" he asked, hoping Senior behaved.

His mom smiled. "It's Valentine's Day, and I convinced your father to take me out. We didn't expect to run into you." She glanced at Starr, then cast a curious look at Brady. "Aren't you going to introduce us?"

"Sorry about that. Starr Dehl, meet my parents."

The picture of politeness, she offered a friendly smile. "It's nice to meet you, Mr. and Mrs. Barton."

"Joe and Sandra," his mom corrected. "You as well."

A rare smile from Senior astonished Brady. "I know that name. Do you still have the ring I designed for you and your sisters?"

Starr nodded and held out her hand. "We never take them off. Thank you for making them."

"It was my pleasure. I designed them but didn't craft the rings. I see that you take good care of yours. Your sisters live in town, and you're visiting, is that right?"

Another surprise. Brady hadn't mentioned Starr at all. How did his father know?

"Yes. I've been here since early January and have been busy making Dahlia's bridal gown and the dresses for the wedding party. Brady kindly rented his guesthouse to me, which I'm sure he told you."

"Is that so?" his mother said.

His parents shared an undecipherable look that made him uncomfortable. He could almost see the wheels turning. *Brady's seeing someone.*

Time to change the subject. He cleared his throat. "She made the dress she's wearing now."

His mom looked impressed. "From what I can see, it's stunning. Don't you think so, Joe?"

To Brady's surprise, before Senior could answer Alfonse

and an attractive woman stopped at the table. "Sorry to interrupt, but I wanted to say hello and introduce you to my wife. This is Beth Anne. Meet Brady, the talented artist I told you about. And Joseph and Helen."

After Senior and Alfonse exchanged greetings, Brady introduced Starr to the couple.

"Your son is a talented artist," Alfonse said, and briefly chatted with his parents.

Moments later, the gallery owner and his wife moved on. His father said, "Our table is waiting, too. We should sit down."

"Of course." Brady's mother smiled. "It was lovely meeting you, Starr."

Senior nodded. "Good to see you out and about, son. I'll talk to you in the morning."

About what?

"Your parents are nice," Starr said. "And it was so cool to meet Alfonse."

"Yeah. My parents were on good behavior, even my dad." Brady shook his head. "He knows how to act when other people are around, but tonight he outdid himself. I don't know what came over him."

"Maybe you'll find out tomorrow."

* * *

WHEN BRADY GOT out of the shower the next morning, Starr was still asleep in his bed. They'd been up late and she was a heavy sleeper. Not wanting to wake her, he penned a quick note and crept downstairs. His father's comment about wanting to talk made him both curious and wary, and he was anxious to reach the store first. After a quick stop for to-go coffee and a breakfast muffin at Lolli's Place, he arrived.

Senior showed up some minutes later. "Good morning, Brady."

"Morning. I've already done the daily sign-in and printed out yesterday's sales. We're ready to open."

"Not for another twenty minutes, plenty of time for a conversation." His father gestured toward the room where Brady did his design work. "There are two chairs in here. Let's sit."

Bracing for who knew what, he followed the man into the little room. They took seats across the work table.

"Starr seems nice. I enjoyed seeing Alfonse, too."

So that's what this was about. Brady nodded. "She's great, and seeing Alfonse was a nice surprise."

"How long will Starr be in town?"

"She leaves the day after the wedding."

"Which is when?"

"In nine days. Why are you asking?"

"Curiosity. You haven't been interested in a woman for a long time. Or if you have, I wouldn't know."

"You never asked. Is that what you wanted to talk about?"

"Partly. I'm impressed with the changes you've been making at the store lately, and I think she's a good influence on you."

"That's all me, sir, but she has been encouraging."

"She's good for you."

"You're right. I'm good for her, too."

"I suppose she as a job to get back to."

"At the moment, she's between them."

"Does she have to leave?"

"I don't know." Would the man get to the point? Brady checked his watch. "We open in less than ten minutes."

"This won't take long. I'm still getting used to you speaking your mind. I'll speak mine. I've been thinking about some of the changes I want."

The man who didn't like change wanted more of them? Brady frowned. "What else do you have in mind?"

"I'm talking about you and me. I don't like being addressed as sir. Just call me Dad, all right?" A few seconds passed, then his father shook his head. "You can pick your jaw up off the floor, Brady."

"I never expected... Where is this coming from?"

"As I said, lately you've impressed me with your take-charge attitude. You know how hard change is for me. I've been focused on operating the business the same as always. The improvements you've insisted on and implemented have been a long time coming. The business is in good hands, and I'm ready to fully turn it over to you. I trust you, son."

Words Brady had never expected to hear. "No way."

"I mean it."

"What about you, Dad? You like to be here."

"And I'll come in from time to time, but nothing like before. Your mother wants me to try something new. She's going to teach me how to play bridge, and we're talking about traveling overseas."

"It's about time." Brady couldn't quite take it all in. Wait'll Joe heard about this. "You do remember that I'm doing a gallery show in a few months?"

"I do, and I believe you're quite capable of handling your artwork so that it doesn't interfere with the jewelry business. You heard Alfonse say he's impressed with you. You wouldn't be having a show if he wasn't. Your mother and I will be there to see it. I'm sure Toni will handle the business competently while you're away."

Elated, Brady grinned. "I don't know what to say except thanks, Dad."

"My pleasure." His father checked his watch. "It's about time to open. I'm heading home now. Sell up a storm."

CHAPTER 30

Over the remaining days before the wedding, Starr finished the dresses, helped put gift bags together, and ran myriad errands as the big event neared. Life seemed to speed by. On the Monday before the wedding, she met Robin and Savannah at the Corner Café. It was a slow night at the restaurant and they were able to sit at a window table.

"How are things with Brady now that he's come to his senses?" Robin asked.

"He's like a new man, smiling almost all the time."

"Of course he is— he's having sex regularly with you. You have no complaints, either. You're glowing."

Starr laughed. "Rightly so." Not just sex, *great* sex. Lots of it. Sometimes slow and tender, other times fast and hot.

Both friends were staring at her, and she went back to what she'd been saying. "It's not just sex that has him smiling. His father finally retired." Brady had full leadership and control of the business. The two men seemed to have turned a corner in their relationship. His father's acceptance of him made all the difference.

The server delivered mouth-watering food, and for a while the conversation was limited to moans and exclaiming over the deliciousness.

Until Savannah let out an envious sigh. "I'm happy for you and jealous. I remember when Ian and I were mad for each other like you and Brady are. We couldn't keep our hands off each other. Then we had kids. We still have sex, but not like that."

"Don't forget about me," Robin said, feigning a hurt look. "Harrison's great in the sack, too. The other night, he used the L word."

"Get out!" Savannah said. "Who knows, you could be engaged soon."

"Not that fast. I'm crazy about the guy, but this time around I don't want to make any mistakes."

They paused to eat more. Starr dreamed of being where Robin was. Sometimes, she—

"Suddenly, you look very serious," Robin said. "What's on your mind, sweetie?" Both women had set their forks down with concerned expressions.

Starr beckoned them closer and lowered her voice. "I have no complaints about how Brady treats me. He's considerate and wonderful, and we talk about everything— except the future."

"Not at all?" Savannah asked. "Not even once?"

"There was the one time after we made up and decided to be together. That was after I resigned from my job. He asked where I planned to live after Dahlia's wedding. I said I didn't know, that it depended on the job situation."

"That would've been a perfect time to discuss the future. How did he respond?"

"Something about if we have a long-distance relationship, we'll figure it out."

"That's promising," Robin said.

"I thought so, but it's been two weeks since the subject came up. I get that in the grand scope of things that's not much time, but he knows I'm leaving the day after the wedding." Worried, Starr bit her lip.

For a moment, neither of her friends commented. She didn't blame them. What could they say?

Then Savannah spoke. "Couldn't hurt if you brought up the subject."

"I would, but I don't feel comfortable pressuring him."

"Why not?"

Because Starr had never had a relationship like the one with Brady. She loved him deeply, and the thought of losing him was overwhelming. "If he doesn't want a future, I'll crumple up in a ball of misery," she admitted in a small voice. "With the wedding soon and everyone so excited and joyous, I can't risk it."

Robin sighed and shook her head. "If you can't talk to him about it, maybe things aren't that good after all."

"But they are," Starr argued.

"Then ask him about the future. If it were me, I would."

"Me too, and soon," Savannah added. "You only have a few days left in Miracle Falls. Have you searched online for work in LA?"

Starr had. "I found a few possibilities, but nothing that excites me."

"Then live here. That'd be so great."

"So great," Robin echoed.

"There's nothing in town, at least that I know of. I'll probably sign on with a company in LA." Living there was easier than selling the townhouse and packing up when there was no work for her here. But still...

Robin rubbed the space above her nose. "What happened to that glow you were wearing? To repeat what I said when you and Brady had a falling out before, the man doesn't move as fast as you do. He probably needs a push."

Talk about a push. Both Starr's friends were pushing her to do something. "I hear what you two are saying. All right, I'll talk to him, but not till after the ceremony. I really need to know. I also need dessert."

"Fortify yourself with sugar— atta girl."

THE NIGHT BEFORE THE WEDDING, Brady and Joe Skyped. "How's it going?" Joe asked. "Are you happy in your new role at the store?"

"I like it a lot. Getting used to Dad isn't bad, either. He can be a pretty decent guy."

"Amazing, isn't it. So, you and Starr are together. And?"

"She's the one, Joe. I love her."

His brother grinned. "It's about time you admitted it. What happened to moving slowly?"

Brady chuckled. "Wild, huh?"

"Best news I've had in months. I heartily approve. Have you told her?"

"Not yet. I'll do that right after the wedding."

"Good venue for it. Women like when a guy gets romantic. Jessica sure does. Nervous?"

"No, believe it or not. I'll let you know how it goes."

The wedding was beautiful, but Brady had eyes only for Starr. She'd made awesome dresses for herself and the rest of the bridal party. People gasped when they saw Dahlia all decked out, and he heard compliments about the outfits that Starr, Sunshine and Addie wore that made him puff up with pride.

In the printed program handed out, Dahlia thanked Starr for making them all look good. At the reception later, several women came up to her. Eager to get her alone and declare his love, Brady interrupted the chit chat. "Pardon me, ladies, while I talk to my woman. I'll get her back to you shortly."

Starr's eyes widened. "Your woman?"

"That's right. It's noisy in here. Let's find a more private place."

He grasped her hand and headed for a deserted room, then shut the door. "This is better."

"It was a lovely wedding, wasn't it?"

He nodded. "You were the most beautiful woman at the altar. I couldn't stop looking at you."

"What about Dahlia and everyone else?"

"They looked great, but I only have eyes for you." He started to kiss her but she pushed him away. She wasn't smiling, either. "You okay?"

"I don't know, Brady. We need to talk."

"Now you're scaring me. But yes, we do."

"Me first. I'm leaving tomorrow, and we still haven't talked about the future. Do you want a future with me or not?"

He loved the way she pursed her lips when she was upset with him. "You know I do."

"How? I can't read your mind. You haven't said anything about it, not one word. I—"

He stopped her with a look. "Slow down and give me a chance to speak my piece."

"Yes, sir. If you're going to end things, please get it over with," she said and squeezed her eyes shut.

"End things? Woman, you have it all wrong. I'm crazy in love with you." She opened her mouth again, but he wasn't finished. "I said I wanted to move slowly and take my time, but like you once said, when it's right, you know it's right. You're my destiny. I want to build a life with you and make beautiful babies together. Does that work for you?"

"It's about time you said it. I want the same thing. I love you so much, Brady. I have for a while now."

His heart about swelling out of his chest, he reached for her. They shared a tender kiss filled with promise. "Do you want to get married?" he asked, still holding onto her.

"Absolutely, but not yet." She paused. "Where am I going to live?"

"With me. I have plenty of room."

"It's too soon. I need my own place."

"Then stay on at the guesthouse. I won't charge you rent."

"If you don't charge me, I'll move."

"Stubborn woman. Suit yourself."

"I will, and I'd like to stay there. An amazing thing was happening when you pulled me away from the reception. Those women who crowded around me saw my name in the program and knew I made the dresses. I could kiss Dahlia for that! They all want me to design outfits for them."

"Like the woman who came up to you at dinner on Valentine's Day. I know others will, too, once they find out about you. Dahlia gave you a good start. She and Jake can boost your career quite a bit if that's what you want."

"I think I do."

"You're not moving away. Yes!" Brady pumped his fists in the air, à la Rocky Balboa.

Dahlia laughed. "I still have to fly home and pack up."

"There are people who'll do that for you."

"I know, but I want to cull through my stuff and figure out what to keep and what to sell. Building a business here could take a while. I hope I don't run out of money."

"Don't worry, I have plenty."

"I don't want to depend on you for that, Brady. I have Keith Jamison's card. If I need funds for the business, I'll contact him about a loan. I may not need to— when the townhouse sells, I should net a decent amount. The toasts will start any time now, and we ought to get back to the party."

"We will, but first let's walk over to the falls so I can kiss you there. After all, we'll be together for the rest of our lives."

"It's lit up at night, too. I love that you're so romantic."

"Women like that," he said. "Or so my brother tells me." He was teasing, and as expected she laughed. "I can't wait to introduce you two."

"I look forward to it."

He kissed her again. Then hand in hand, they headed outside and into a bright future together.

The End

ALSO BY ANN ROTH

Ann Roth Classics

A Place to Belong

Father of the Year

Another Life

My Sisters

Dunlin Shores

Book 1 Just the Way You Are

Book 2 Wedding Bell Blues

Book 3 Falling for Mr. Wrong

Book 4: A Special Kind of Love

Firefighters

Book 1 Mr. January

Book 2 Mr. February

Book 3 Mr. March

Book 4: Mr. April

Book 5: Mr. May

Book 6: Mr. June

Book 7: Mr. July

Book 8: Mr. August

Book 9: Mr. September

Book 10: Mr. December

ABOUT THE AUTHOR

Ann Roth is an award-winning author of 40-plus contemporary romance and women's fiction novels, as well as novellas and numerous short stories. Her first novel was published in 2000 by Harlequin Special Edition and was nominated by *Romantic Times* as best first book. Ann lives with the love of her life in the Greater Seattle area and enjoys creating flawed characters and putting them in challenging situations that help them grow and ultimately find love— whether or not they're looking for it.

Find out about new releases!
Sign up for my newsletter

Or visit my website www.annroth.net